AND THEN THE FIRE WITHIN . . .

Shadows from the fire danced on her body, taunting and tempting. Wynne straightened beneath his gaze . . . a woman answering a man's unconscious command.

Cole stood up slowly. His blanket dropped away but he ignored it as he drew her to him. Their bodies met and he held her against him tightly as he buried his face in her hair.

"Don't be afraid," he murmured. "I won't hurt you." With those simple words, his mouth gently sought hers. He kissed her tenderly, his tongue teasing her mouth open to receive his again and again.

The ache deep within her had begun to build. She touched him, moving her palms against his firm flesh. She wound her fingers through the dark hair on his chest and held on to him tightly as his kisses started to deepen. She had lost all sense of propriety, forgot everything . . . except the tide of passion that threatened to sweep her into oblivion.

Avenging Angel

Lori Copeland

A DELL BOOK

Published by
Dell Publishing
a division of
The Bantam Doubleday Dell Publishing Group, Inc.
1 Dag Hammarskjold Plaza
New York, New York 10017

Dell ® TM 681510, Dell Publishing,
a division of the Bantam Doubleday Dell Publishing Group, Inc.

ISBN: 0-440-20200-0

Special Dell Edition
Printed in the United States of America
Published simultaneously in Canada

June 1988

10 9 8 7 6 5 4 3

KRI

Dedication

To the many dear friends who lent me their encouragement and unfailing support in this new endeavor. I wish I had room to call you by name, but I want you to know you have a very special place in my heart.

To Lydia E. Paglio, for her continuing faith in me and who virtually made this book possible. I hope I never fail you, babe.

To Denise Marcil, who found a home for my new baby. It's been a pleasure working with you.

To Olivia Ferrell, for taking my hand and leading me through the unknown. I'll never forget your friendship.

To Norma Brader, who has been with me from the beginning, strengthening, sustaining, and always there with a kind word or a pat on the back when none was due. Thank you is so inadequate, but I want to say it anyway.

And to my wonderful family for putting up with me. Lance, Randy, Maureen, Rick, Kathe, Russ, Opal, James, and Joseph. You're my whole world and I love you   . I love you . . I love you.

AVENGING ANGEL

Chapter 1

July 1865

Wynne Elliot coughed and dabbed her handkerchief daintily at her nose as another cloud of choking dust swept in through the stagecoach window. She smiled for what seemed like the hundredth time at the gentlemen across from her and fervently wished the tiresome trip were over.

Gazing out the window, she compared this almost harsh Missouri countryside to her own beloved Georgia. It was July, a time when flowers were blooming back home, when the breezes were moist and balmy, and when moss was draped through the trees to create a kind of fairyland picture.

Here the ground was hard, the grass depressingly dry from lack of rain. And while there seemed to be little evidence of the kind of death and destruction which her dear South had suffered, there were still scars.

The farther they traveled, it seemed, the more rugged the contour of the land became. The Ozark mountain country, she'd been told, was a land where people either survived or didn't, and given the landscape, she could well imagine why.

She could see low mountains with virtually untouched forests in the distance. And the road they were traveling over twisted and snaked through gaps and valleys, revealing endless walls of shale and limestone.

On at least two occasions the coach had stopped so the driver and guard could remove fallen rocks from the way. Why, it seemed that at any turn a group of outlaws could have been hidden behind those massive boulders to waylay the coach. At the last station she had heard mention of the name of Alf Bolin and his men, an unsavory group that seemed to relish jumping out at unwary travelers, and the men's casual conversation had made Wynne's pulse flutter nervously.

Of course, since her journey began in Savannah, she'd heard many such shocking tales. The men at the way stations seemed to delight in relating such stories to stun and distress the lady passengers.

But anything she had been told had failed to

prepare her for Missouri's rugged beauty. And it was beautiful, Wynne admitted reluctantly. Great oaks and maple trees, which by their size had to be a hundred years old, lifted strong arms out over the trail and sank roots into soil which was alternately black and rich clay red, but so stony that no plant could hope to survive. Still, inhabitants of the area seemed to eke out an adequate living from the earth. And apparently in Springfield, a regular metropolis she'd heard, there were thriving businesses. She had been told just yesterday that the railroad as well as more stores, and hotels would be there soon. But if this were true, then Missouri would come out of the great conflict in much better shape than her own beloved Georgia.

She sighed as the stagecoach continued to toss its passengers about. How much farther could River Run possibly be? Her bones felt as if they were coming through her skin. Traveling by coach had not been easy, what with the jostling about, the dust, and the heat. How she longed for a bath, a long, hot bath, with scented soap, and a shampoo. . . . She sighed longingly. Revenge could indeed be tedious at times.

Absently she rubbed the smooth, strange-colored stone she'd grown accustomed to carrying in her pocket. Cass had given it to her. Odd that she hadn't rid herself yet of this one last painful reminder of him. But the trinket had become a kind of worry stone, worn smooth by the continual wash of river water. Her thumb fitted perfectly in the little hollow which looked as if it could have been carved for just that purpose. Her fingers had moved over it for the past few months in a kind of silent litany: *I'll get him . . . I'll get him if it's the last thing I do . . . I'll get him. . . .*

But it had been a long, tiresome journey to fulfill that promise, and it wasn't over yet. She tried to bolster her sagging spirits with the promise that it wouldn't be much longer. As soon as she caught that devil . . .

Wynne wiped ineffectually at the small trickle of perspiration that escaped from beneath her hairline, then adjusted her hat.

Her attention settled on the flamboyant young woman in red sitting next to her. Now there was an interesting example of womanhood.

Miss Penelope Pettibone was on her way to a new job at Hattie's Place.

According to Penelope, Hattie's Place was where a man could go for a drink, a hand of cards, and "other gentlemanly pursuits." At the mention of "other gentlemanly pursuits," Wynne's eyes had widened knowingly, and her face had flushed a pretty pink. Never in her nineteen years had Wynne ever met one of . . . "those" women, and she had found she had a certain unwilling fascination with Miss Pettibone, one that made her wonder how it would be if she were the one headed for the job instead of Penelope. Wynne fanned herself more quickly at the titillating thought and then turned her attention to the reason for her trip to Missouri.

Only that scoundrel, the dishonorable Cass Claxton, occupied her thoughts now. The mere thought of that man left her breathless with anger. Not only had he left her standing at the altar in complete disgrace, but he'd also managed to walk away with every penny she had except the small pittance she kept in a tin box under her mattress for extreme emergencies.

True, she'd been foolish to fall in love with a man she knew so little about and even more foolish to offer financial assistance on a business venture he was about to embark upon, but Wynne had always been one to put her whole heart into everything—especially in matters of love.

If it hadn't been for the war and her suspicion that Cass had enlisted the day they were supposed to marry, she would have tracked him down long ago and put a bullet straight through his thieving heart for doing her the way he had.

Her temper still boiled when she thought how gullible she'd been. Well, she was no longer gullible, and the war was over now. Quite by chance she'd been told by a close acquaintance of Cass's that he had indeed enlisted, and survived, and had been seen in Kansas City a few weeks ago. The friend had said Cass was en route to his home in River Run and should be there any day now.

Wynne clenched her fan in her hand; her eyes narrowed pensively. It had been a long time coming, but Mr. Cass Claxton would soon pay for his sins, she vowed. A satisfied smile crossed her pretty, heat-flushed features. Yes, very soon Cass would rue the day he'd ever heard of Wynne Elliot.

If there was one lesson she'd learned from this, it was that *no* man could be trusted, and though she wasn't necessarily soured permanently on men, she would certainly never allow herself to be fooled by one again.

The coach lurched along as Wynne studied the two male passengers dozing in the seat across from her. Undoubtedly they were no different, she speculated.

She did have to admit, though, she liked to

watch the way stuffy Mr. Rutcliff's fat little jowls jiggled every time the stage hit a rut in the road. But when it came to women, she'd bet he was just as unpredictable as all men, even if he was nearly seventy years old.

She'd had to cover her mouth with her handkerchief to keep from laughing out loud a couple of times when a bump had nearly thrown him out of his seat. He'd snorted himself awake and angrily glanced around him to see who had been the culprit that had dared interrupt his napping.

Henry McPherson, the other gentleman traveler, was younger than Mr. Rutcliff and boringly polite. He constantly tipped his hat and said, "Yes, ma'am," and, "No, ma'am," in response to any comment either she or Penelope made.

Actually Wynne had the impression the two men had been scared to death of Penelope since they'd overheard her discussing her destination with Wynne.

The coach began to pick up speed, and Wynne glanced out the window at the scenery that was now swiftly rushing by. "Does it seem to you we're going faster?" she asked of no one in particular as a frown creased her forehead.

"We can't go fast enough for me," Penelope said with an exasperated sigh. "I can't wait for this trip to be over." She made another useless effort to knock the layer of dust off her dress and grimaced in distaste when it only settled back on the light material.

Puzzled by the increasing speed of the coach, Wynne leaned her head out the window and immediately jerked it back in. "Hell's bells! I think we're about to be robbed!" she blurted out in disbelief, almost instantly wincing at her own statement, one of many of her father's salty expressions.

At her exclamation both men's eyes instantly flew open, and Mr. Rutcliff craned his neck out the window to verify her statement. "Oh, my! I do believe you're right!"

Penelope sent up an instant wail. "I knew it! I knew it! We'll all be killed!"

Wynne shot Penelope an irritated glance. Over the past few days she'd noticed that optimism did not seem to be the girl's strong point. "Penelope, really! I'm sure we are well protected." There was the guard, the driver, and the two male passengers. There was certainly no cause for alarm; besides, the coach could probably outrun the outlaws without the slightest problem.

But a few minutes later her optimism sagged. Her heart was beating wildly as the sound of gunshots filled the air and the riders drew steadily closer.

Glancing worriedly at the gentlemen seated across from her, she noticed they didn't look overly optimistic either. "Shouldn't we do something?" she asked fretfully. She clutched the worry stone in her hand as the two men peered out the coach window apprehensively.

"There's nothin' to do but pray," Mr. Rutcliff replied in a barely audible voice.

Pray? Wynne blinked back a sudden urge to cry as she realized that all of them just *might* be killed.

Pray! Suddenly she found herself doing just that as the masked riders slowly but surely gained ground on the wildly swaying coach.

Like a flat iron on a hot stove, the noonday sun bore down on the two dusty riders as they sat atop their horses on a small rise looking out across the land.

Only a faint, teasing wisp of a breeze grazed their horses' manes. The heat was so stifling it was hard to draw a deep breath.

"Just look at it, Beau. We're finally home." The baritone voice, husky with emotion, spoke first.

The two men sat on tired horses overlooking the

rolling hills of their southwest Missouri home, savoring the smell and feel of being back.

"It looks good, doesn't it?" The older one almost breathed the words reverently. Letting his reins go slack, he slumped wearily in the saddle as he relaxed for a moment, his eyes hungrily drinking in the familiar sight spread before him.

The gently sloping terrain was no longer the lush, fertile green that would have met their eyes if it had been spring. The blazing summer sun had taken its toll on the land and burned it to a dry cinder. But it was still a delectable sight to one who had seen nothing but death and destruction for the last few years.

Four years. Four years of hell. Four years of never knowing if they would ever see home again. Four years of watching men die by the thousands and wondering if they would be next, living with the unspeakable horrors of war day after day after day . . .

Home. The word held a new and even more precious meaning to the two men as they breathed silent thanks to their Maker for bringing them intact through the carnage and destruction.

"You know, Cole, there were times when I thought I'd never see this again," Beau confessed.

"I know," his older brother answered quietly. "I had those times too."

"We were lucky, you know. There are so many who won't come home—"

"Hope Ma and Willa have some of those chicken 'n' dumplin's waitin' for us," Cole interrupted. He'd had enough dying and sorrow to last him a lifetime. All he wanted to do was forget the last few years, not relive them.

Anxious to forget the past himself, Beau released a long sigh of longing as he thought about his ma and the Indian housekeeper's delicious cooking. Willa had been with the family since he was a baby and as much of a mother to the three boys as their own ma had been. When the family had moved from Georgia to Missouri back in the late forties, they'd established a home and hoped to build a new life. Unfortunately their father, Samuel, had died early, leaving his wife with three young sons to raise. No one could argue that Willa had been nothing short of a godsend to Lilly.

"I want six pans of corn bread and three dozen fried apple pies before I even hit the front door." Beau's mouth fairly watered at the thought.

"Yes, if I were you, I'd eat the pie and corn bread even before I went over to see Betsy." Cole teased him with a knowing wink.

"You're right," Beau said solemnly. "That would be the only sensible thing to do." Then they broke out in laughter. Both knew the first place Beau would head for was old man Collins's place. Beau and Betsy had been about to be married when the war intervened, and now the wedding would take place as soon as possible.

"Who wants ol' Betsy when they can have Willa's cookin'?" Beau grinned mischievously, his eyes twinkling. He'd always been the "scamp" of the family, as Willa put it. "You know, now that the war's over, you ought to think about settlin' down, too, Cole."

His brother chuckled softly as his gaze returned to caress the valley below them. "Betsy's the prettiest girl in the county, and you're claimin' her. Who would I marry?"

"Aw, come on." Beau chided him. "You know you wouldn't marry Betsy if you could." Cole and Betsy had always gotten along well together, but Beau knew that no woman had ever captured Cole's heart. "I'm beginnin' to worry about you, Cole!"

Cole chuckled again. "Well, don't. Now that the war's over, when the right woman comes along, I might give marryin' some serious thought."

"It'll never happen," Beau said, knowing that

finding the right woman for his overcritical brother wasn't going to be an easy task. "You're never going to find a woman who'll suit you because you're too picky."

"I'll run across her someday. I just happen to like a woman with a little spirit," Cole said distractedly as his eyes continued to drink in the familiar surroundings. The war had been an ugly, evil blight on the land, but mercifully here the scenic hills of Missouri had remained virtually untouched. "And I haven't met her yet." This was a familiar argument, one his whole family had memorized. Cole's mother and Willa were fond of questioning when he, the eldest, was going to marry and produce offspring.

"Spirit, huh? Well, what about Betsy's sister, Priscilla? Now there's a fine figure of a woman if I ever saw one." Beau grinned at his brother. "She's strong as a bull moose, healthy as a horse, and sturdy as a oak fence post. Why, I've seen her and her father cut a rick of wood in a couple of hours and never raise a sweat. She'd make some man a fine wife," Beau said encouragingly. "Got a *lot* of spirit too," he added for insurance. "Saw her hand-wrestle an Indian brave once, and she didn't do bad!"

Cole's mouth curved in an indulgent smile. "She didn't win, did she?"

"No, she didn't win, but she didn't do all that bad," Beau insisted.

Cole smiled wider at the younger man's sincerity. "Beau, somehow the thought of a woman hand-wrestlin' a brave, cuttin' a rick of wood in a couple of hours, and never raising a sweat just doesn't appeal to me."

"Well, *what* does? I've seen you go through more women than I can count, and not one of 'em suits you. You're just too damn picky!" Beau repeated sullenly.

Cole shifted in his saddle. His bones ached, and he was dead tired. "Don't start naggin' me, Beau," he said good-naturedly. His little brother could nag as hard as any granny when he set his mind to it, and Cole was in no mood for a lecture on women. "When I find a woman who can wrestle the Indian brave and *win*, then turn around and be soft as cotton, smell as pretty as a lilac bush in May, and forget all about being a lady in bed, that's the day you can stop worryin' about me."

Beau shook his head in exasperation. "I've never known a woman to smell like a lilac bush in May after she wrestled an Indian brave!" he complained.

Cole chuckled, took off his hat, and wiped away the sweat on his brow. The clear blue of his eyes carefully scanned the valley below, then narrowed and lingered on the cloud of dust being kicked up in the far distance.

"Looks like the stage comin'," he noted.

"The driver's sure got the horses whipped up." Beau leaned forward slightly in his saddle, his eyes narrowed in his handsome face. "Will ya look at that!"

Leather creaked as the horses moved restlessly beneath the men's weight. Their gazes followed the path of the coach barreling along the dusty road. The driver was whipping the team to higher speed, and the coach careered crazily as it tried to outrun the small band of riders galloping toward it.

Beau released a low whistle under his breath. "Looks like they're in trouble."

Putting his hat back on his head, Cole took up his reins and glanced back over the hillside at the frantic race. "We'd better see what we can do to help."

Both men spurred their horses into action, and the powerful steeds sprang forward. The horses covered the ground with lightning speed, steadily gaining on the swaying coach.

By now six masked riders had brought the stage to a halt and the passengers were filing out with their hands held high above their heads.

The leader of the motley pack had dismounted hurriedly. While he held a gun on the driver and guard, the others began pulling luggage off the top of the coach.

"Don't nobody make a move and you won't get hurt," the second rider informed them in a gravelly voice. "Driver! You and shotgun throw down your guns and the gold box."

The driver and guard looked at each other, then foolishly made a move to pull their guns. Two shots rang out. The women screamed and covered their eyes as the bodies of the two men fell from their perch. Even to the inexperienced eye, it was apparent they were dead by the time they hit the ground.

Three of the bandits immediately returned to dragging valises off the top of the coach and ripping through the contents in search of valuables.

The passengers watched in dismay as their personal items were strewn about in the frenzied search. Wynne stood in shock. Her undergarments were being handled by rough, dirty hands, the lace pieces thrown into the dust with no regard, ripped and torn.

In a vain effort to stop the robbery, Penelope stepped forward and batted her eyes coyly at the leader. "Really, sir, we have nothing of any value. Won't you please let us pass—"

The man angrily pushed her aside. "Out of my way, woman." As he shoved her, his hand caught the large emerald broach pinned to the front of her dress and ripped it off harshly.

Wynne gasped at his audacity. For a moment she forgot her own paralyzing fear and rushed over to stand protectively in front of the sobbing girl. "You brute! Why don't you pick on someone your own size?"

Wynne's heart thumped loudly in her chest as the robber's eyes narrowed angrily. It nearly stopped beating altogether when the bandit jerked her up close to him and made a thorough search of her body with his beady eyes. He quickly relieved her of the pearl ring on her left finger, scraping her knuckle painfully in the process. Rummaging in her purse, he removed all the coins, then focused his attention on her. "This all you got, lady?"

The snapping green of her eyes met his coolly. "I am not a fool! Of course, you have it all . . . and please get out of my face." Her nose tilted upward in an effort to avoid his offensive odor.

Thank goodness he had a mask over his face to dull the stench of his odious breath!

"Aww, am I offendin' Her Majesty?" He chuckled wickedly and jerked her closer, lifting his mask above his mouth. The sight of his yellow, tobacco-stained teeth made her stomach lurch.

Slowly his greedy gaze lowered to the gentle swell of the décolletage of her emerald-colored dress and stopped. "What's the matter, honey? Ain't I pleasin' 'nough for you?" He laughed mirthlessly as she continued to keep her face averted from his rancid smell. "Hot damn. You're a pretty little thing." He breathed against her ear. "How's about givin' ol' Jake a little kiss?"

"See here! Rob us if you will, but I must insist on your treating the ladies with respect!" Henry McPherson stepped forward in Wynne's defense. He was promptly knocked unconscious by the butt of a gun wielded by one of the masked men.

His body slumped quietly to the ground as the assailant waved his pistol menacingly. "Don't no one else try nothing foolish if you don't want to get hurt."

"Come on, Jake! Cut the crap and get on with it," one of the riders ordered, casting an apprehensive glance at two riders fast approaching from the west. "We got company comin'."

28

Jake laughed once more and shoved Wynne away from him. "Sorry, honey. We'll have to make it another time."

"In a pig's eye we will," Wynne said scoffingly but retained enough sense about her to do it under her breath.

The bandit paused in his work, and his evil eyes narrowed menacingly. "What'd you say?"

She grinned weakly. "I said, yes . . . some other time . . . maybe."

"Damn, Jake! Would you quit socializing and come on!"

Jake forced his mind back to the business at hand. After another sweep of her body with his cold dark eyes Jake brutally ripped the fragile gold chain from around Wynne's neck. She winced, then straightened her small frame into an angry stance. "You give that back!" she screeched, and snatched at the necklace. But he stuffed it into the bag he was carrying and laughed at her again.

"Sorry, Red, but I just got a sudden hankerin' for little gold chains." He chuckled again and strode in a rolling gait over to his horse and mounted quickly.

"That necklace isn't worth anything," she protested angrily, "except for sentimental value to me! My father gave that to me just before he died—"

Her words fell on deaf ears as the man tipped his hat to her in a mocking salute. Then the six riders spurred their horses back into action.

"Well, okay then! Take the necklace, but I won't forget this!" she shouted into the cloud of dust their horses kicked up.

Stamping her foot in exasperation and grabbing at her tilting hat, she stared at the robbers' retreating backs. *Damn-damn-damn,* Wynne muttered under her breath. Seconds later two other riders appeared over a rise and quickly took up hot pursuit of the culprits.

The dazed passengers stood about stupidly as Wynne rushed over to kneel beside the injured Henry. He was just beginning to come to and moaned before opening his eyes to look around in bewilderment. "What happened?"

"Just lie still, Mr. McPherson," Wynne said, reaching for one of the pieces of scattered clothing to place under his head. "You were knocked out by one of the ruffians, but they're gone now." Glancing around, she saw the others hadn't moved at all. "Someone had better check the guard and driver," she said briskly.

Mr. Rutcliff snapped out of his stupor at the

sound of her voice and knelt between the two shot men. Shaking his head sadly, he glanced back to meet Wynne's questioning gaze. "Dead as a doornail. Shot 'em both clean through the heart."

Penelope collapsed in tears, and Wynne absently reached over and patted her shoulder. "It's all right, Penelope. They're gone now. Why don't you go sit under that tree until you get yourself under control?"

"But we all could have been killed," Penelope wailed. "I tried to stop them, but you saw what happened—"

"Yes, but we weren't killed," Wynne said in a soothing tone. "Mr. Rutcliff, are you all right?"

The elderly man looked pale and mopped at the perspiration trickling down inside his collar. "Why, yes, I believe so. Quite a disturbing turn of events, wouldn't you say?"

"Yes, I would say that," Wynne replied blowing in exasperation at the wisp of hair that had escaped from beneath her hat and hung loosely in her face.

As Wynne and the other travelers tried to gather their wits, Cole and Beau were pushing their horses to the limit, but the gang of riders had already disappeared into the distance. The long legs of the brothers' animals swiftly ate up the dusty miles, but the other riders had too much of a head start on them.

"What do you think?" Beau shouted a few minutes later as he reined up beside Cole.

"We're not going to be able to catch them. We'll only wind the horses," Cole responded as he pulled his mount to a halt.

Beau's gaze continued to follow the cloud of dust in the far distance until it topped a rise and disappeared altogether. "No, I suppose not. Well, let's go see what we can do to help the passengers."

They pulled their mounts around abruptly and started back toward the stage.

When the two riders came back into view, Wynne paused in picking up her scattered clothing. She watched warily as they approached. Spying one of the guns still lying on the ground, she picked it up and carefully leveled it on the approaching pair. One robbery a day was all she was going to put up with, thank you. If these two ruffians had come for the same purpose, she was going to be the one to take care of them this time.

Penelope was beside herself with fright and would be no help at all. She sat under a nearby tree, crying and fanning herself. Mr. Rutcliff was

trying to comfort the injured Henry McPherson.
That left only Wynne to defend what was left of
their meager possessions.

Beau glanced over at Cole worriedly, then back
down both barrels of the twelve-gauge shotgun
she was pointing at them as they rode up and
cautiously reined to a halt.

"Throw your guns down, gentlemen," she commanded in a firm voice.

"Now, ma'am," Beau said patiently, "we don't
make a habit of partin' with our guns—"

"Now!" She hefted the shotgun up an inch
higher on her shoulder.

Beau looked at Cole and sighed. Both men
slowly unbuckled their gun belts and let them
slide to the ground.

"Now your rifles."

"Ma'am . . ." Beau protested again. He wasn't
about to let the Springfield .58 caliber be taken by
this slip of a girl. He almost laughed. There she
stood, her collar torn, dust smudges on her face,
and that silly hat! A wide-brimmed thing with a
bird in a nest. And it kept tipping forward so she
kept nudging it back, causing the gun to wave
dangerously. And no matter what she said, that
charming southern drawl took out a great deal of

the sting. He'd heard enough of that speech pattern to know she was Georgia born and bred.

"I said throw down your rifles." The gun waved menacingly again.

With a tolerant glance at Cole, Beau slid his beloved Springfield carefully to the ground. Only then did she lower her weapon a fraction. "Now, state your business; then be movin' on."

"Afternoon, ma'am." Swiping off his hat, Beau flashed what he hoped was a winning smile. "Me and my brother was wonderin' if everyone was all right here."

In Wynne's opinion, this newest set of strangers didn't look a whole lot better than the last ones. They were rumpled and dirty, both in need of shaves and haircuts. The only difference she could discern between these two and the other band of unsavory hoodlums who had just fled was that they didn't smell as bad—at least not quite.

Both men were large in stature and impressively muscular, if one liked that sort of man. But they were the exact opposites in coloring. They were still wearing the ragged blue uniforms of the North. Wynne prayed that on top of everything else this rotten day had brought her, she hadn't had the misfortune to meet up with two carpetbaggers.

She studied them carefully. The one who had been doing all the talking had hair streaked whitish blond by the sun and dancing blue eyes. He sat in his saddle with a rakish air. The second man was older, his skin toasted to a deep nut brown, and his hair was jet black with just a trace of unruly curls softening his rugged features. Wynne swallowed hard and tried to steady her hand as she kept the gun directly turned on the miscreants. Lordy, the thing was unbelievably heavy!

"Don't come any closer," she warned as the men's horses edged nearer.

"Ma'am, why don't you put the gun down?" Beau said in his most persuasive tone. "Someone might get hurt."

She narrowed her eyes and took a menacing step forward to show them she was not in the least intimidated by their presence. She meant business.

"It's quite possible someone might—namely, you. Now, I'm warning you, mister, you'd better not rile me. You'd best state your business and move on, or I'll have to use this."

"I really don't think that'll be necessary." Beau turned slightly in his saddle so he could see Cole's face. It was expressionless, but Beau noted that Cole was keeping an uneasy eye on the woman's trigger finger. "I think I'd better state our business, Cole."

Beau started to dismount and stopped short as the girl's voice rang out again. "Just stop right there!" she demanded.

Deciding she'd better let them know in no uncertain terms who had the upper hand, Wynne marched forward with a steely glint in her eye. Unfortunately a discarded valise was in her path. After hitting her shin painfully, Wynne pitched forward. Still clutching the gun, she twisted to one side and fell to one knee.

Cole and Beau ducked frantically as the gun went off, sending a spray of buckshot zooming over their heads. For a moment confusion reigned as Wynne fought to gain control of the gun and her destroyed composure as well as her feet. Beau and Cole rolled out of their saddles onto their knees while still hanging on to the reins of their horses, which were wide-eyed and dancing by now.

Seconds later Wynne was primly straightening her gown, grumbling a pretty unladylike "hell and damnation" under her breath, but the gun was firmly back on her targets.

"Gentlemen, don't be misled." She cautioned them in her most superior, even if it was shaky, voice. "I assure you I *do* know how to use this gun and shall not hesitate to do so if the need arises. So I suggest you move on. My fellow passengers and I have nothing left but our clothes in the road, so you're wasting your time if you've come to rob us."

Wynne glanced uneasily at the dark rider who was slowly coming to his feet. His face was grim, and his eyes narrowed. She didn't like the set of his mouth.

She hoped she wasn't making a complete ass of herself. But after all, she had the gun and he didn't.

The electrifying blue of the man's eyes was directly on her as he studied the scene before him and remounted his horse.

"Ma'am," Beau protested with a weak grin, "I think you've got the wrong idea. We're here to help, not rob, you."

"Oh, really?" Wynne's eyebrows lifted skeptically. He did have a point, though. These two men had chased the robbers off, but it could very well have been for their own evil purposes.

"Honest," Beau declared solemnly. "We're only sorry we weren't in time to prevent this unfortunate mishap." A little of his southern heritage came through as he swept his hat off and bowed gallantly. She was once more the recipient of his radiant smile.

"That may be so, but you're still a Yankee!" She spit the words out as if they left a vile taste in her mouth. "And I wouldn't believe a thing a Yankee said!"

"Ma'am," he said coaxingly, "the war's over. Can't we let bygones be bygones?"

"That's easy for you to say," she pointed out. *"You* won."

Beau shrugged his shoulders. "True, but I had some help," he said modestly.

Wynne shot him a dirty look. He wasn't taking this whole situation seriously. Beau slowly eased his way over to her. "Now, why don't you just calm down and let me and my brother take you and the other passengers on into town?"

Wynne surveyed the lifeless bodies of the driver and guard and realized she was at this man's mercy even though she was holding the gun. It was obvious that neither she nor Penelope could drive the stage, and the two other men were in no condition to attempt such a feat.

"Well . . . maybe that would be a good idea, but bear in mind I'll have this gun pointed at you all the way in case you try something underhanded." She shot the other man a warning look. "And that goes for you too."

Cole shook his head in disbelief at the way his brother was handling the situation. He calmly took a cheroot out of his shirt pocket and lit it. If it had been up to *him*, he'd have taken the gun away from her ten minutes ago and turned her across his knee.

"What's the matter with him? Can't that pompous ass talk?" Wynne whispered crossly, motioning with her head to Cole. All the man had done since he arrived was stare at her as if she were a raving maniac!

Beau glanced over his shoulder toward his brother. "Who, Cole? Sure, he talks, when he wants to." Then his gaze returned to focus on her, studying the hat, which was tilting dangerously again. "You don't have to be afraid of us," he told her reassuringly, noting the cautious look in her eye. "Do we look like the type of men who would take advantage of a lady?"

Wynne's eyes studied him for a moment, then drifted involuntarily over to the other man. His eyes and stance remained aloof as she met his direct gaze.

No, this one didn't seem the type to take advantage of a woman, but the other one certainly looked questionable.

"Nevertheless, you've been warned," she stated simply, then turned toward the stage. Once again fate intervened. Her feet became entangled in one of Penelope's stray petticoats lying on the ground. Her own skirt wrapped itself around her legs, pitching her forward. When she threw out her hands to keep from falling, the gun spun in the dirt and landed at Beau's feet. Dust puffed up into her nose, and she sneezed, barely halting the automatic move to rub her nose. As she looked up from her prone position, the first person she saw, naturally, was that dark man watching her as if she were something in a sideshow.

Fortunately it was Beau's boots that were right in front of her face. With a courtly bow he reached down and handed the gun back to her with a polite smile. "Allow me, ma'am."

"Thank you . . . sir." She felt her face flood with color. After scrambling to her feet, she snatched the gun back and reached up to straighten her hat, which had gone askew in the turmoil. She had no idea why she was so clumsy today! "I'll just get the other passengers in the stage," she announced.

"That would be fine, ma'am," Beau drawled with a grin.

He made his way back over to where Cole sat on his horse watching the fiasco.

"What do you think you're doing?" Cole asked calmly.

"Gettin' ready to escort the stage back to town," Beau answered innocently.

"Why did you give that gun back to her?"

"Oh, that," he scoffed. "She's not gonna shoot anyone. She's just scared."

"I *know* she's not going to shoot anyone intentionally," Cole growled, "but I think we're in serious danger of getting our heads blown off by her stupidity!"

"Come on, Cole. Look at 'em. They're—they're helpless." Beau's gaze returned to the shaken passengers, beginning to climb back into the coach. "Let her feel like she's runnin' the show. It's not gonna hurt a thing."

Cole took a drag on his cigar and studied the situation for a moment. In his opinion, everything was under control and one of the men passengers could take the stage on into town.

"Boy, you're a born sucker when it comes to a pretty face," he said accusingly. The woman undoubtedly was a looker. She stood barely five feet tall with the prettiest red hair and snapping green eyes Cole could ever recall seeing, but she still seemed like a menace to him.

"No, I'm not," Beau said. "I just think it's our duty to get 'em into town safely. Look at 'em, Cole. Neither one of those gentlemen looks like he could handle a team of horses, and I know the women can't."

Cole wasn't heartless, nor was he inclined to spend one more moment with a gun waving in his face. He had made it all the way through the war without an injury, and he wasn't about to have some snip of a woman ruin his perfect record less than ten miles from home. "There's no reason for us to get mixed up in this," Cole contended. "We can send someone out here to help them when we ride through town."

"No, I don't want to do that," Beau argued. "We can't just ride off and leave the ladies out here to fend for themselves. It won't take long to escort them back to town, and then we'll be on our way."

"I still say we stay out of it."

"Okay. If you don't want to help, then I'll do it myself."

Beau could be stubborn as a Missouri mule, and no one was more acutely aware of that fact than

Cole. "All right, all right. But I don't like it," he said.

"Thanks." Beau grinned with relief. "I just wouldn't feel right about leavin' them alone." He watched as the last passenger clambered aboard the coach. "Now, you drive the stage and I'll load the driver and guard on our horses and be right behind you."

Cole dismounted with a grumble and strode over to the coach as Beau took care of the dead men.

Gripping the cheroot between his teeth, Cole had planted his foot on the wheel of the stage and started to climb aboard when the cold barrel of a gun tapped him on the shoulder. He tensed and turned around to meet Wynne's calculating eyes.

"Don't forget. I'll be watching you." She reminded him as curtly as her southern accent would allow.

He bit down on the end of the cigar impatiently. "Ma'am, I'm quivering in my boots," he drawled in a mixture of Georgia softness and Missouri twang.

Well, Wynne thought irritably, he could talk! Then her eyes suddenly narrowed. There was something vaguely familiar about him, although

she was certain she had never met this man before. In spite of herself, she found herself noticing
how very even and white his teeth were, and
though he had obviously been riding for some
time, he was not nearly as dirty and offensive as
the bandits had been. The heat had curled his dark
hair attractively around his tanned face, and his
eyes—well, she had never seen such a strikingly
clear blue color before. . . . For a brief moment
she tried to imagine what he would look like with a
shave, a haircut, and clean clothes, and the new
image was of an extremely handsome swain.

She shook the disturbing image away. But she
couldn't shake the feeling that he reminded her of
someone else.

"Good. See that you remain that way." Wynne
primly tucked herself and the gun into the coach
and slammed the door. But a moment later an
ominous steel cylinder was slid out of the window
and carefully positioned in the direction of the
driver's seat.

Cole shot a dirty look at Beau, who had just
ridden up on his horse. "I don't know why I let you
talk me into these things!" he snapped.

Beau was still grinning as Cole climbed aboard

the stage. With an impatient whistle and a slap of the reins he set the stage in motion and, the barrel of a shotgun pointed straight at his head, headed for town as fast as he could.

Chapter 2

The stage pulled into town with a loud jangle of harness and a cloud of boiling dust. The townspeople, surprised to see Cole seated in the driver's seat, ran to meet the new arrivals.

"Cole, boy!" Tal Franklin, the town sheriff, climbed aboard the coach and slapped him soundly on the back. "Good to see you, son!" Cole could have sworn Tal's eyes grew misty for a moment before he dragged out a large handkerchief and wiped hurriedly at his nose. The last few weeks the townsfolk had seen the sons of River Run return home—at least the ones who had survived the war—and it had been a heartwarming sight.

"Good to see you, Tal." Cole grinned widely, clasped the man's hand, and pumped it affectionately. Words seemed very inadequate for the feelings that swelled within him as he looked at the familiar face he'd known for most of his thirty years. God, it was good to be home!

"Looks like you come through without a scratch." Tal beamed; then his smile faded a little. "Have you seen either of your brothers?" Tal hated even to ask the question, dreading the answer he'd heard too often in the past few months. So many of the boys who had made it home were nearly destroyed by their experiences of death. They were bone-weary and disillusioned.

"One of 'em's right behind me." Cole smiled and set the brake before leaping off the driver's seat. "I ran into Beau about a couple hundred miles back, and we rode home together."

"Aw, your ma's going to be beside herself. Two of her boys comin' home the same day!" Tal slapped him on the back again. "But what in the world are you doing driving the stage?"

At that moment Beau rounded the corner by the saloon, leading Cole's horse with the bodies of the stage driver and shotgun guard draped across the saddle.

A buzz of excited voices reached the sheriff as he turned to peer over his shoulder. "What's going on here?"

"The stage was robbed about five miles back,"

Cole reported as he walked back to open the door of the coach and help the first passenger down. He waved at the sound of several friendly voices that called out to him, and his heart swelled with happiness at being back among familiar faces.

There was old Nathan at the blacksmith shop, grinning at him with his gold tooth shining in the afternoon sunlight. Nute Walker was sweeping the front porch of his general store and watching all the commotion that was taking place. A holiday mood was evident in the crowd.

Mary Beth Parker, the town spinster, sat in the window of the post office and waved her handkerchief at him. He remembered her smile from when he was a small boy and his ma would send him in town to pick up the mail each month. Mary Beth had been the postmistress of River Run for more than fifty years, and it wouldn't seem right to see anyone else sitting in her place.

Familiar sounds, familiar faces—how good it was to hear and see them all again.

Jerking open the stagecoach door, Penelope stepped lightly into Cole's waiting arms. He swung her small frame down easily, then quickly doffed his hat in the first show of manners Wynne had seen from him. "Ma'am, I hope the ride wasn't too uncomfortable for you."

Penelope's sultry gaze took in the width of his shoulders and the broad expanse of his chest as she removed her arms from around his neck ever so slowly. She batted her eyes at him demurely. "Why, thank you, sir. I surely do appreciate your bein' such a gentleman. I'm feelin' much better now, thank you." Her soft southern accent floated lightly on the air, along with the enticing scent of her jasmine perfume.

Cole felt his smile widening to a silly grin, and he mentally berated himself for getting so flustered in the presence of a pretty girl. But it had been awhile since he'd been so close to a female, and he could feel his body reacting accordingly.

His grin was still spread all over his face as he reluctantly set Penelope aside and turned to the next passenger. Instead of warm flesh, his hand came in contact with the cold metal of a gun. And his grin died a sudden death.

Wynne forced the burdensome gun ahead of her as she tried to work her billowing skirts and the hatbox she was carrying out the narrow doorway. Naturally the brim of her hat scraped the doorframe, and it tilted alarmingly. She had watched the sickeningly courteous treatment the dark, silent man had bestowed on Penelope, and when he just stood back and watched her struggle out of the coach on her own, Wynne's irritation became evident.

Intent on maneuvering herself, her purse, the hatbox, and the gun out the narrow door, she missed her footing on the bottom step. The hatbox crushed against the doorframe, and the gun barrel reared upward as she came flying out nearly head-first.

All effort at trying to remain graceful disappeared while she concentrated on not killing herself by falling out of the high-set stage.

An unwilling witness to this minifiasco, Cole ducked quickly to one side and automatically flinched against the blast he expected to hear as Wynne's gun waved about wildly. He straightened just in time to see her plop into the dust, flat on her fanny, the gun and the hatbox beside her, her purse dangling from her wrist. Her face flamed a bright red when she glanced up to see the definite smirk on his face. This had to be the most humiliating day of her life! What must this man think of her when she kept falling all over the place like a complete idiot?

Cole drew a deep, resigned sigh, then picked up his hat and dusted it off on his thigh. Jamming it back on his head, he walked over to Wynne and leaned down until his face was level with hers.

With as serious an expression as he could muster, he spoke in a perfectly controlled voice. "Excuse me, ma'am. Could I assist you with your hatbox?"

Swallowing the peppery retort which sprang immediately to mind, Wynne allowed something like a growl to escape her tightly compressed lips. Struggling to her feet, she steadfastly refused to look at the gathering crowd. There were definitely a few smothered chuckles, and she felt like a total fool. This was absolutely the last straw! She had no idea why she was being besieged by such bad luck today, but she was beginning to resent it highly! "Thank you . . . sir, but I believe I can manage by myself." She certainly had done so up to now with no help from him at all!

He'd helped Penelope out of the stage like a porcelain doll, then let *her* fall out on her face. She was completely mortified, but she wasn't about to let on that she'd noticed the difference or that it bothered her.

She shook the dust from her skirt and was reaching for the hatbox when Cole's hand snaked out. Before she knew what was happening, he'd snatched the gun away. "Please, I insist on bein' of service, ma'am. At least let me carry your gun."

His blue eyes danced determinedly, and again her face flushed brick red as she thought about how bumbling she had been during this whole ordeal. With some effort she gathered the shredded remnants of her composure, squared her shoulders, and lifted her small chin. "Yes . . . well, thank you. That would be most helpful." She acceded gracefully, her nose tilting up a fraction. Lifting the hem of her skirt and holding her purse, she swished past him in her most haughty manner. Assuming she and the other passengers were perfectly safe now with the sheriff present, she could afford to let down her guard a little.

Tal Franklin stood with Beau, discussing the details of the robbery, as Wynne approached. "I'm certainly glad to see you, Sheriff," she confessed, dropping her hatbox onto the ground beside him. "Do you think there's any possible way you can catch those thieves and return my money today?" She peered up at him hopefully while adjusting the precarious tilt of her hat and tucking up stray strands of hair which trailed over her dusty, damp face.

Tal had witnessed the whole performance of this young woman's getting off the stage and wondered about the obvious animosity between her and Cole. And that hat she was wearing! Eastern fashions were slow to get to the Midwest, and generally the ladies were interested in seeing the new styles; but he'd bet his last dollar not one of them would wear that bird's nest. "Well, I'll try my best, ma'am, but they've got a pretty good head start on me. One of my men's roundin' up a posse right now. We'll be on our way soon as they get here."

Wynne's shoulders slumped. "I'd hoped you'd know who they were."

Tal's heart immediately went out to her. "From the description Rutcliff gave me, sounds like it's the Beason gang. They been giving us a peck of trouble lately. If it is them, they'll head straight for the hills, and it'll be a mite hard to get to them," he said in a resigned voice.

"But you'll have to get to them," she replied. "They took every cent I have plus my jewelry. I haven't anything left except my clothes!"

"Sure sorry, ma'am. We'll do everything we can." His attention was diverted momentarily, and he stepped over to help one of the men lift the lifeless body of the guard off Cole's horse.

Wynne sank down dejectedly on her hatbox to think for a moment. The sun beat down unmercifully, and the dust hung in the air. Her dress stuck to her moist skin, and she fanned her heat-flushed face with her handkerchief as she tried to think. Without any money she didn't have the slightest idea what to do next. She'd been carrying every last cent she had left, but at best it would have been enough to see her only through a few months. By then she'd planned to have her revenge on Cass Claxton and be on her way home to try to sell the only asset she had left in this world: the land her family home had been built on.

Now she was stranded in a strange town, penniless, and without the vaguest idea of what to do next. Since her father's death the only family she could claim was a distant aunt in Arizona, and she didn't think her aunt would even remember her name, let alone wire money to her. She could get a job, but she wasn't trained for anything other than being a lady.

After spending the last few years at Marelda Fielding's Finishing School for Young Ladies in Philadelphia, she knew all the genteel manners and actions befitting a proper lady, but Miss Marelda had hardly prepared her to be sitting in the middle of the street on her hatbox, alone and flat broke.

Wynne fanned herself harder and forced down an almost hysterical giggle. Miss Prim and Proper Marelda Fielding would positively swoon if she could see the fine mess Wynne'd gotten herself into this time.

Cole and Beau were talking in undertones when

she glanced in their direction. Somehow she had the feeling they were discussing her situation, and it unnerved her.

"What are we going to do about her?" Beau asked worriedly.

"Penelope told me she's here to work at Hattie's," Cole said. "She didn't say, but I assume that's where the crazy one's headed too. So you can stop playing mother hen."

Beau's gaze studied Wynne's small, wilted form, and he felt disappointment as Cole's words registered. "Oh? I wouldn't have thought she'd be one of . . . those kind of women."

"Well, apparently she is, so let's just play it smart and move on." Cole resettled his hat and turned toward his horse. "If you want to spend time socializin' with her in the future, you can always ride back to town."

"The devil I can," Beau said, but he sounded awfully wistful to Cole. "Betsy would wring my neck."

The sheriff motioned to Cole as Beau strolled back over to where Wynne sat and knelt beside her. "I think we're just about through here. The sheriff will notify the families." He paused and surveyed her worried face. "Are you gonna be all right?"

Wynne sighed and plucked absently at the drawstrings of her purse. She was indeed in a pickle and needed someone to advise her on what she should do now. After debating the question, she had decided that this man seemed harmless, even though he had fought on the wrong side during the war.

"To be honest, Mr. . . ." She paused, searching for a name. There'd been no time for the pleasantries of exchanging names.

Remembering his manners, Beau swept off his hat gallantly. "You can just call me Beau, ma'am."

"Thank you, Beau. And my name's Wynne Elliot, but you may call me Wynne."

"Wynne. That's a right pretty name, ma'am."

"Thank you . . . Beau . . . but as I was saying, I'm afraid this robbery has left me in quite a quandary." Taking a deep breath, she shot him a timid smile.

"Oh?" Beau was instantly sympathetic. "Well, I know you must have been real scared, but you're safe now," he assured her.

"Oh, I'm not concerned for my safety," Wynne answered quickly. "It's just . . . well, they took all my money, and now I'm not quite sure what

I'm going to do." With tears precariously close to the surface, her drawl became more pronounced.

Wynne couldn't help noticing the abrupt way his gaze dropped from hers, almost as if he were suddenly embarrassed. "Oh, uh, why, I don't imagine you'll have to worry none about your keep." He consoled her rather weakly. "Hear tell Hattie takes right good care of her . . . girls."

Wynne stared at him vacantly. "Hattie?"

"Yeah . . . you know, Hattie Mason . . . she runs the local saloon and . . . well, you know, the lady who owns Hattie's Place—"

Suddenly what Beau was implying dawned on Wynne. "Hattie's Place!" She sprang to her feet indignantly as Beau's head snapped back.

He rose more slowly. "Well, yeah . . . Cole said he thought you and Miss Pettibone were headed for the same . . ." His voice trailed off meekly when two red flags of anger bloomed high on her cheeks.

"Oh, he did, did he?" She shot a scathing glance in the direction of the gossipy culprit. "Well, you can just tell *him* he'd better get his facts straight before he starts maligning my good character!" she snapped.

"Now, ma'am," Beau said, trying to pacify her hurriedly, "my brother didn't mean no harm. He just sort of assumed since you and Miss Pettibone were traveling together . . . you know, you two being such pretty women and all—"

She stamped her foot angrily. "Well, he assumed wrong!"

"Yes, ma'am. I'll tell him." Beau agreed quickly, suddenly realizing what a nice, even-tempered girl his Betsy was.

Shooting visual daggers at Cole, who was still talking to the sheriff and Penelope, Wynne snorted. "Hattie's Place! How dare he!" She stamped her foot in disgust, again raising a cloud of dust.

Cole glanced in Wynne's direction at the sound of her upraised voice, and she glared at him bitterly.

"Now, don't you be frettin' yourself none, ma'am." Beau hastened to change the subject. "Cole and me will be happy to take you to your folks, and in a few days the sheriff will find the men and return your money and then ever'thing will be all right again."

She was barely listening to his optimistic predictions as her angry gaze bore into the tall dark-haired man, who had returned to making idle conversation with Penelope in front of the saloon. She seriously doubted if Cole would be too thrilled about Beau's generosity.

Her temper continued to simmer when she noted the polite way he was treating Penelope. She couldn't help comparing his courteous manner toward the petite blonde with his arrogant manner toward her a few moments earlier. His gentility had taken wing when he had let her fall out of the coach on her fanny and make a complete fool of herself for the second time today!

"But you don't understand." She interrupted hastily as Beau tried to soothe her ruffled feathers. "I don't have any family out here."

Surprise flickered briefly in his eyes. "You don't?"

"No," Wynne said in confirmation. "In fact, I really don't have any family . . . anywhere."

"You're not from around here?" He knew he hadn't recognized her, but a lot of things had changed, he was sure, since he'd been away.

"No, Savannah is my home . . . or was until Papa died a few months ago."

"You're from Georgia?" Beau asked, surprised. "Well, what on earth is a young lady like you doing traveling out here all alone?"

"I'm . . . looking for someone," she said vaguely.

Beau looked relieved. "Good, at least there's someone. A lady friend?"

"Wellll . . ." Wynne shrugged her shoulders lamely. "Not really. I'm looking for a man. I heard his home was in River Run. Even though I know he's been off fighting the war, I understand he's coming back here now that it's over."

"Oh." A devilish light twinkled in Beau's eyes. "A beau, huh? Well, take heart, Miss Elliot. Me and Cole have lived in these parts all our lives, so we know just 'bout everyone around here. If he lives around here, no doubt we can help you find him."

Wynne's face lit up expectantly, her cares suddenly seeming much lighter. "Do you think so?"

"Why, sure!" Beau affirmed. "And as for you havin' no money, don't worry about that! We'll just take you home with us," he said. "Ma always has room for one more, and she'd be ashamed of us if she found out you was in trouble and we hadn't done our Christian duty."

"Oh, no. Really, I couldn't impose on you like that," Wynne protested.

"Impose!" Beau warmed to his idea. "We'd be right proud to have you come along with us. Soon as me and Cole get settled in, we'll start lookin' for your man." His face creased in one of his irresistible grins as he offered Wynne his arm. "Now I don't want to hear no more arguments. You're coming home with us."

He picked up Wynne's hatbox and escorted her to his horse, assuring her all the while that everything would work out. "You can ride with me," he said. "I'll get Cole to carry your bags."

Wynne wasn't at all sure she was doing the right thing, but she suddenly found herself being lifted up and placed firmly on the back of his horse.

Her relief wavering, she leaned over to catch Beau's arm. "Uh, Beau, don't you think you should check with your brother before you offer to let me go with you?" She could well imagine what *his* reaction was going to be to this latest piece of news.

Beau swung his large frame up behind her and grinned in encouragement. "Oh, don't fret none. He won't care. After being gone four years, all he wants to do is get home. He don't care who goes with him."

"I still don't think he'll be too happy about all this," she protested.

"He won't care," Beau insisted.

Beau nudged the horse's flanks gently and set them into motion. Seconds later they ambled up beside Cole and Penelope. Cole glanced up, and surprise flickered across his face when he saw Wynne mounted in front of Beau.

"You about ready to go?" Beau inquired pleasantly. "Wynne's coming home with us."

Wynne could have sworn Cole's mouth dropped open for a minute before he quickly recovered from his brother's casual announcement.

"I thought she was headed for Hattie's," Cole blurted.

"Well, it just so happens you thought wrong!" Wynne answered curtly. Then she proceeded to bestow on him one of her loveliest and snootiest smiles, one Miss Fielding would have been proud of. "Your brother has kindly offered the hospitality of your home until I can regain my money." She batted her eyes in obvious flirtation, just to see that look of irritation sweep across Cole's features. "Beau said you wouldn't mind carrying my valises." She crossed her hands over her breasts in mock admiration. "My, you're such a wonderful gentleman."

Cole glanced at Beau sharply, then back at Wynne with a grim set to his mouth. "If you ladies would excuse us for a minute, I'd like to have a word with Beau."

Beau obediently slid down off the horse and

handed the reins to Wynne with a knowing wink. "Be right back."

The two brothers walked around the corner of the building while Wynne said her good-byes to Penelope.

The minute the two men were out of sight, Cole grabbed Beau's arm and demanded, "What in the hell are you doing this time?"

"Hey, just calm down," Beau said cajolingly, glancing back over his shoulder worriedly to see if they could be heard. "I knew you wouldn't be too happy about this arrangement, but the poor girl's up a creek, Cole."

"I fail to see where that's our responsibility," Cole replied stubbornly. "Let Hattie take care of her!"

"She told you. She wasn't coming to work for Hattie," Beau said patiently. "Penelope is the only one going to work there."

"Then what is she doing out here all alone in the first place? Damned crazy woman—" He broke off in a grumbling voice.

"She's looking for some man."

Cole snorted. "God help him! Let's hope, for his sake, she doesn't find him."

"What have you got against her?" Beau asked.

"She hasn't said ten words to you, and you act like she's done something wrong."

"She's careless and a little addlebrained, don't you think?"

"No, I don't. So she doesn't know how to handle a gun very well. Lots of women don't. Betsy and Priscilla don't—"

"I don't want to hear any more about Priscilla! Okay?"

"Okay, okay. But you can't hold not being able to handle a gun well against Wynne," he pointed out. "For the life of me, I can't understand why you're so dead set against helping her. You're usually a little more gentlemanly when it comes to women," Beau added. "Ma would be ashamed of you."

"I think you're asking for trouble," Cole argued. "I think we'd better turn her over to Tal and be on our way."

"I can't do that."

"You can't do that," Cole repeated in exasperation. "Why can't you do that? It means nothing to us one way or the other. We stumbled on a robbery! We didn't take her to raise!"

"I know, but somehow I sort of feel responsible for her, Cole. Don't ask me to explain. I'm gonna take her home to Ma for now, and then I'm gonna help her find the man she's looking for," he stated flatly. "All I'm asking you to do is carry her valises on your horse. Now, is that askin' too much?"

"Yes, it is, and you're a fool," Cole grumbled, pulling his hat off and wiping his forearm across his forehead.

"Maybe so, but that's the way I'm gonna do it. Now, are you gonna carry her bags, or am I gonna have to make another trip back into town to get them?"

Cole raked his fingers through his dark hair in annoyance. "I don't know why I let you talk me into these things," he muttered. "She's only gonna be trouble for us. You mark my words."

"I'm marking as long as you're carrying her bags." Beau grinned and slapped him on the back good-naturedly as they walked back around the corner.

"I'll tell Tal she'll be out at our place if he needs her," Beau announced. "I won't be but a minute."

Cole grunted an answer and went over to pick up the two bags sitting on the ground in front of the stage. After hefting them up onto his shoulders, he went back to his horse and started tying them on.

Wynne sat on Beau's horse and watched him work, noting he did so with very little enthusiasm.

She fanned herself energetically, trying to lessen the growing heat and distract the flies that were buzzing around her head. She almost envied Penelope, who had disappeared into the cool interior of Hattie's Place. Almost envied her, but not quite.

Even though this Cole had not made the slightest effort to be pleasant from the moment they met, Wynne decided as she got off the horse that she should at least introduce herself if she was going to be spending the next few days in his company.

"Excuse me," she said.

Cole glanced up, and once more she unwillingly noted how very strikingly blue his eyes were. Against the deep tan of his skin they looked as blue as a cloudless sky on a bright summer day. And he was handsome, Wynne had to admit. Devilishly handsome—although he had the temperament of an old goat.

Strange, but she suddenly had the nagging feeling again that she had met him before. There was something about him that jarred her memory, yet she couldn't quite put her finger on what it was. Before she could pursue the puzzling thought, Cole returned his attention to his work, totally dismissing her.

Wynne cleared her throat and tried again,

thinking perhaps he'd not heard her the first time and had glanced up only accidentally. "Uh, sir?"

This time he stared at her, and Wynne smiled back timidly.

"Are you talkin' to me?" he asked curtly.

Her smile faded. "Well, of course, I'm talking to you," she stated. "Who did you think I was talking to? The horse?"

"It wouldn't surprise me none." He went about his work, making no effort whatsoever to continue the strained conversation.

Swallowing her exasperation, Wynne tried again. "I, uh, I thought since we would be in each other's company for the next few days, we should introduce ourselves."

He grunted something unintelligible again.

"Uh, I'm Wynne Elliot." She extended her hand.

"And I'm Pompous Ass," he replied evenly, cinching the rope around her bags tighter and ignoring her hand.

A flush of embarrassment rose from her collar, and her gaze slid away in embarrassment. "Oh, my, I didn't know you heard that."

"I heard," he said tersely.

"Well, I must apologize—is it Cole?"

He shot her another irritable look and continued his task.

"I suppose this whole ordeal has unnerved me, and I have completely forgotten my manners." Once again she extended her hand toward him in a friendly gesture, forgetting that it was covered in dirt from her fall out of the stage earlier. "My name is Wynne Elliot, but you may call me *Miss* Elliot." She was going to give only so much until he showed a greater interest in being civil.

Cole stared at her slightly grubby hand and, after a moment of hesitation, gingerly accepted it. "*Miss* Elliot." He bowed mockingly. "I wish I could say it was an honor to make your acquaintance," he said dryly.

She ignored his continuing despicable manners. "I'm . . . sorry about calling you a pompous ass."

"And I'm sorry I called you . . . what I did," he said generously.

Her forehead wrinkled in a frown. "What did you call me?"

" 'Addlebrain' and 'careless' are the two that come to mind right off," he confessed with a grin playing about his lips.

Her frown deepened. "Addlebrained! You called me addlebrained!" She jerked her hand out of his. "I suppose you think I'm addlebrained just because I dropped the gun and tripped over it!"

"No, I think it was because you fell out of the

stage," he said blandly, controlling the grin with some effort. "Then I added 'careless.'"

He watched with amusement as she shook her head angrily, causing her hat to slip down over her nose. She shoved it back on her head impatiently, and the bird rocked precariously in its nest.

"Well, I can assure you I am *not* careless or addlebrained," Wynne sputtered. "You just happened to catch me at a bad moment!"

"If you say so . . . Miss Elliot." Cole picked up the reins of his horse and swung into the saddle as Beau came out of the sheriff's office.

"I'll follow you," Cole called as Beau, holding his horse's reins, walked up behind Wynne. "Let's try to make it home for supper."

"Sounds like heaven to me!" Beau whistled as he helped Wynne up onto the horse and lifted himself up behind her. He gave a loud rebel yell as he kicked his horse into action.

Wynne shot one more cross look in Cole's direction, then held on for life as the trio rode out of town in a cloud of dust.

Addlebrained indeed!

Chapter 3

Funny how life held such strange twists and turns. Not so very long ago the only thing Wynne Elliot had to worry about was the color of her next ball gown.

As she bounced along on Beau's horse, she thought about how wonderful life had been back home in Georgia before both Mama and Papa had passed away. She had been an only child, raised in an affluent home by doting parents. Moss Oak had been one of the biggest cotton plantations in the South before the war broke out. The plantation had been in the family for generations, and her father, Wesley Elliot, had run it as he had run his family, with a firm but loving hand.

Then the war had come, and Papa had sent her away to school. For a while she could ignore the rumors of the terrible atrocities going on and con-

centrate solely on learning the fine art of being a
lady, which Papa thought she sorely needed. She
was a little too independent for his liking. Since
she'd followed him about the plantation from
when she was a child, she'd picked up a few habits
he disapproved of—like his penchant for swearing.

But all too soon her idealistic bubble burst, and
she was faced with the harsher realities of life.
Mama had taken ill with a strange sickness, and
Papa had brought Wynne back home to comfort
her.

With a feeling of complete helplessness, Wynne
and her father had stood by and watched as each
week Rose Elliot struggled to overcome the devils
that were ravaging her body. There was nothing
anyone could seem to do to still the nausea and the
swift weight loss that beset her. Then came the
terrible pain. Wynne was still tormented by the
sound of her mother's soft sobbing in the night and
her father's agonized voice trying to ease her torment and contain his own. Weeks seemed like
years then.

At times Wynne would spend hours praying that
the good Lord would relieve the suffering and
take away the agony they all were experiencing.
How she longed to hear laughter and the sound of

gaiety rumbling through the old mansion once more instead of the hushed whispers of the servants and the almost tangible smell of death. At other times she would cast away her own selfish feelings and cry out for someone, anyone, to give her mother peace.

When the end came, Rose Elliot simply went to sleep and never woke up.

If Wynne had thought her mother's sickness was heartbreaking, it was nothing compared with her father's grieving his life away after her mother's death. He roamed the halls at night in search of something that Wynne never quite understood. Her heart broke even more when she passed his study late in the evening and heard the tortured weeping of a man who had suffered an unbearable loss, one he could not seem to cope with. The day Rose died, she took the biggest part of Wesley with her. Left behind was the lonely shell of a man merely serving out his time on earth until they could be together once more.

It was then that Cass came into Wynne's life. He was a gentle, loving man who helped her through that terrible time with his sunny disposition, quick wit, and unusual charm.

She'd met him through a mutual friend at a Christmas ball. When she questioned why he hadn't enlisted in the southern cause, Cass had explained that since he had family obligations, he had paid someone to take his place. While it bothered her that he had paid the $400 for another man to fight on his behalf, she conceded that it was customary practice for men of means to do so.

And undoubtedly Cass came from an affluent and prosperous family. At the time he was in Savannah, visiting relatives, prominent, wealthy pillars of the community, and Wynne had been so totally captivated by his impeccable manners and his courtly ways that all else faded from her mind.

It was such a rare treat for the belles of Georgia to have such a fascinating, eligible young man in their midst that Wynne simply forgot about the war and let her heart be won by the dashing young man whose pretty words dripped off his tongue like rich, warm honey—lying, deceitful words that she still didn't believe she had actually been gullible enough to believe!

A scant six weeks after Rose's death Wesley chose to join her. Wynne had heard the shot ring out as she lay in her bed that fateful night. For months she had heard the reverberation over and over again. . . .

She was left totally alone and more frightened than she had ever been in her life.

The Yankees came through and burned Moss Oak and all the surrounding buildings. Mercifully they had left the main house standing, but they had ransacked and stolen all the furnishings as Wynne and the servants had stood by and surveyed the devastation in stunned silence.

The loyal family servants had stayed on, erecting makeshift housing to live in so they could work the land for her, but it was hopeless. The fields were charred and desolate, and it would be a long time before cotton would blossom there again.

"Are you comfortable?" Beau's voice broke into her painful thoughts and brought her quickly back to the present.

Immersed in her sad memories, Wynne had almost forgotten her uncomfortable perch in a saddle too large for her and the closeness of the man riding behind her. She plucked at the material of her dress, attempting to allow some air to circulate against her skin. The sun was a ball of fire in the sky, making her nearly limp with heat, and she was anything but comfortable; but considering how kind Beau had been, she decided it would be ungrateful on her part to complain.

"I'm fine, thank you." She shifted slightly, increasingly aware of the pressure of Beau's arms around her as he held the reins. Surely it couldn't be much farther. "Are we almost there?"

"Just another three miles or so," he answered. "We can stop and let you rest a spell if you'd like."

"No, that's all right. I'll be fine."

She was most appreciative of what this man was doing for her. Not all men would have taken her under their wing the way he had.

She turned her head slightly, her eyes fastening on the rider trailing a safe distance behind them. He certainly would have left her for the buzzards.

Her mind unwillingly brought Cass, another tall, handsome devil, to the surface once more, and the picture set her to seething all over again.

The only good thing Cass Claxton had done for her was to be there for her to lean on during the most tragic time of her life. And in all honesty he had never failed her once back then. He helped her face reality, always there for her when she swore she couldn't, wiping at her tears and telling her that she could. For a young man of twenty-two, he readily admitted he didn't know all the answers, but together they would find them.

Then one day Cass was offered an opportunity to go into business with one of his cousins. They wanted to buy a business that manufactured gunpowder, and Wynne was ecstatic. It meant Cass would be staying in Savannah.

She immediately began dropping hints of marriage, seeing that as a way of salvaging her broken life. In further enticement she offered the money from her inheritance as bait for such a venture, and it wasn't long before she was able to persuade Cass to accept her generosity. The night before they were to be married, Wynne gave him all her money—with the exception of a meager amount she kept in a small tin box under her bed—assuming his business venture would be concluded early the following morning.

Looking back, she wondered if Cass ever really loved her or if he had asked for her hand in marriage simply to appease a girl for whom nothing in life had gone well lately. Certainly his family could have lent him the money to go into business, but instead, he had asked Wynne to marry him.

A shiver of embarrassment rippled through her as she recalled her wedding day. It had dawned cold and gray with the promise of rain in the air. Tilly, her mammy since childhood, had lovingly dressed Wynne for the ceremony, fretting over her like a mother hen.

Wynne had smiled and glanced at herself in the large looking glass she was standing before. The soft, delicate folds of her mother's ivory wedding gown billowed out around her and swept to the floor. Her eyes grew misty as she stared back at the reflection that could have been Rose's nineteen years ago.

"Do you think Mama and Papa would have approved of what I'm doin', Tilly?" she had asked softly.

Tilly had heaved a big sigh and patted her shoulder reassuringly. "You got to do what you think best, baby." Seeing that Wynne's face still held worry, she added tenderly, "I'm sure your man will be real good to you, darlin'."

And she was right. Cass probably would have been good to her—if he had made it to the wedding.

The pain and humiliation still stung sharply as she thought about how she and the guests had waited at the church for him to arrive that day. They had waited and waited and waited. . . .

The very next morning Wynne had returned to Marelda Fielding's Finishing School, a feeble effort on her part to put her life back to what it once was.

But never again had she found the carefree life she had known. The death of her parents, the war, and Cass's rejection—all had taken their toll. And it seemed to her she just had to take some sort of revenge.

Slowly a plan—a very simple plan to avenge her pride and uphold the Elliot name—began to take root. She would find Cass Claxton and kill him for what he had done to her. Not only had he stolen her blind, but he had made her the laughingstock of Savannah in the process! Surely such parody could not go unpunished.

Wynne jerked her thoughts back to the present, assuring herself that Cass Claxton had not seen the last of her. She would find him if it was the last thing she did, and before she killed him, she would demand an explanation for his despicable behavior.

Squinting against the glaring sun, she turned her attention back to the man riding behind them, trying to make out his dusty features beneath the dark beard. It was either her vivid imagination, or else *he* even *looked* like Cass. No, that couldn't be. They only looked alike because she had been thinking about her former fiancé, she thought as she fanned herself rapidly.

But her imagination wasn't playing tricks on her. Now she realized why she had thought she'd met him before. Both men had similar characteristics. Cass had the same blue eyes and curly black hair as Cole. Unwillingly she found herself leaning back in the saddle, peering more closely at the trailing brother. Even the set of Cass's chin suggested the same stubborn streak she now saw in Cole's. Her eyes skimmed down his face and paused at the opening of his uniform. Thick wisps of the same dark hair on his head peeped out of the opening of his shirt, and her pulse quickened.

Powerful and ruggedly virile, Cole sat his saddle with the same aura of authority that Cass had, and for a moment Wynne found her heart thumping at the remembrance of being pressed against the broad expanse of a chest much like the one she was now practically ogling.

Her eyes narrowed speculatively. *I wonder what* he *would look like with his shirt off. . . .* She caught herself shamefully. Whatever made her think a thing like that?

She wasn't quite sure what made her gaze lift suddenly; but it did, and she found herself staring into a set of mocking blue eyes that held ill-concealed amusement at her disgraceful surveillance of him. Her face flooded with color, and she hurriedly snapped her head around to face the other direction.

That moron! She could practically feel his arrogant eyes boring a hole in the back of her head, but she refused to give him the satisfaction of looking at him again.

She was sure her face was bright red as she thought of what Cole must be thinking!

"Did you say something?" Beau called.

"No, nothing!"

For the remainder of the ride she carefully kept her eyes straight ahead and her thoughts a complete blank. When the two riders finally turned into a winding lane and let their horses have their head, Wynne breathed a great sigh of relief.

The horses thundered down the lane as Cole and Beau grinned at each other mischievously and reverted to their childhood days, when they would try to outrace each other home. Wynne held on as tightly as she could, fearing they both had taken leave of their senses.

With a burst of speed, Cole's horse shot by them and raced the remaining half mile to the farmyard. With a whoop of sheer joy, he sprang out of his saddle before the horse had even stopped and enfolded in his arms the woman who had just run out the door to see what all the excitement was about. Lifting her high above his head, he swung her around and around, his face breaking out in a wreath of smiles. "Hi, Ma! I'm home!"

"Cole!" Tears of relief filled the woman's eyes as

her laughter joined his, his words of greeting re-sounding through the air. How long she had yearned to hear those words again.

Her eyes searched her son's face, looking for signs of the young man who had left home four years ago. She found none. The familiar features greeted her, but she could see he had grown much older in the time he had been gone and she couldn't help noticing the age lines gathering around the corners of his eyes. He looked so much like Sam it was all she could do to remember this was her firstborn, not her deceased husband, who stood before her.

"Beau? Have you heard from Beau?" she questioned.

"Beau's with me, Ma." Almost before the words had left his mouth, Beau and Wynne came riding into the yard.

There was a second round of shouting and laughter as Beau tumbled off the horse and wrapped his mother in his arms. With two burly men as sons, Lilly didn't have a chance to stand on her own two feet. Beau tossed her up into the air and nearly broke her bones as he caught her back in his arms and hugged her tightly. He then gently set her on her feet.

"Beau and Cole! Back home in the same day.

Praise the Lord!" The tears in her eyes spilled over as she reached over to clasp her arms around Cole's neck and hug him tightly.

"It's so good to be home, Ma," he confessed in a husky, emotion-filled whisper.

"And your brother . . . have you seen or heard from him?" Her eyes pleaded for the answer she longed to hear.

Cole met her question with surprise. "No, isn't he here with you?"

"No—no, I got a letter a few months ago. Said he had joined up—"

"Damn!" Cole said irritably. "I thought he was gonna stay here and help you!"

Wiping at the corners of her eyes with her faded apron, she tried to defend her youngest son. "I know, but you know he always had a wanderin' streak in him . . . just like your pa."

"Well, don't worry, Ma. Now that the war's over, he'll be ridin' in any day." Cole tried to console his mother, but Wynne noticed his face was unusually solemn.

Lilly's arms went back around her boys' shoulders, and she hugged them simultaneously again. "Well, I thank the Lord you're here. I can't believe you're both home at the same time. When we heard the war was over, we started looking for you

82

to come home, but since we hadn't heard anything from either one of you in so long, we didn't know what to expect."

Beau and Cole hung their heads sheepishly. "I would have wrote, Ma," Beau said apologetically, "but I figured I'd probably get here before the letter did."

"And what's your excuse?" Lilly put her hands on her hips and turned on Cole those accusing eyes that only a mother can conjure.

"Ah, Ma . . . you know me. I never was good at writing letters." Cole grinned with a lame shrug.

For the first time since all the excitement had broken out, Lilly glanced up at Wynne and smiled. "Land sakes! All this excitement, and we plumb forgot our manners. Who have you brought home with you?"

"Ma, this is Wynne Elliot." Beau walked over and lifted Wynne off his horse and set her down on the ground. "She was on the stage to River Run when it was robbed. They took all her money, and since she don't have no kin around here, we brought her home to stay with us for a few days."

"Robbed! Why, that must have been real frightenin'." Lilly reached out and pumped Wynne's hand warmly. "I'm glad Beau brought you home. You're welcome to stay as long as you like."

"Thank you," Wynne murmured gratefully. "I should be able to move on in a few days." She purposely avoided meeting Cole's eyes. "The sheriff is out looking for the bandits right now."

"Well, don't you fret yourself none. Tal will find them if anyone can. He's a good man. Now, come along, and let's all go in the house," Lilly suggested, wrapping her arms around her sons' waists and giving them another motherly squeeze. "It just so happens Willa and me have a big pot of them chicken and dumplin's you're so fond of simmerin' on the stove. Course, you're not either one goin' to sit at my table till you shave and wash some of that road grime off you." She tugged affectionately at Cole's beard.

Beau's face lit up happily. "No kiddin', Ma? You really got some chicken and dumplin's! I was just tellin' Cole this morning how I hoped you'd have some."

"Luck!" Lilly scoffed, hugging him tighter. "Why, we've had a pot of them chicken and dumplin's on the stove since the day we heard the war was over. We've just been a prayin' and waitin' for you two to come home and eat 'em!"

As suddenly as it appeared, the laughter drained out of her voice, and her eyes grew misty. "I guess I'm just gonna have to stay down on my knees an extra long time tonight and thank the good Lord he seen fit to send you back to me." A tear suddenly slipped through her veil of happiness as she grinned and pinched Cole's cheek once more. "It's good to have you back, boys."

Cole looked down at his mother and said in the most heartfelt voice Wynne had ever heard, "Thanks, Ma. It's sure good to be here."

Chapter 4

Lord a'mighty, it was hot! he thought as he mopped his forehead again with a lank handkerchief. The blazing late-afternoon sun beat down on the lone rider without mercy as he entered the hot, parched streets of Springfield.

Bertram G. Mallory reached up and took another swipe at his dusty brow as he cast his eyes upward for some sign of rain, but there was none in sight. Only the endless blue of a summer sky met his gaze as his weary horse plodded along. It had been more than three months since it had rained in these parts, he'd heard. Too long. The countryside was brown and scorched, and the man's patience was wearing thin—not only with the weather but with Wynne Elliot.

Every time he got near the damn woman, she somehow managed to slip through his fingers. But she wouldn't do it again. He ran a long, lean hand over his dirty face. No, sir, he'd make sure of that this time.

He reined in the horse, with a low, painful groan slid out of the saddle, and hitched the animal to the rail. His hand automatically went to shield his still-tender left side. The result of the untimely accident he'd experienced a few weeks ago was still sensitive to the touch, not to mention the thought.

Bertram's eyes narrowed as he recalled the harrowing incident that had left him with three busted ribs and a splitting headache for days.

At the time it had seemed like a good idea to hop that train. After all, when he'd heard that Miss Elliot was reportedly attending a finishing school for ladies back east, he had been riding for days and been bone-tired. He would have tried anything to make the trip shorter.

But when he'd finally arrived at Marelda Fielding's Finishing School for Young Ladies in Philadelphia, he'd been told by Miss Fielding that Wynne wasn't there. Apparently the Elliot woman had decided to pay a visit to Missouri. River Run, Miss Fielding had said. Well, he knew right then that meant a peck of trouble unless he could get to her before she got there.

River Run was a good several weeks' travel from Philadelphia by stage, but not by train. Since it was imperative that he catch up with her as soon as possible, and with the least amount of discomfort on his part, he decided to hop the first train going south and hoped it would carry him to within a reasonable distance of Missouri.

With a sense of elation he'd quickly sold his horse and pocketed the money. He figured when he arrived in Missouri by train, several days ahead of her, relaxed and completely rested, he would buy another horse while he waited for Wynne Elliot's arrival. At the time he'd grinned smugly.

It was a good plan, he decided. And there was no need to waste his money on a ticket. He'd simply wait until the train passed under a big bluff and then jump on the top of the car and ride there until the conductor collected the fares. Then he would casually blend himself in with the other passengers and enjoy the ride.

He flinched as he again felt the sharp, excruciating pain ripping through his side. It would have worked, too, if his timing hadn't been a fraction off and if the train had run as far as Missouri.

He'd jumped just as he'd planned. He'd hit the top of the rail car with the speed of a bullet, but the train had been traveling faster than he'd calculated. Not much—but just enough to throw off his rapid descent.

The jolt splattered him painfully into a spread-eagle position flat against the top of the fast-moving train. Then his eyes had widened as he frantically clutched for some sort of a hold and the train shot around a bend in the track. Even now Bertram could almost feel all over again the terror he had felt as his fingers began to slip and he'd realized he and the train would soon be parting company. Even his toes had dug in for support. At the deepest bend of the curve he lost his grip. He was ruthlessly flung off the side of the car, and his life had flashed before his eyes as he'd been hurled through the air. His poor body was flung like a rag doll to the ground, where he rolled for what must have been fifteen minutes down a deep, briar-blanketed ravine.

When he regained consciousness, there had been an old prospector bending over him. It was dark by then, and he was certain every bone had been broken in his throbbing body. Bertram winced again as he recalled the agonizing ride to town, slung over the back of the old man's donkey. The prospector left him with the doctor and, after waving off Bertram's gratitude, disappeared out the front door.

But to Bertram's amazement not quite every bone had been broken. He'd come out of the harrowing brush with death with only three cracked ribs and a cracked head, but they had been enough to lay him up at the local hotel for several weeks.

To add to his embarrassment, he'd found out that all the pain and inconvenience had been for naught.

The train had gone only twenty miles down the road before service ended. How was he to know that? Because of the difficulty merchants were experiencing throughout the country trying to get their goods overland by wagon, not to mention the financial loss of trying to cope with losing their animals to injury as the result of the terrible road conditions in most states, almost every town had railroad fever. Tracks were springing up all over the country, and the city fathers were crying for rail service. He'd been certain he could get to Missouri with no problem. . . .

The unexpected hotel expenses, having food brought in, and doctor's fees had taken the meager amount of money he'd brought with him, so he was faced with yet another costly delay while he found a job. He worked long enough to buy another horse, and then once more he set off in pursuit of the elusive Miss Elliot.

To begin his search anew, he'd been forced to go back to Miss Fielding's Finishing School for Young Ladies, hoping that by now she might have returned. He'd listened with a sinking knot in the pit of his stomach as Miss Fielding told him she had not seen Wynne since he had last been there and she assumed Wynne was still visiting in Missouri.

Bertram had sagged against the long white column on the porch as the door closed and fought the overwhelming feeling of yet another failure. He could smell the roses that were twining up the columns in a red blaze of color, and drifting tantalizingly through the air was the mouth-watering smell of someone baking corn bread.

He wondered again why he didn't just give up and go back home to Savannah. It would certainly be the sensible thing to do. But he knew he wouldn't give up. Bertram released a long sigh and pushed himself away from the column. He'd give anything for a bath, a shave, and a soft bed to sleep in tonight. And a woman to keep him company. That would be nice. A soft woman to hold in his arms and ease his aches and pains.

But he had given his word, and Bertram G. Mallory was a man to whom a promise meant something. He would go to any lengths to fulfill an obligation. But by the good Lord, this one was almost more than he could cope with. Yet a promise was a promise. And his promise was to find Wynne Elliot, no matter how long it took.

Wearily Bertram pulled himself back into the saddle, and once more he pushed himself and his horse hard. By his calculations he knew, now that he was in Springfield, his mission was finally nearing an end. And none too soon. He winced painfully as his hand went to shield his side again. River Run was just down the road apiece. By late tomorrow afternoon, he hoped he and Miss Elliot would meet face-to-face.

But tonight he'd rest a spell. He sure wished he had the money to find a good, clean hotel and have the bath, the shave, the hot meal, and maybe even the woman he had been longing for. But he knew that was foolish wishing. He certainly didn't have the funds for that sort of luxury. No, he'd settle for a cold beer or two, then camp somewhere on the outskirts of town for the night.

Bertram glanced around him, surprised to see so much activity on the streets at this hour. Pulling a watch from a side pocket, he noted it was getting close to 6:00 P.M. Most folks would be home taking supper about now. He rewound the stem, then carefully placed the watch back in his pocket.

He was right proud of that watch. His grandfather had given it to him many years ago, and even through the thick of battle he'd managed to hold on to it.

These big towns must have a faster way of life, he decided as his gaze lingered momentarily on a group of ragged-looking women who were standing next to the livery.

Although it wasn't unusual to see hundreds of Confederate female refugees swarming about the towns, looking for food and shelter, it still worried him. They were a destitute, heart-wrenching sight, and he didn't like to think about their being so alone. Women should be taken care of, pampered and held gently. It always saddened him to see those women. After what he'd experienced during the war, he'd have thought he would have become accustomed to the poverty and degradation that had been brought upon the people, but he hadn't. He guessed he never would. He had fought for only a few weeks, then been wounded and sent back to Savannah. But it was all he'd wanted of the killing.

Picking up the reins of his horse, he threaded his way along the fringes of the crowd that milled about, talking in low tones. They all seemed to be waiting for something. He wondered if one of those medicine shows might be coming to town.

Suddenly the hushed murmurs stilled. Everyone stood quietly waiting. His puzzled gaze studied the small crowds gathering in the doorways and alleys surrounding the square, and his brow furrowed with interest.

As far as he could tell, there was nothing unusual happening, yet the crowd seemed apprehensive and watchful.

He threw the reins over the nearest hitching post and stepped up onto the porch of the general store, where he spoke to one of the old-timers leaning back in a chair, whittling on a piece of wood. "Howdy."

The old-timer's knife paused as he glanced up at the newcomer and gave him a friendly grin. He had a battered old hat on his head and a snow-white beard that was stained with tobacco juice, and from what Bertram could tell, he didn't have a single tooth left in his head. "Howdy," he answered, then leaned over the rail and spit a long stream of brown liquid into the dust.

Bertram stepped back out of the line of fire, then pushed his hat back on his head before he hunched down beside the man's chair. "Hot, ain't it?"

"Sure is."

"Could use some rain."

"Yep." The old-timer leaned over and spit again. "It'll rain soon, though. Saw a black snake in a tree this mornin'." He spit once more and wiped at his mouth with the sleeve of his shirt. "Hit's a sure sign rain's on the way."

"Yeah. Sure is." A black snake in a tree was about as accurate prediction of rain as Bertram could think of, with the exception of birds flying low or walking on the ground. They always meant rain, and he was grateful for any small sign the drought would soon be over.

"You're a stranger to these parts, ain't you, boy?"

"Just passin' through."

"Humph." The old man grunted, then leaned over and spit again.

Bertram surveyed the scene in the square. "What's going on out there?" He nodded his head toward the people still gathering on the street, his curiosity aroused once more.

"Gonna be a shootin'," the old man stated calmly, his gnarled hands gently rubbing the piece of carving he was working on.

Bertram wasn't sure he'd heard right. "A shootin'?"

"Yep."

Once more his worried gaze sought the milling crowd. "Who's gonna be doing it?"

The old-timer looked up and gave him his toothless grin again. "You ever heared of Wild Bill Hickock, boy?"

Bertram blinked in surprise. "Hasn't everyone?" It was a well-known fact that Wild Bill's reputation and skill with a gun had made him the constable of Monticello Township, Illinois, when he was still a teenager. Rumor had it that he had been working as a Union sharpshooter and scout during the past few years, and Bertram had even heard speculation that Wild Bill had been a spy for the Union, posing as a Confederate throughout southern Missouri and Arkansas.

"Well, Wild Bill's gonna git his watch back today," the old-timer announced gleefully.

Bertram frowned. "Someone took his watch?" He let out a low whistle under his breath. That sounded mighty daring to him. Most men gave Wild Bill a wide berth when they met him. He couldn't imagine anyone being foolish enough to steal the man's watch.

"I guess you could say that. Him and Tutt ain't

exactly the best of friends. They've had hard feelin's over Savannah Moore, a woman they both had a hankerin' for, but that's not what they're fightin' about."

"Oh?"

"Nope, they ain't fightin' over her this time. They were aplayin' cards the other day, and after Hickok had won most of Dave's money, Dave reminded him of the thirty-five dollars Wild Bill still owed him from another time when they had been aplayin'. Well, Wild Bill said he owed him only twenty-five dollars, and he laid it on the table in front of Tutt."

The old man warmed to his subject, his fingers fondling the piece of carving as he ran the sharp knife blade over the soft wood. "Now Tutt took his money all right, but he also took Wild Bill's gold watch that was alayin' there, saying that he figured that would about make up for the other ten Wild Bill owed him."

Bertram was completely engrossed in the story the old-timer was telling. Having heard of Wild Bill's reputation, he'd have sworn that Tutt would have been a dead man before he could have gotten the watch in his pocket. "And Wild Bill let him have the watch?"

"Oh, I wouldn't say that exactly. Bill jumped up

and told Tutt to put the watch back down on the table. But Dave jest ignored him and left with the watch anyway. Th' air's been real thick betwix the two ever since."

"And that's what's the shootin's gonna be about?"

"Yep. Wild Bill warned Tutt not to wear the watch in public, but he paid Bill no heed. He went ahead and wore it anyway. We knowed somethin' was bound to happen, and sure enough, it has."

A stream of tobacco flew across the porch and raised dust beside the walk. "Some of Tutt's men sent word to Wild Bill that Dave would be acrossin' the square around six o'clock tonight if he wanted to try and get his watch back. Hickok sent word back that Dave couldn't be carryin' his watch across the square unless dead men had started walkin'."

Bertram fumbled in his pocket and hastily withdrew his own watch, noting with dismay that the appointed hour was upon them. "It's six o'clock right now. Why, Dave Tutt's a fool for tauntin' Hickok like that. He'll kill him for sure."

The old man leaned over and spit once more. "Maybe, maybe not. Dave Tutt ain't 'zactly shabby with a gun hisself. But there's one thing for certain. All hell's agonna break loose in a minute."

If there was one thing Bertram had no desire for, it was to become remotely entangled in a shoot-out on a public street with two known gunslingers. Even watching the spectacle held no interest for him. "Well, I think I'll just mosey on—" His words were interrupted as a breathless hush fell over the crowd.

Up the street to one side a bearded man stepped into view of the crowd. About the same time another man with shoulder-length dark hair and a long brush of mustache appeared on the opposite side. The flat-crowned hat, black coat, and tucked shirt identified the second man as Wild Bill Hickok.

"You'd better stay on that side of the square if you want to live, Tutt," Hickok warned.

Bertram could do nothing but watch now as Tutt made no effort whatsoever to reply. Bertram held his breath, watching the men as if he were watching a play. Except it wasn't one. One of these men would be dead in a few minutes.

But Dave Tutt didn't dally. He merely stepped out into the street, drawing his gun as he went. As he drew, so did Hickok, and both men fired at the same time.

The bullet from Hickok's gun went straight

through Dave Tutt's heart, and he fell dead in a crumpled heap in the dusty street.

Hickok quickly whirled around and pointed his gun in the direction of Tutt's friends, who by then had drawn their own guns. "Put your arms up, men, or there'll be more than one man dead here today."

Bertram had seen enough. As if Hickok's words had freed his paralyzed body, he spun and started for cover. But as luck would have it, his foot caught on a loose board. As if a hand had come out of the sidewalk and grabbed his ankle, he was jerked to a sudden halt. The momentum was such that Bertram reeled off the porch into the street. He landed with a thud beneath the watering trough, his ankle throbbing with excruciating pain. He swallowed a painful moan, and his eyes squinted shut with agony.

The old-timer jumped up from his chair on the porch and peered over the trough. On the square Tutt's men slowly holstered their weapons and melted into the crowd.

With one final glance around him Wild Bill calmly walked over to Tutt's body and recovered his gold Waltham watch and chain, then turned and walked to the courthouse to surrender his pistols to the sheriff.

"Here, boy. Let me help ya. Are you bad hurt?" The old man rolled Bertram over onto his back.

Bertram groaned and held on tightly to his rapidly swelling ankle. If he didn't get that boot off soon, he knew he'd have to cut it off, and he couldn't afford another pair of boots.

"I think I busted my damn ankle." Bertram gritted the words out. The pain was a searing heat, and he was having trouble breathing, let alone talking.

The old man squatted beside him and gingerly rotated Bertram's foot.

"Aaagh!" Bertram screamed.

"I believe you're right," the old-timer said. He motioned for some of his cronies still sitting on the porch, whittling, to lend a helping hand. "We'll have to git you over to Doc Pierson's and let him have a look-see."

"Damn! Damn! Double damn!" Bertram railed. A broken ankle! That was all he needed now to lay him up again for another who knew how many weeks!

He was still cursing a blue streak as four elderly men gathered around him. They seemed hardly strong enough to support their own weight, let alone budge him, but each one dutifully scooped up an arm or a leg. He bit down as they unceremoniously hauled him across the street to the doctor's office like a wilted sack of flour and folded him onto the doc's operating table.

"Take care o' my horse," Bertram shouted as the old men melted back out the doorway.

"Sure will. He'll be at th' livery," his one new friend assured him.

Bertram groaned again. Now a livery bill! What else?

The doctor leaned over him. "Now, son, let's see what's happened here."

A firm hand clasped his boot as Bertram closed his eyes in renewed agony and prayed to pass out.

Chapter 5

"Yes, the war's over, but there's still men out there in the bushes who don't know that yet." Cole glanced up and smiled at his mother, who had just cut him another thick slice of gooseberry pie. "Lord, Ma, you're going to have me so big I can't get back on my horse," he complained good-naturedly, but Wynne noticed he had no trouble polishing off the second serving of dessert.

"You're as thin as a shitepoke," Lilly said, then quickly turned to slip another piece of pie onto Wynne's plate before she could stop her.

Wynne eyed the man sitting at the table across from her, and the thought that she wouldn't describe him as thin skipped through her mind. He was powerfully built, with broad shoulders and an expansive chest beneath the blue chambray shirt he was wearing this evening. Now that he was freshly bathed and cleanly shaved, Wynne had to admit he was quite a handsome man. It was only his deplorable disposition that spoiled everything.

"Thank you, Lilly, but I really couldn't eat another bite," Wynne protested. For two days she had sat at the dinner table and nearly burst. Willa's meals had been large and plentiful. She was surprised at such an abundance of food on the table each day, especially when it seemed every other homestead she had passed while riding the stage seemed to be in a depressing state of shortage of even the barest essentials.

She had been surprised by the house too. True, whitewash and repairs were needed, but it reflected an affluent life-style she'd not expected to find. The house was quite large with the parlor and family rooms on the main floor and the upstairs five bedrooms, each furnished with a double bed, clothespress, nightstand, and full-length mirror, again much like her own at Moss Oak.

There was also a gentility present, almost a southern flavor to their life-style. Meals were at set times, and manners were observed religiously. Like tonight, china, glass, and silver had been used on the night of Cole's and Beau's return.

Suddenly Lilly's voice wafted through her thoughts. "Nonsense. It wouldn't hurt for you to have a little more meat on your bones," she told Wynne as she busied herself refilling their cups with the dark chickory coffee that Wynne had come to despise. It was tangy and bitter, and she would just as soon do without than to have to drink it. "Praise the good Lord the garden's doin' well," Lilly murmured, almost as if she had read Wynne's mind. "And Elmo Ferguson's been seein' that we have fresh meat on the table at least twice a week."

"I'll have to stop by and thank Elmo for lookin' out for you," Cole said with a mischievous twinkle in his eye. "But I bet he's been invited in for a piece of sweet potato pie every now and again."

"Oh, occasionally I've had one cooling on the windowsill," she said absently. "So, you're a captain now." Lilly's eyes shone once again with pride as she hurried to change the subject. She didn't like to be teased about Elmo, and Cole knew it. "I'm real proud of you, son."

"Thanks, Ma, but I'm lookin' forward to bein' just a plain farmer again."

He glanced over at Wynne as she quietly pushed the second piece of pie aside. She didn't want to offend Lilly, who had immediately taken her in and treated her as part of the family, but she was stuffed as tight as a tick. "If you don't mind, I think

I'll save this for a little later on," she murmured as she saw the way he was looking at her.

A cool, distant set of blue eyes locked obstinately with hers for a moment before they dropped back down to his plate. "A lot of people would be glad to get that pie, Miss Elliot," he said curtly.

For two long days Cole had purposely gone out of his way to ignore her, speaking only when forced to and, in general, treating her as if she were something he had picked up on his boot in the barnyard instead of a houseguest.

Because he was beginning to fascinate her, she had taken the opportunity to observe him and his relationship with his mother. With her, he was kind and thoughtful, even nice.

And the relationships between Lilly and her son still amazed Wynne. Cole and Beau treated their mother with the utmost respect, while there was a genuine, honest warmth among them, evidenced daily by the continual bantering that volleyed back and forth in the household.

If one were around Lilly very long, it wasn't hard to see where Beau had gotten his soft heart and sense of humor. Wynne only wished some of that goodwill had washed off on Cole.

The tension between them had seemed to grow

with each passing day, even though Wynne had gone out of her way to be pleasant to him. Well, if not out of her way, then she had at least made a conscious effort to be polite to him, far more than he had done for her.

"I'm aware there are people going to bed hungry tonight," she said challengingly, daring him to look her in the eye again, but when he complied, his eyes stern, her hand reached feebly back for her fork. "Well . . . maybe just a few more bites."

"That's all right, dear. I'll put the pie in the warming oven, and it will be there when you get hungry again." Lilly took her place at the end of the table and reached for her cup. "I wish Beau and Betsy would hurry up and get back."

Lilly smiled when she thought about her middle son and his intended bride. She heartily approved of the woman Beau had chosen to be his wife.

When Beau had found out that his fiancée had taken a teaching job in a small community about fifty miles from River Run and was over there cleaning her schoolroom for the fall session, he had immediately set out to bring her back home for a few days.

Lilly reflected sadly on how the war had affected all of them. There had been a state of martial law in many areas during the past several years. Schools had closed, and churches had disbanded. But the small community of Red Springs, where Betsy taught, had not been directly affected by the fighting during the war. Although the community could barely afford to provide a roof over the new teacher's head and three meals a day, it wanted its children's education to go on uninterrupted, and Betsy had answered the call.

She was a woman to be proud of, and Beau was a lucky man, Lilly thought with delight. She only wished Cole could find a woman who would be as suited to him.

"Stop frettin' now. They should be back anytime," Cole said when he finished off the pie and pushed away from the table.

Outside, the sound of hoofbeats shattered the peaceful silence of early twilight as several riders rode up to the house and reined to a halt.

"Now who could that be?" Lilly frowned. "It's nigh on to dark, and I can't think of a neighbor who would come callin' at this hour."

Cole automatically reached for his gun belt hanging on a peg next to the back door as Lilly hurried over to pull the curtain aside to peek out.

"Why, it's the sheriff," she announced, her face breaking out in a friendly smile. She pulled the door open and hurried outside onto the porch, leaving Cole and Wynne to follow.

As Lilly stepped off the porch, Tal Franklin smiled at her, and she felt her pulse give an excited little extra beat.

No one could argue that at fifty-two the sheriff of Laxton County wasn't still a fine figure of a man. His six-foot-three frame sat in the saddle with an air of undisputed authority. There was just a suggestion of gray in his sideburns now, but his dark, hazel eyes were as clear and sharp as they had been thirty years before. His body was honed as hard as steel, and the elements had tanned his skin to a deep bronze. It was no wonder he could make the ladies of River Run blush with delight when he turned his smile in their direction, and Lilly was no different from the rest.

"Evenin', Lilly." Tal tipped his hat politely, his warm gaze taking in the soft curve of her breast against the worn calico dress. She always looked fresh, and she always smelled good. Even now he knew that if he were just a bit closer to her, he would be able to smell that faint lemon smell she always had about her.

Wynne had followed Cole out the back door, and she watched with growing amusement as Lilly's face blushed vividly pink when her eyes met

the handsome sheriff's. It wasn't hard for her to
see there was an attraction between the sheriff
and Cole's mother, and somehow that didn't surprise her.

The two looked about the same age, and they
both were unusually attractive people. Cole's
mother still had a youthful, trim figure, beautiful,
laughing blue eyes, and pretty dark blond hair
with only a few threads of gray running through it
to give away her age. Wynne thought she was
beautiful.

It was plain to see the sheriff was of the same
opinion. She wasn't sure, but if she were to hazard
a guess, she would say that Elmo Ferguson wasn't
the only one vying for Lilly's attention.

Lilly was busy discreetly fussing with her hair as
Tal slid out of his saddle and handed the reins to
one of his deputies.

"Are the sheriff and your mother . . . attracted
to each other?" Wynne asked in a whisper when
Cole came to stand behind her. She certainly
wasn't on good enough terms with him to discuss
such personal matters, but it was plain for all to see
that Lilly and Tal were looking at each other in
that special romantic way.

Cole glanced at her coolly. "I wouldn't know."

"Oh, they are," she said. "Can't you see the way they're lookin' at each other?"

The revelation took Cole by complete surprise. He had never thought about his mother's looking at another man that way—at least no one other than Elmo. And he wasn't at all sure he liked the idea.

"No, they're not," he said curtly.

Lilly's and Tal's heads snapped up at the sound of his annoyed voice. "Did you say something, dear?" Lilly called.

"No." Cole gave her a weak grin and lowered his voice to a deep growl next to Wynne's ear. "You have an overactive imagination, Miss Elliot. And remember, that's my mother you're talking about."

Wynne glanced at him over her shoulder. "I know it's your mother. I wasn't casting any aspersions on her." The man obviously didn't have a romantic bone in his entire body! "I was only making a simple observation."

"Well, stop. It's gettin' on my nerves."

Doesn't everything? she thought resentfully, but decided to hold her tongue.

Cole reached in his pocket and withdrew a cheroot as he watched her flounce away. He stuck it between his teeth and angrily lit a match with the end of his thumbnail. His pa had died in a hunting accident just after his youngest brother had been born, and as far as Cole knew, Lilly had never looked at another man except old Elmo, and that was purely in a friendly manner—nothing more. Leave it to Miss Elliot to make more of it than it was. The bird on her hat must have pecked a hole in her brain.

"Won't you and your men come in and have some supper with us?" Lilly asked as Tal reached for a small leather pouch tied to his saddlehorn.

"No, thanks, Lilly. The men are wantin' to get on home before dark. I just stopped by to bring Miss Elliot something." He was holding the bag in his hand now, but his attention was still centered solely on Lilly as Wynne approached them.

"You have something for me, Sheriff?"

Diverting his attention from Lilly slowly, Tal colored slightly before he was able to get his mind back on the business at hand. "Uh, yes, Miss Elliot, ma'am." He quickly extended the small pouch to her. "We brought your ring back."

Wynne's face lit with relief as she hurriedly undid the bag and dumped the pearl ring out into the palm of her hand. "Oh, this is marvelous! Where did you find it?"

"Down the road apiece from where the stage

was held up," he explained. "Must have dropped out of the bag when they was tryin' to make their getaway." He nodded at Cole, who had stepped off the porch to come stand beside Wynne. "Evenin', Cole."

"Evenin', Tal." Cole glanced down at the ring in Wynne's hand. "Was this all you were able to find?"

"I'm afraid so. They seemed to have gotten clean away this time. But just as soon as me and my men get a little rest, we're going to go out again."

Wynne's newfound hopes were suddenly dashed as she realized with a sinking sensation that she would probably never recover the rest of her belongings. It had already been two days since the robbery had taken place, and the men were probably long gone by now. "Well, thank you anyway, Sheriff." She sighed. "I'm grateful that you were able to recover my ring."

"As I said, ma'am, as soon as me and my men rest up, we'll try to pick up their trail again," he told her.

"You sure you won't come in and at least have a cup of coffee with us." Lilly invited him again, but he swung up into his saddle.

Wynne looked over at Cole and grinned smugly. He shot her a disapproving look.

"I'd love to, Lilly, but we have to be getting along. Some other time, I promise."

"Thanks for your trouble, Tal." Cole shook the older man's hand.

"No trouble. Just wished I could have gotten the rest of the little lady's things back for her," Tal said. He tipped his hat politely at Wynne and Lilly. "Evenin', ladies."

Wynne watched with a heavy heart as the small group of riders left the yard in a cloud of dust.

Cole and Lilly had already started back to the house when Wynne's gaze dropped to her tightly clasped hand. She opened it slowly, feeling a mist rise unexpectedly to her eyes. One little pearl ring: That was all she had left of her personal possessions. All her money was gone. Her other jewelry, which would have been worth much more than the ring, was lost. Of course, there was still Moss Oak, but that was of no value at all right now. It was merely a piece of land with charred fields and no owner to care lovingly for it. Even sadder was the fact that she didn't have one soul to care, much less to help her with her plight.

She sighed wistfully. What in the world was she going to do now?

Chapter 6

It was late Saturday afternoon before Beau returned from Red Springs with Betsy. He lifted his fiancée down from the buckboard as carefully as if she were a rare jewel and stole a brief but thorough kiss before he set her lightly on her feet.

Her face blushed a pretty pink, but her eyes shone with the same radiating love as his while she primly straightened her hat and tried to pretend disapproval of his rowdy ways. But she loved him for it. Beau's spontaneity and zest for life had been one of the first things that had attracted her, and she wouldn't have him any other way.

Lilly made a big fuss over Betsy, telling her how much she had missed seeing her in church on Sunday mornings and taking her around to the side of the house to show her how well her flower bed was doing this year.

"I have to water it every evenin'," Lilly confessed. "If it don't rain soon, I'll have to stop. I can't have the well goin' dry, and the vegetable garden's goin' to need waterin' more than these ol' flowers do." Lilly sighed and leaned down to touch a delicate lavender petal lovingly. "They sure are pretty, though." The world had seen too little beauty since the war began. Too little beauty, too little happiness, too many tears, but thank God it was over now, Lilly thought.

"They're truly lovely," Betsy said as Beau joined them. He'd taken care of the horse and buckboard quickly, and his stomach was reminding him he hadn't eaten since early this morning.

"Hope we haven't missed supper, Ma."

Lilly laughed. "No, Willa's frying chicken, and I was just gettin' ready to put the biscuits in the oven."

Beau sniffed appreciatively as the aroma of meat sizzling in hot fat filled the air. "I hope she's fixed enough." He'd never forget that when he was fighting, long days had gone by with bare rations and little or no meat.

They started for the house, catching up on the news as they walked. "Cole rode into town this morning to see what kind of supplies he could buy. He should be back anytime now," Lilly told them.

"Oh, it will be so good to see him again." Betsy smiled. "Beau says he's fine."

"He is. And he looks real good." Lilly beamed. "Thin, like this one here, but I'll have 'em both filled out in no time at all."

"Is Wynne still here?" Beau asked. He'd told Betsy about the girl he and Cole had befriended on their way home, and she was anxious to meet her.

"Yes. She's in the house helping Willa." Lilly shook her head thoughtfully. "Don't know what's gonna happen to the poor little thing. Tal hasn't been able to recover any of her money. But he did find the pearl ring she was wearing and brought it back to her."

"Well, that's more than I thought he would find," Beau said.

"What about her family?" Betsy questioned.

"Don't seem to have any. Her mama and papa're dead. She says there's an old mammy she can go to back in Savannah, but she don't seem inclined to want to do that just right now."

"No, she's lookin' for someone," Beau said.

"Oh? Who?" Lilly asked.

"I'm not real sure. Some man, but she never did get around to tellin' me who."

"Well, that's a relief," Lilly said. "At least when

she finds whoever it is, she'll have someone to take care of her."

The three went inside and found Wynne busy setting the large oak table in the dining room. Introductions were made, and Betsy decided she liked Wynne immediately. She asked Wynne to accompany her upstairs so she could freshen up before dinner, and Wynne complied willingly.

Sitting on the side of the bed, she listened attentively as Betsy chattered on about how she had known all of Beau's family since she was born and how she had been in love with Beau for as long as she could remember.

Cole rode in from town just as they were starting back down the stairway.

"Now that's another man that's going to make some lucky woman a fine husband one of these days," Betsy confided in hushed secrecy. "Isn't he about the most handsome devil you've ever seen? I mean next to my Beau, of course."

The part about his being a "devil" Wynne was more than inclined to agree with, but she hesitated to dash Betsy's high opinion of Cole by telling her she wasn't impressed with Beau's older brother in the least.

"I suppose he would appeal to some women," she replied evasively.

"Some women? Are you serious?" Betsy laughed, a delightful clear, tinkling sound. "My older sister, Priscilla June? Why, she would absolutely faint away if he would give her the time of day."

"Really?" Wynne forced her tone to remain pleasant. "What's the matter? Can't Cole tell time?"

Betsy looked blank for a moment, then broke out in a fit of giggles. "Oh, Wynne, you're so funny!" Her blue eyes widened expectantly. "Listen, are you spoken for yet?" Maybe the man she was looking for was her fiancé.

"No." Wynne smiled. "Not yet." Maybe when she got to know Betsy a little better, she would feel inclined to tell her about Cass. Somehow she sensed Betsy would understand and sympathize.

"You're not?" Betsy's grin widened.

"And I don't care to be," Wynne added quickly. "I've decided to be an old maid." She had even given serious thought about going into a convent as soon as she found Cass and took her revenge. By then she would have a whole list of grievances to be forgiven for.

Betsy's face wilted with disappointment. "Oh, my, what a shame. . . ."

Willa was setting huge platters of fried chicken

on the table when the two women entered the dining room and took their places.

Beau smiled at Betsy as she picked up her napkin and placed it in her lap daintily. Cole picked up a bowl of potatoes and completely ignored Wynne as she took the chair opposite him.

"We'll have prayer first," Lilly admonished sternly, and Cole set the potatoes back down promptly, and they all bowed their heads.

"Lord, we thank you for this bounty we are about to receive and for giving us another beautiful day of life," Lilly said softly. "We thank you that you've seen fit to put a stop to this terrible war, and I want to tell you again how much I appreciate you looking over Cole and Beau and sending them back home to me, safe and sound. I'm mighty beholdin' to you, Lord. If it wouldn't be no bother, I'd ask that you send my baby home real soon, 'cause I'm worryin' about him something real powerful, too, Lord. But I know you must have a lot of things on your mind now, and I want you to know I'm not demandin' anything. I just wanted to remind you 'bout my baby in case you might have forgotten. If you have time, Lord, we could sure use some rain. Garden's gettin' awful dry, and the well's threatenin' to do the same.

"Well, guess I'll close now. Supper's gettin' cold.

Just wanted you to know we love you and hope you'll forgive us for anything we might have done today that you wouldn't be right proud of. We didn't mean you no harm, Lord. You've been mighty good to us, and we won't be forgettin' that. Amen."

"Amen." Cole and Beau solemnly added their deep voices to hers.

"Now"—Lilly looked up and smiled—"you may pass the potatoes, Cole."

"You know, Wynne, I've been doing some thinking about that robbery," Beau announced while he spooned pole beans onto his plate. "You think you could recognize those men if you ever saw them again?"

Surprised, Wynne glanced up. "I guess so. Why?"

"Well, I was just wonderin' . . . Cole, you don't think Frank and Jesse had anythin' to do with it, do you?"

"Frank and Jesse?" Lilly answered before Cole could. "Why, those boys wouldn't do anything like that!"

Cole spared his mother an indulgent look. "Ma, Frank and Jesse's been ridin' with Quantrill's Raiders and they certainly ain't been holdin' Sunday school picnics."

"Cole, since when have I gone addlebrained? Their pa was a preacher, if you remember. And those boys were good boys, at least they was until th' Jayhawkers took it in their heads to persecute 'em."

Wynne's mind was not solely on the conversation but rather on how she was going to get through another meal without popping the buttons on her dress. "Who are Frank and Jesse?" she asked, passing the bowl of potatoes on.

"Frank and Jesse James." Beau repeated the names as if they should mean something to her.

She smiled. "Sorry, I've never heard of them."

"Well, of course, she hasn't," Betsy said. "The James boys live up around Jefferson City. In fact, they live only a couple of miles from my aunt Marabelle. When I was a small girl, I used to visit my aunt during the summer, and me and Jesse would play together—that is, until their mother, Zerelda, married that horrible Ben Simms."

"Terrible man," Lilly murmured sympathetically.

"Yes, he was. Ben Simms was some sixteen years older than Zerelda, and he treated Jesse and Frank terrible. In fact, he was downright cruel at times," Betsy said. "I remember Aunt Marabelle telling how he whipped Frank so bad one time that he had to miss school for several days."

"How awful," Wynne commented. Cruelty was foreign to her. Wesley Elliot had rarely raised his voice, and Rose Elliot had always preferred talking rather than a leather strap. "Is that when they started to get into trouble?"

"No. Ben Simms died, and then Zerelda married a doctor named Samuels—Reuben Samuels, I believe his name was. He was from Kentucky and a kind man, but"—Betsy laughed—"Zerelda was a woman who ran her own house, and I don't know if he was a happy man or not."

"Zerelda had a hot temper, is what she's tryin' to say." Beau grinned. "And she passed that temper on to Jesse. Frank, now, is more like his real pa —calm, slow to anger . . . more brainy. But Jesse is actually the clever one."

"The boys were fairly ordinary farm boys," Betsy remarked as she buttered a biscuit. "Jesse was real religious, like his pa. But when the war was first brewin', there was a lot of bitterness about the border warfare bein' waged between Kansas and Missouri. It was over whether Kansas should come into the Union free or slave."

Lilly shook her head thoughtfully. "Family

against family, brother against brother, just like the Good Book says."

"The people of Missouri were mostly southern sympathizers," Beau told Wynne. "They would up and march right over the border and kill all the Kansans they could find. Of course, the Kansans didn't take right friendly to that sort of doin's, so they up and marched right back and knocked a few Missourians' heads together. Missouri men were called bushwhackers and the Kansans were called Jayhawkers or sometimes Redlegs—"

Cole glanced up from his plate and commented dryly, "Or sometimes sons of bitches."

"Cole!" Lilly exclaimed. "Watch your language! There are ladies present at this table!"

Cole and Beau grinned at each other as Beau continued. "The Redlegs were not attached to regular uniformed forces. They operated on their own, rode and robbed and slaughtered as they pleased. Quantrill is a Missouri leader of one of those forces."

"And Frank and Jesse James ride with him?" Wynne asked.

"Frank rides with Quantrill occasionally, but Jesse rides with one of Quantrill's rebel bands," Cole said.

"Well, anyway, durin' the war they were attackin' farmers. Just out of the blue they'd swoop down and demand to know if there was anyone there from the other side. If there happened to be, they'd up and kill him."

"How horrible!" Wynne gasped, her whole attention focused on the story now.

"It is awful," Betsy said. "But probably no more so than all the other things that happened durin' that miserable war." It was still hard to believe it was over.

"Actually just two Missouri counties were real actively involved in the war," Beau continued. "And one of them was Clay County, where Frank and Jesse and Betsy's aunt Marabelle lives."

"You see, Frank and Jesse's mother was originally from Kentucky," Betsy added. "And she was a confirmed southerner. With that temper of hers and her set ideas, she wasn't shy about sayin' what she thought either. To her, Union sympathizers were scoundrels, and southerners were God's people.

"Unfortunately she had northern neighbors, and Zerelda told 'em where they could go—on more than one occasion. When Fort Sumter was fired upon, Frank decided to join up. He was eighteen at the time. I remember hearing he was at Wilson's Creek for a while. He came back home all full of victory and pride 'cause his regiment had won that battle. But Aunt Marabelle said it wasn't long after that before he was seized by the Unionists and took to Liberty to jail."

Betsy laughed. "But his ma came to his rescue real quick. She went to the commander of the Union forces in the county and asked him to release Frank. He said he would if Frank would sign an oath of allegiance and if the Stars and Stripes were flown in the yard of their house. Frank finally signed the oath, but the commander was transferred shortly after that, so the flag never flew over Zerelda's house."

"You forgot to tell her that the new commander tried to recapture Frank and that he had to go back into the bush," Beau pointed out. "From what I've heard, that's when he decided he couldn't go back with General Price again, so he joined Quantrill's guerrillas."

"Jesse was at home, farming while this was goin' on," Betsy said. "And, one day a squad of Union soldiers rode up to the Samuelses' cabin. Dr. Samuels was busy out back, but he must have heard the horses comin'. He came around front and asked what they wanted. They said they wanted him and his wife—that they'd been talkin' too much. Zerelda was out back makin' soap and didn't know what was goin' on. So the Unionists got a rope, seized the doctor, and bound his hands behind his back. The rope then went around his neck, and they marched him to a coffee-bean tree and threw the end over a limb. They jerked him off his feet and left him hangin' there."

Wynne suddenly felt faint. "How . . . horrible."

"That's not all," Betsy said soberly. "As soon as they left, Zerelda ran around the house and cut him down. Amazingly he survived, but he was in bad shape for a long time. The men thought Jesse was hid in the barn. They finally found him in the field plowin'. Now, mind you, he was only fifteen at the time. Two of 'em seized Jesse, and a third tried to beat him to death with a rope. Finally, they went back to the house, and when they discovered Samuels wasn't hangin' in the yard, mercifully they rode away."

"What happened to Jesse?" Wynne whispered.

"Jesse finally managed to get to the house. He was hurt bad, and so was the poor doctor. Zerelda took care of the both of 'em, wouldn't hardly leave their side until she was sure they were gonna make it. Aunt Marabelle says that's when Jesse changed. He went off to join one of Quantrill's bands right after that. All through the war the

Unionists kept comin' to the Samuels house, lookin' for Frank and Jesse, keepin' the family on edge all the time."

"So Jesse finally decided to ride with Quantrill," Wynne murmured. "Can't hardly say I'd blame him any."

"No, he didn't." Cole patiently tried to keep the facts straight. "He had to be seventeen before he could ride with Quantrill. So he joined one of the side commands under the direction of Quantrill, Bloody Bill Anderson."

"You sound as if you know them personally," Wynne said.

Cole shrugged. "Our paths have crossed a few times."

"Frank and Jesse floated in and out of Missouri all durin' the war," Beau told her. "There's not a better place to hide than in some of these hills and hollers. We got some of the roughest country you'll ever see. A man could get lost a hundred feet from his cabin in a few of those valleys, and down around the White River country is about the best place to start. There's where you'll see Frank and Jesse, if you're lookin' for 'em."

"Well, I'm not," Wynne affirmed. "And I hope I never have the occasion to meet up with them."

Lilly shook her head again thoughtfully. "Next thing you know, they'll be robbin' banks."

Beau gave Betsy another moonstruck smile and picked up the bowl of poke greens and extended it to her. She shook her head and smiled back at him winsomely.

"Well, have you and Betsy thought about a date for your wedding?" Lilly inquired pleasantly, hoping she could change the depressing conversation.

"We was thinking about maybe the last Sunday in October." Beau grinned. "It'd be kinda coolin' off by then."

Betsy's face flamed bright scarlet as she hurriedly groped for her water glass to avoid choking on the bite of food she had just put in her mouth.

"I mean . . . well, what I meant is . . . I just thought . . ." Beau stammered, his face turning as red as his fiancée's.

"I think we know what you meant, Beau," Cole said dryly.

"Well . . . no . . . you see what I meant was—"

"What he meant was he and Betsy want to wait until early fall to get married so that Cass will be back home by then." Lilly intervened mercifully. "There'll be no marriage in the Claxton family unless the whole family's present to wish Beau and Betsy well."

The sound of Wynne's fork clattering off the side of her plate caused four pairs of eyes to rivet on her all at one time.

Cass Claxton! Had she heard wrong? She fervently prayed she had.

"Is there something the matter, dear?" Lilly's fork paused in midair as she peered over it anxiously. Wynne's face had suddenly turned as white as a ghost.

"No . . . I . . ." Her mind was churning with confusion. Had she actually heard Lilly say Cass Claxton was her son? No. She couldn't have, yet Lilly had clearly said *Cass* would be home and the *Claxton* family would be together. Hell's bells, fickle fate had dropped her right into the viper's own nest this time.

"Wynne?" Betsy's concerned voice slowly seeped through Wynne's stupor. "Are you ill?"

Even Cole had stopped eating now, and she could feel his probing eyes on her as she removed her napkin from her lap and carefully rose on shaky limbs. "Uh, if you'll excuse me, I think I need a bit of fresh air."

She turned and bolted out of the room without

another word, leaving them staring at one another in bewilderment.

"My word, what do you suppose happened?" Lilly asked worriedly.

"Why, I just can't imagine!" Betsy exclaimed.

"Maybe all that talk of war and Frank and Jesse upset her," Beau said anxiously.

"Well, I'd better go see about her—"

"Let her be, Betsy!" Cole's voice sliced authoritatively through the air.

Betsy whirled and faced him. "But, Cole, she might be ill. . . ."

"Go ahead and finish your supper," he commanded tautly. "If she had been sick, she would have said so."

Betsy glanced at Lilly expectantly.

"He's right, dear. Maybe the past few days have finally caught up with her and she just needs some time alone," Lilly said. "Why don't we give her a few minutes to herself and then one of us will go check on her?"

Betsy wasn't at all sure that was the right thing to do, but one look at Cole's stern face and she began to sink back down in her chair obediently. "Well . . . maybe just a few minutes, but then I'm going to see about her."

The remainder of the meal was finished quickly

and in strained silence. When Willa brought dessert, Cole stood up and excused himself curtly, then left the room. A few moments later they all were relieved to hear the back door open and snap shut.

Chapter 7

The air was still warm and humid, so heavy it was almost difficult to breathe. A slight stirring of the wind touched Wynne's flushed cheeks as she stepped out the back door of the Claxton farmhouse.

She stood on the porch, her hands clenched together. She paced without knowing it, looking around helplessly, seeing nothing. *Where do I go from here?* she asked herself. *Oh, why?* Why did it have to be Cass's brothers who had befriended her?

Swiping angrily at the tears that suddenly threatened her composure, Wynne stepped off the porch. She looked up at the sun, which was just sinking in a big, fiery orange ball behind the grove of cherry trees on the west side of the house and headed in that direction.

When she was a little girl, she'd healed small disappointments and cried out her frustrations in the arms of a gnarled tree at Moss Oak. Somehow she'd drawn strength and security from that old tree. The cherry grove here seemed to beckon invitingly as if it would offer a refuge for her inward turmoil, a haven for the chaos that had again come upon her unexpectedly.

Once she'd reached the shelter of the grove, Wynne sank down in a thick carpet of grass beneath a tree. Above her, fruit was sparsely scattered about the branches. The aroma of dry grass, sweet cherries, and the sultry end of a summer day taunted her senses. Overcome with sadness and defeat, Wynne dropped her face into her hands.

After a few minutes she managed to regain control of herself. Sniffing and rubbing the backs of her hands across her cheeks, she stared around. Lilly was right, she thought dismally. If it didn't rain soon, everything was going to dry up and blow away. She hiccuped. Maybe, if she were lucky, the wind would take her right along with it.

Throwing her head back, Wynne stared up at the clear blue sky through the tree branches. *Fool! Fool! Fool! You've done it again! Made a complete fool of yourself by stumbling right into the arms of Cass's family,* she berated herself. She raised her face and chuckled mirthlessly, then irritably snapped a loose thread off the waist of her dress. *Literally thousands of people between here and Savannah, but who does Lord Providence send to rescue her?*

She laughed out loud. *Cass Claxton's brothers! That's who.* If it hadn't been so ironically funny, she would have bawled.

She leaned back against the tree and rested her head against its trunk. A hopeless sigh escaped as she pondered the disturbing similarities in Cass and his family. No, not his whole family. Lilly was nice, and so was Beau. But that rotten Cole was just like his brother—cold, calculating, and totally heartless. He'd never done anything spontaneous in his life, she'd bet. And he thought her the most foolish thing in the world—and he just might be right.

She was always reacting without thinking things out. But she'd thought out well what she'd do to Cass Claxton. And nothing would stop her, Wynne decided again.

It didn't matter that his family had taken her in when she had no one else to turn to. Cass Claxton couldn't toy with her feelings and steal her money without paying for it! And she could no longer delay putting her plan into effect.

For days she had been hoping that Sheriff Franklin would be able to recover her money. But now that she knew she was staying with Cass's family, she would have to move on. Oh, granted, she should just sit right here and wait for the rat to return to his nest. That would be the easiest way to handle the situation. Cass would undoubtedly return home one day soon, and she could shoot him and then be on her way. Her hand absently toyed with her worry stone. But she had to face facts. If she stayed around until Cass returned, it was possible she would let slip what she was about to do, and then Cole would try to intervene in her plan. She shot a dirty look toward the house. That would be just like him!

No, the pearl ring the sheriff had returned would have to be her ticket to freedom. She would go into town first thing tomorrow morning and see if the bank would accept it as collateral on a small loan.

Wynne felt better now that she had a plan. The bank would lend her a small sum. She'd need only enough to live on for a few weeks while she continued her search for Cass. It wouldn't take a great deal. Only enough for food and lodging, and she would assure the banker that she ate very little and required a minimum amount of sleep. She was aware it was a rather slim hope that she might encounter Cass while he was on the trail, but at this point she really had little other choice.

And who knew? Maybe she would be lucky and locate him right away. Wynne sat up straight. Maybe she would get even luckier and he would still have a portion of her money on him. After all, she was overdue for a stroke of luck. Long overdue.

Her stomach turned slightly queasy at the prospect of removing personal belongings off a dead man, for that's exactly what Mr. Claxton would be when she found him: dead as a doornail.

Once her mission had been accomplished, she could return to Savannah and try to rebuild her life or maybe even enter that convent. A life of servitude would be her penance for killing a man even if he did deserve to die for what he'd done.

Oooh! Why had she not realized immediately that Cole was Cass's brother? Why had she thought it was just her imagination? They looked so much alike it was almost scary, but she had been so preoccupied with all her other problems she never dreamed fate would throw another Claxton in her path!

Her ears picked up the sound of a match being struck. Before she could turn to see who it was, the fragrant aroma of cigar smoke filtered softly through the evening air.

"You didn't finish your supper," a man's deep voice stated dryly.

Wynne started at the unexpected intrusion, then stiffened with resentment. The last thing she needed was to put up with *his* company. "I suddenly lost my appetite," she answered curtly.

"So I noticed." He took a long drag off the cheroot and leaned against the tree opposite her. Smoke curled in a tiny blue furl around his head as his gaze narrowed on hers suspiciously. "I hope it wasn't anything we said that caused your sudden . . . indisposition."

She eyed Cole squarely. "Certainly not. What would make you think that?" She might be in the serpent's nest, but they weren't aware of it and wouldn't be if she had anything to say about it.

"Oh, no reason," Cole replied easily. He stood with his hat tipped back on his head, his arms crossed over his chest, quietly studying her.

Feeling uneasy beneath his penetrating gaze, Wynne looked down at her hands, which were now folded primly in her lap. Distressingly long moments passed before she finally lifted her head back up to meet his unnerving scrutiny.

"Do I have something on my face?" she snapped.

"No."

"Then why are you staring at me like that?"

Cole shrugged. "I was just wondering how you could keep such a straight face and lie the way you do."

Her gaze dropped back to her hands guiltily. "I have no idea what you're talking about."

His tongue made a clucking sound as he shook his head disapprovingly. "Now, now, Miss Elliot. Didn't that fancy school you went to back East teach you that a real lady never tells stories? At least not the big whopping ones you've been tellin' lately."

Her eyes blazed with fury and frustration when she looked at him again. "Mr. Claxton, did you want anything in particular, or did you just come out here to annoy me?"

"Annoy you?" He took another thoughtful drag on his cheroot. "I don't think I'd waste my time doing that. A prissy little old thing like you 'annoys' too easy."

"I'm not prissy." She pouted, locating another loose string around her waist. She jerked at it angrily again, and it unraveled a bit further. Hellfire and damnation! Now her clothes were even trying to come apart on her! She turned her eyes upward guiltily. *Papa, I am sorry for all this cursin', but you can surely see I'm bein' sorely tested,* she thought in apology. She felt better then. Actually Papa would have been saying things much worse, she rationalized, if he'd been in this revolting predicament.

Cole studied her, sitting under that tree, picking at a string on her dress. Soft hands, pale skin, had never done a day's work in her life. All fluff and ruffles and a bird on her hat. His mouth quirked in near disgust. He pitied the man who hitched up with her, and it was on the tip of his tongue to say so; but he wasn't inclined to start another argument. He had more important issues to discuss with Miss Elliot.

He pushed away from the tree and edged over to where she sat wrapping a loose thread around her finger absently. "Mind if I set a spell?" he asked casually.

She shrugged.

"Gonna be a nice night," he observed pleasantly as he sat down on the ground next to her.

She shrugged again.

"Willa can sure fry chicken, can't she?"

Wynne hazarded a sideways glance at him. Why

was he being so pleasant all of a sudden? She jerked another string off her dress. "I suppose."

He removed his hat and laid it on the grass beside him. Wynne couldn't help noticing what nice hair he had. It was coal black and had a nice, healthy sheen. The high humidity caused the curls to roll up in tight little kinks around his neckline and damp little loops in the front where his hat had creased them almost flat. Tonight he was bathed, clean-shaved, and dressed in freshly washed denims and a steel blue chambray shirt that turned his eyes almost the exact same shade, a far cry from the first time she'd seen him.

He leaned back against the tree trunk, gazing off into the western sky, which was ablaze with purples and oranges and golds, and he sighed contentedly. "It's good to be home."

The words were said wistfully, thankfully, and it put Wynne a little more at ease with him. "Were you away long?"

"Yeah, four years, but it seemed like forever."

"And Beau was gone that long too?"

"Yes, we left about the same time."

"Oh."

Cole studied her from beneath lowered lashes. "But my youngest brother, Cass, hasn't returned yet."

Wynne's back stiffened perceptibly at the despised name. "How sad. Where has he been?"

"Fighting, just like we have."

Wynne's mouth dropped open in surprise. "He's been in the army?"

"So Ma says." Cole hunched down more comfortably. "I was surprised when I heard about it. When I left, Cass was supposed to stay around and help her with the farm. We even paid to have a man fight in his place, but it seems he took off awhile back to visit family in Savannah and then all of a sudden decided to join up." He glanced at her. "You sounded a little surprised yourself, Miss Elliot. Any particular reason?"

So she had been right! Cass must have hightailed it to the first regiment he could find and joined up after he'd left her standing at the altar.

"No, I—I'm just a little surprised. I thought he was just away somewhere."

"No, he's been in the war," Cole repeated. "He didn't join until late in the conflict. Ma's pretty worried about him. You heard her at the supper table. She's hoping he'll come ridin' in any day now."

Wynne pulled at another string on her dress. "She hasn't heard anything from him lately?"

"No, but he'll not keep her worryin' for long," he said.

Ha! He had not been nearly as gracious with her! "How gallant of him!"

Cole's eyes snapped up to meet hers again. "Gallant?"

Realizing how sharp she must have sounded, Wynne immediately set out to rectify her hasty observation. "I mean, that will be very considerate of him," she said. "I hope he's fared as well as you and Beau have." She had to strain to get that particular lie past her lips.

Cole momentarily turned his attention back to the glorious sunset. "Yeah, that's what we're all hoping. How old are you, Wynne? Seventeen, eighteen?"

"Nineteen," she said curtly.

"Nineteen? Hmm, I didn't think you were that old. That's about Cass's age. He's twenty-two."

"I suppose he followed your leadership and became one of those damn Yankees." She turned her gaze on him accusingly, bitterly remembering the blue uniform Cole had been wearing the first day she met him.

Cole continued to study her as he drew on his cheroot. "Damn Yankee?" He shook his head tolerantly. "No, as a matter of fact, Cass chose to fight for the South. If you'll recall, Missouri was a little divided in its opinion of the war, and so were the Claxton men."

"Cass was the only one of you who knew right from wrong!" she said defensively, but that was only where the war was concerned. Otherwise he'd been a real jackass. "He worried about the war all the time, even though he'd paid someone to fight in his place and how it was goin' and about gettin' back to take care of your mother. . . ." Her voice trailed off lamely as she realized what she'd said.

"Oh?" Cole's brow lifted thoughtfully. "Do you know my brother?"

"Oh, heavens, no," she said quickly.

"Then how do you know what he thought?"

"I was . . . just guessing." She laughed nervously.

"Amazing." His lips pursed thoughtfully as he studied Wynne. "For a moment there it sounded exactly like you might have met him. You did say you were from Savannah, didn't you?"

"Yes . . ."

"And Cass was in Savannah for a while," he said thoughtfully.

"Really, Cole." She gave another cheery laugh. "Savannah is a large city. I couldn't possibly know everyone who goes there." Her fingers flew over her worry stone nervously.

In the blink of an eye the cheroot was gone, and she was in the grass, held down by strong arms across her shoulders. His blue eyes locked angrily with her startled ones as he demanded in the deadliest voice she had ever heard, "Then what in the hell are you doing with his worry stone?"

"His . . ." Her mind churned feverishly as the stone dropped out of her hand like hot lava.

Good grief! How stupid could she get! She had been sitting there with the blessed thing in her hand, talking to him!

Wynne peered up at Cole while her mind worked furiously. Should she continue to lie her way out of this newest crisis, or should she just tell this overbearing, conceited, boorish clod the truth about his precious brother?

Cole's voice was menacingly low when he spoke again. His face was so close she could feel the warmth of his breath on her face, see the tiny lines fanning out from the corners of his eyes. His body on hers was hard and masculine, yet she took no pleasure in its tantalizing presence.

"Come on, Miss Elliot. I'm dying to know how you happen to have my brother's worry stone, yet you say you've never met him." Cole's steely gaze bore into hers relentlessly as his fingers pressed into her shoulders.

"You're hurting me," Wynne said between clenched teeth. She struggled, attempting to break his hold, but the effort was useless. He had her pinned solidly to the ground, and she could barely breathe, much less dislodge his weight.

He shook her to emphasize his words, and her head bobbed crazily. "I'm waiting, Miss Elliot."

"You're hurting me!"

Once more they glared at each other defiantly, each gaze a silent stalemate. His breath was soft and sweet against her face, and he smelled fresh, like soap and water and shaving cream.

He threatened her again in a stern voice. "I can stay here as long as you can, lady."

Wynne twisted beneath him then and succeeded in getting her hands free from between them. With a lurch her curved fingers clawed at his face. They struggled again, and Cole easily caught her wrists and, while holding her body still beneath him, thrust her arms up over her head and pinned them to the ground.

"Ohhh, let me go!" Wynne demanded. She would dearly have loved to spit in his face, but he'd have probably spit right back at her! She decided on another approach. Feminine wiles had never worked in the past with him, but maybe they would now. At least she had to chance it.

Forcing her body to go limp, Wynne feigned sudden, subdued submission. "Oh, all right." She batted her big green eyes at him prettily. "Is all this brute force necessary, Cole?" She made sure her voice was soft and her drawl as sugarcoated as possible. It made her sick to do it. "I do declare, you're crushin' the little ol' life right out of me." She blinked her wide eyes again coyly. "Surely a big, strong man like you doesn't have to pin a poor innocent girl to the ground to ask her a simple question."

He blinked back at her mockingly. He was absolutely the most maddening man. "Innocent? Like hell you are! You tell me where you got Cass's worry stone and I'll let the 'poor little innocent girl' go about her business—but not until she learns to tell the truth," he snapped. "If she doesn't tell the truth, she just might get her pretty little ol' fanny whipped right here and now."

"Why, you big jackass! Get off me!" Feminine wiles flew right out the window right along with her temper. Because he was momentarily surprised by her lurch, Cole's grip was knocked loose. Overcome by her own fury, Wynne rolled over on top of him and pounded her fists on his chest.

Deciding retreat was the better maneuver at this point, Cole covered his head with both arms. When her blows continued to rain on his chest, he lost all patience and with one swipe of his arm knocked her aside. But before he could pin her down, Wynne had twisted away and was on her knees.

Once again her long skirts were her undoing. Before she could get to her feet, Cole had caught her around the waist and pitched to one side, pulling her with him. Determined to escape, Wynne twisted again. This time she lost her balance and rolled over the edge of a slight incline. But before her momentum could give her any advantage, Cole's arm snaked out and flipped Wynne over onto her back again. His forearm resting against her chest and his powerful leg thrown across hers successfully halted any further escape attempts.

"I am sorely getting out of patience with you!" he grunted as he planted himself squarely in the middle of her squirming body.

"Get off me, you big—" He was crushing her for sure this time.

"I will," he said pleasantly, "just as soon as you answer one simple question." He reached into his shirt pocket, withdrew another cheroot, and lit it while she seethed angrily beneath him. "Where did you get Cass's worry stone?"

"What makes you think that silly stone belongs to your brother?" she grunted.

"Because I gave it to him and Beau and I each have one to match. I found all three of them in a riverbed not too far from here when I was just a kid. Cass would never willingly part with it, so save yourself another lie."

"He gave it to me!" she shouted in a most unladylike display of temper.

Cole's face exhibited brief surprise at her outburst. "He *gave* it to you?"

"That's right. He gave it to me." She pushed at his heavy weight once more and grunted painfully. "Now get off me!"

He studied her hot, flushed face thoughtfully. "Not yet. When did he give it to you?"

"In Savannah. Two days before we were to be married."

This time there was no doubt of his surprise. His mouth went slack, and his hold on her loosened. Wynne quickly seized the opportunity. Pushing with all her might, she pulled away from him, and Cole let her go. Drawing in a deep breath of fresh air, Wynne brushed damp tendrels of hair off her face as Cole stared at her in disbelief.

"Cass was going to marry you!" he said.

"That's right." She sat up and irritably tried to straighten her hair, which by now was tumbled about her head wildly. He made it sound as if he thought his brother had completely lost his mind. "But don't worry, Cole. He didn't marry me. Your precious little brother left me standin' at the altar," she said bitterly. "But not before he made off with almost every cent I had in the world."

By now Cole had managed to regain his composure and was looking at her as if he didn't believe a word she said. "Now I know you're lying. Cass wouldn't steal anyone's money, let alone a woman's," he said sharply.

"Well, that just goes to show how much you know. He *did* take my money," she contended. "And when I find him, I'm going to shoot him first, ask questions later."

Cole's eyes narrowed in sudden realization. "Then Cass is the man you're looking for?"

"That's right." Her defiant gaze met his steadily.

"And you're going to shoot him when you find him?"

"That's right!"

"So . . . that's what you're doing out here," Cole said musingly, "looking for my little brother."

"So I can blow his thievin' head off," she said.

"I doubt that."

"Don't. I'll do it. I promise."

"Not if I can help it, you won't."

"You won't be able to do a thing to stop it," Wynne stated smugly. "First thing tomorrow morning I'm going to take my ring to the bank and secure a small loan. Then I'll buy another stage ticket and be on my way. Unless you want to trail me all over the countryside, there's not one blessed thing you can do to stop me."

She knew as well as he did that he wouldn't follow her.

"Just where do you think you're going to find Cass?" Cole asked. "None of us know where he is."

Wynne pushed herself to her feet. At the tone of Cole's voice her bravado wavered. "I—I know that, but I've been inquiring about his where-abouts everywhere the stage stopped, and I know he was seen in Kansas City a few weeks ago and he was supposed to be on his way home. That's why I came to River Run. But obviously he hasn't made it yet, so now I'll just head toward Kansas City and hope to find him somewhere along the way."

Cole's face sagged with relief. "Then he's alive?"

She glanced at him guiltily. "Yes. He's alive—for now."

Cole shook his head warily and thrust long fingers through the riot of thick, damp curls which framed his face. "Ma will be relieved to hear that."

"Are you—" Wynne straightened her spine defensively. "Are you going to tell Lilly about me?" she demanded. She'd hate to hurt the woman. Lilly had been awfully good to her, and so had Beau. She wouldn't want to cause them any more worry, yet Cass had caused her more than her share of heartache.

Cole studied her for a moment, then chose his words carefully. "I don't know what happened between you and Cass, but I do know my brother is an honorable man. Whatever he's done, he had good cause to do it. That's why I'm not gonna say anything to Ma about any of this, but not because of you. Number one, I don't want her to worry any more than she already is. Number two, I think my brother can take care of himself"—his eyes ran over her coldly—"especially when it comes to little eastern finishin' school girls."

She stamped her foot at him irritably. "You'd better fear for his life!"

"Cass can take care of himself," Cole stated flatly, rolling to his feet. "And number three, you haven't a prayer of findin' him in the first place. In case you haven't noticed, lady, there's a lot of territory between here and Kansas City, and a woman travelin' alone is just askin' for trouble."

"I'm nineteen years old, and I am perfectly capable of taking care of myself. I made it out here alone, didn't I?" Wynne pushed again at her hair, which seemed determined to fall in her face. Somewhere strewn about the grass were the rest of her hairpins.

"You did—just barely. But I'd have to argue with you about bein' able to take care of yourself."

"Why?" Her mouth firmed, and her chin raised automatically as she challenged his statement.

"For one thing, you're standing there in nothing but those frilly little breeches you women wear—"

"Frilly breeches! What are you talking about?" Wynne's gaze dropped to her waist, and her mouth dropped open with astonishment.

The skirt of her dress had slipped to the ground and lay in a puddled heap around her feet. Apparently the loose strings she had been jerking away at had been there for a purpose, and in all the scuffling the material around the skirtband had completely given way, leaving her standing in nothing but her linens!

"Oooooooh! How dare you!" Her face flamed as

crimson as her hair as she swooped down to pick up her skirt and step back into it, shooting him a glare that would have felled an ordinary man. "I hope you were enjoyin' yourself!"

A smile played about his lips as Cole observed her growing frustration with maddening composure. "No, as a matter of fact, I wasn't. And if you call gettin' robbed and bein' stranded in a strange town without a penny to your name takin' care of yourself, then I guess you have," he said, going right back to the conversation as if nothing unusual at all had happened. "But next time you might not be so lucky. Next time you might run into highwaymen who are lookin' for a little more than money or you might meet up with bushwhackers who haven't seen a woman in a few months or there're still splinter groups of Quantrill's raiders ridin' in these parts. One of them might take a fancy to a pretty face and want to bring her back to camp for all his friends to enjoy."

The more he talked, the more uneasy Wynne became. "You're—you're just trying to scare me!" Still, she couldn't help recalling the earlier conversation at the dinner table about such men.

"You think so?" Cole's face was as solemn as a preacher's now. "There're a lot of men ridin' these roads nowadays, Wynne. Most of 'em have been away from home for a long time, and they wouldn't be too particular who they took their ease with."

A rosy blush flooded Wynne's face at his bold insinuations. "You can talk all you want, but I'm leaving tomorrow morning," she said firmly.

"All right." He shrugged indifferently and reached down to pick up his discarded hat. If she wanted to be bullheaded about it, then it was her skin she was risking, not his. "Have it your way." He turned and started to walk away, then had second thoughts. "Oh, by the way. Tell Cass, if you happen to see him, Willa's keepin' his supper warm."

She wasn't about to give that dirty scoundrel any message, Wynne thought resentfully as she watched Cole turn once more and head back to the house. But she'd cheerfully tell Mr. Cole Claxton a thing or two! One being that the next time *he* saw his baby brother he'd be in a pine box!

And with that Wynne gathered the waist of her skirt in one hand, the hem in the other, and marched to the house behind Missouri's *second* biggest scoundrel.

Chapter 8

Dawn was just breaking over the horizon the following day as Wynne tripped lightly along the rutted path, carrying her two brown valises with her. Her heart was lighter than it had been in several days.

It was going to be another scorcher, but she comforted herself with the thought that it couldn't be a very long walk into town and she would enjoy the peace and solitude.

She almost laughed out loud when she thought about the way Cole had accused her of not being able to take care of herself. She could take care of herself as well as the next person. Maybe even better.

If he could see her now, he'd certainly have to change his mind. She was properly dressed in a pale blue sprigged dress with tatted lace trim, the waist nipped in to emphasize its narrowness and the fullness of her bosom, her hair was brushed up with small curls nested at the crown of her head, and she was on her way into town to take care of her own affairs. She was a woman well versed in the business affairs of running a plantation. Papa had made sure of that, so dabbling in the business world was not new to her.

Granted, the overseer at Moss Oak had been experienced and especially conscientious, considering that many overseers had up and deserted the plantations during the war, leaving their employers helpless in the care of the servants staying behind and the crops in the field. Many owners had simply sat and watched their heritages disintegrate before their eyes.

But Moss Oak had survived, not without a great many problems plaguing it, but the land was still there and in the Elliot name. The fields were parched, no crops in the ground other than the small truck garden which fed the servants who remained on the place, but someday it would be brought back to the fertile land it once had been. She'd see to that. And she sincerely hoped that whoever bought the land would love it as much as Wesley Elliot had.

She sniffed disdainfully. The nerve of Cole Claxton trying to tell her she couldn't take care of herself.

Mercy, it was hot! Wynne glanced skyward at the sun, beating down pitilessly. Already the lace around the collar of her dress was clinging to her skin. Her black, high-top, buttoned shoes were certainly fashionable, but they were not meant for walking any distance. When she had progressed a few miles down the road, that fact was achingly plain.

Even the perky bird sitting serenely on top of her hat looked slightly more wilted than when her journey first began, and her hair was beginning to straggle down her neck.

Wynne had lain awake half the night, thinking about her predicament. But having firmly made up her mind, she'd risen early and tiptoed around her room. She'd hurriedly washed and dressed in her Sunday best and pushed her clothing into the two valises. She wanted to be out of the Claxton household before anyone noticed her absence.

While she didn't want to create a scene by leaving as the family gathered for breakfast, she couldn't just disappear without any explanation, and she didn't want to hurt Lilly. Cass's mother had been so giving, so accepting. Penning a neat note to Lilly, Wynne said that she had decided to

resume her search for the man she had been looking for and had left the house early because she
didn't want to disturb Lilly's rest. Explaining that
she was going to sell her ring, then take the first
stage out that morning, she cautioned Cass's
mother not to be concerned for her welfare because she was sure it would be only a small matter
of time before she found the man she was seeking.

She thanked her for the kindness that the Claxton household had shown her and forced her pen
to include Cole's name as one of her generous
benefactors. Actually she did feel a certain sense of
loss in having to leave. It would have been lovely
to be able to extend her stay so that she would
have been there to see Beau and Betsy married.
While she was sealing the envelope, it occurred to
her she was going to miss Lilly too. Funny, but she
felt no animosity toward her. After all, she
couldn't help it if she had two loathsome sons.

Nevertheless, Wynne was thankful Cole had remained silent about her past association with Cass.
She assumed, and hoped, he would continue to do
so now that she'd left.

Just remembering how she'd made a fool of herself in the orchard the night before made her
cheeks burn with embarrassment. When she'd returned to the house, Wynne had entered through

the front door and slipped upstairs to make the necessary repairs to her dress before joining the others.

Cole had been sitting at the table eating a piece of pie when she came downstairs thirty minutes later. Although there were a lot of fretful glances coming from Betsy, nothing had been mentioned about Wynne's earlier, somewhat abrupt departure from the dinner table, so she felt certain that Cole would remain discreet to spare his family worry.

The sun was a blazing ball of fire now. Wynne dabbed at the perspiration gathering on her brow with a dainty lace handkerchief.

Although she had only a meager amount of clothing in her valise, it seemed to weigh ten pounds more than it had when she started.

Five more miles down the road a large blister was forming on her right toe, she was hot and thirsty, and her arms ached from carrying the burdensome bags.

Another two miles found her angrily sorting through the two bags and stuffing only the essentials into one, then discarding the other in the middle of the road.

By the time the town of River Run came into

view, her disposition could best be described as something less than sunny.

Behind her the sound of approaching hoofbeats reached her. The animal wasn't coming very fast, just a smooth, ground-covering pace. Curious, Wynne turned to see who might be on the road this early.

Oh, no! she groaned. Him again! She'd recognize Cole Claxton's arrogant posture anywhere. What was he doing out here? Coming to drag her back no doubt. Well, he had another think coming, she thought, seething.

The horse drew nearer as her chin rose a notch higher and she mentally prepared a scathing refusal for when he demanded she return to the Claxton homestead.

When his mount was abreast of her, her mouth shot open to refuse his offer, but damn the man, he rode right past her! Didn't even look her way.

Before she realized it, she had been standing in the road for a full five minutes watching that—that arrogant fool's retreating back. She stamped her foot indignantly. Damnation! That man got under her skin even when he ignored her. To make matters worse, the moron hadn't even asked her if she wanted a ride! Might have known it, she grumbled to herself. The man had the manners of a dolt! And with another muttered oath learned at her father's knee, Wynne picked up her one valise and continued her trek toward town.

Banker Elias Holbrook glanced up from his desk as the tinkle of the bell over the bank door announced his first customers of the morning. Business had been mighty slow since the war began. Some banks had even had to close their doors, but Elias had somehow managed to keep his business afloat.

With pride he watched Nute Walker stride to the teller window to make a deposit. The new owner of the general store was doing well, and here was old Mrs. Groves again this morning. Only butter-and-egg money, but she faithfully put her few pennies in her account every week.

Suddenly Elias blinked. The striking young woman who had made such a town spectacle of herself a few days earlier, getting off the stagecoach, staggered through the door, dragging a dusty brown valise. Her face was flushed as red as one of the stripes on Old Glory, which flew over the courthouse, and she wore a hat with a strange-looking bird on it. The little hat was cocked crazily on the side of her head, and strands of her red hair hung limply from beneath. Her dress was soaked in perspiration, and dust lay heavily on the hem of her shirt. Her lovely green eyes were ringed with dirt, reminding him of a worn-out raccoon.

Wynne dabbed at her cheeks and neck as she sagged weakly against the polished pine railing and let the cooler air of the bank's interior wash over her.

Regaining his composure, Elias spoke to the young woman pleasantly. "It's gonna be a warm one."

She smiled lamely. "Yes, quite warm." It wasn't even nine o'clock in the morning, and the heat was already suffocating.

Moved to compassion by the pitiful sight of her road-stained face and dress, Elias poured a glass of water from a pitcher sitting on his desk and handed it to her. Wynne accepted his offer gratefully. Even the tepid water felt cool to her parched tongue. She emptied the glass in one long swallow, then, drawing a deep breath, returned the glass to the corner of Elias's desk.

Her foot hurt abominably. There was a chair right next to a big oak desk, and without thinking, she sat down and peeled off the offending shoe. The petite foot she withdrew had a blister the size of a silver dollar throbbing painfully on its big toe. Emitting a huge sigh of relief, she tucked the skirt of her dress under her bottom and then brought the injured foot up to her lap to poke gingerly at the puffy spot.

Amazed by her actions, Elias leaned over Wynne's shoulder and peered at the proceedings with growing interest. This was the first time a lady had ever come into his bank and removed her shoes, especially such a lovely young lady.

"My, my. That looks terrible." He clucked sympathetically.

"It hurts like the blue blazes," she said with a groan. Almost immediately she realized what she'd done. Hell and damnation! What must he think of her?

Her foot slid very slowly off her lap, and as circumspectly as possible under the circumstances, Wynne tucked her bare foot and her shoed one beneath the dusty hem of her skirt.

A true lady would never enter a bank and take her shoe off in front of a man! She could just hear what Miss Fielding would have to say about that!

Clearing her throat nervously, Wynne set the shoe in her lap on the floor and crossed her hands in her lap. She pasted an utterly charming smile on her face. "Would you perhaps be the man I would talk to about obtaining a small loan?"

Elias straightened automatically and tugged at

his vest. "A loan?" His face brightened. It had been years since anyone had been in his bank wanting a loan! The war had stopped nearly all transactions of that sort. No one had any money, so no money could be lent.

"Why, yes, my dear! I certainly am." He extended a cordial hand. "Elias Holbrook, here."

"Mr. Holbrook." Wynne accepted his hand with a graceful nod of her head. "How nice to make your acquaintance, sir. My name is Wynne Elliot." Just as she shook his hand, her hat tilted dangerously to one side. Her hand flew up to steady the hat.

Elias smiled at her obvious discomfort. She was a charming, beguiling young woman, and he wanted to put her at ease. "Wynne. That's a lovely name, my dear."

"Thank you."

"You're staying out at the Claxton place, aren't you?"

"Yes . . . I don't know if you heard about my minor inconvenience. . . ."

"Yes, yes, I did. I'm terribly sorry." There wasn't anyone in town who hadn't heard about the stage being held up or who had missed the spectacle this young lady had created by falling out of the stage with her rifle.

"Yes . . . well, about the loan. Your establishment has been quite highly recommended to me," she said hoping he wouldn't suspect how desperate she really was.

Actually the part about someone's recommending his bank was not entirely true. Not one person had suggested she try the bank, but she thought it might sound more businesslike if she took this approach.

"Oh, my. Why, that's wonderful," Elias proclaimed. He scurried around his desk and sat down, reaching for a pen and paper. "Now, what amount did you have in mind, Miss Elliot?" Of course, it would be out of the question for a woman to secure a loan with the bank, he thought fondly, but the Claxton family was a real solid investment, and he could issue the loan in Cole or Beau's name.

"Well . . ." Wynne wrapped her handkerchief around her forefinger tightly. "I think perhaps twenty dollars would be sufficient."

"Hmm . . . twenty dollars . . . yes . . ." Elias was scribbling as they talked. "And what sort of collateral would you be able to offer the bank?"

"Oh, I have this pretty little ring my father gave me for my sixteenth birthday." She hurriedly slipped the ring off her finger and handed it to him. "Isn't it nice?"

Elias stared at the tiny ring lying in the palm of his hand, then glanced back up at her. "This is all the collateral you have?"

She mustered up the most winning smile she had. "Yes, that's all I have with me right now, but it is truly a lovely ring, don't you agree?"

She could see the seed of doubt begin to sprout in Elias Holbrook's eyes, and her heart sank. "Well, yes, my dear. It is lovely, but I would need more than the ring to make such a loan," he said. "Have you nothing else of value?"

"Oh, yes! I have a whole plantation back in Savannah," Wynne answered.

"A plantation!" Elias's face brightened once more. "Well, well. Now that's more like it. May I see the deed, please?"

"Deed?"

"Yes, the deed. You do own the land free and clear?"

"Yes, but I don't have the deed with me," Wynne said.

"Oh?" Once more doubt clouded Elias's face. "Oh, dear me."

"But I *do* own the land and I could send for the proper papers—"

"Yes, but that might take months," he pointed out gently.

"But I still have the ring as collateral. . . ." Her voice trailed off weakly as he began to shake his head negatively, and she realized with a sinking heart he wasn't going to give her the loan.

For the next ten minutes she tried everything she could think of to make him change his mind, but he remained firm. The bank could not issue the loan in her name.

"Miss Elliot, may I make a suggestion?" he said kindly. "Why don't you talk this over with Cole Claxton and then you and he come back in? Perhaps something could be worked out—"

Wynne was on her feet in an instant. "Cole Claxton! Never!"

"Now, my dear"—Elias could see he had said the wrong thing—"it pains me greatly to have to refuse you a loan, but you must realize the bank is not in the habit of making loans to women—"

"It pains me too," Wynne replied angrily. She stuck her foot in her shoe and sucked in her breath painfully as the leather slid across the blister. "Thank you for your time, sir!"

"Miss Elliot . . ." Elias watched feebly as she limped across the bank lobby and snatched up her valise, then slammed out the front door.

"Yes . . . good day, Miss Elliot," he added under his breath sheepishly as he glanced around at the other early-morning customers and smiled.

The temperature felt as if it had shot up even higher than before when Wynne stepped out of the bank.

Oh, yes, Banker Holbrook had thought the ring was lovely but completely inadequate collateral for a twenty-dollar loan just because she was a woman! But it wasn't until he suggested that Cole come talk to him, that perhaps he would be willing to issue the loan in Cole's name, she'd known her goose was cooked for sure.

No matter how she'd argued—presented her case, she amended, for Miss Fielding's sake— Banker Holbrook had not been persuaded. Well, she wasn't beaten yet.

Shifting the valise in her hand, she stepped off the sidewalk and limped toward the general store.

Mr. Holbrook had suggested that she find a private investor. He'd said Nute Walker sometimes made small loans in exchange for personal property. But Mr. Walker didn't need a pearl ring.

Nor did Tom Clayborne or Jed McThais or even Avery Miller, for that matter. It seemed as if not one person in River Run had use for a lovely pearl ring or any money to lend either.

Wynne slumped down on a bench in front of Hattie's Place and glumly surveyed the ring on her right hand. Tears sprang to her eyes. She'd always thought it was the prettiest ring she'd ever seen.

The interior of the saloon was extremely quiet. She supposed Penelope would still be sleeping. For a moment Wynne toyed with the idea of marching right in there and rousing Hattie out of bed and asking for a job. After all, she was completely alone, broke, in a strange town, and didn't even know where her next meal was coming from. It was a time for desperate measures.

She stood up and went over to the saloon door. Standing on tiptoe, she peeked inside. She couldn't ever recall seeing such an establishment before. Papa would have never permitted it, and it was quite possible he was changing positions in his grave right now because of her brazenness.

Barely visible in the dim interior was a lone man sweeping the floor. Chairs were stacked neatly on top of tables, and a low ceiling fan was trying its best to move the stagnant air in the room. The strong odor of stale cigarette smoke and brackish beer filled her nostrils. Her nose wrinkled as she thought about what it would be like to work in a place like this.

If you're going to kill a man, Wynne, then you certainly should be able to give yourself to one in order to survive, she reasoned.

For a moment she felt a mild stirring of apprehension at the thought of actually killing Cass. What would it be like to walk up and point a gun at his big, broad chest, then deliberately, coldly, cruelly pull the trigger? A ripple of revulsion snaked through her. This was the first time she'd ever really stopped to think about the act.

When it happened, would he look at her with amusement, or with scorn, or maybe even with a tiny bit of remorse? Or would that devil throw his dark head back and laugh at her, his even white teeth glistening in the sunlight, having his own revenge, even as he stood at death's door?

With a long sigh she stepped away from the door and sat down on the bench again. Well, she'd never know how Cass would react until she found him, and she couldn't find him until she had some mode of transportation, and she couldn't get that transportation unless she sold her ring.

Across the street a small crowd had gathered at the general store. They were signing up for a wagon train that was due to leave the following morning, heading west. Mr. Walker had suggested she try to sign on, but when she'd inquired about that prospect, she'd been told she would have to have a husband or a guardian of some kind, preferably a family member.

She sighed again, long and wearily. Well, she obviously didn't have a spare "uncle" around, and her chances of finding a husband by daybreak the next morning were about as slim as selling the pearl ring.

Her gaze fell on the livery stable, and it occurred to her that she hadn't tried there yet. Now there was a possibility she hadn't thought of before. Of course, how stupid of her! She probably wouldn't be able to sell the ring there, but perhaps the owner would have a nice horse he would trade for it.

Riding a horse wouldn't be the most comfortable way to travel to Kansas City, but she supposed she could do it if she had to. She'd ridden nearly every day on the plantation before she'd gone away to school. And other women braved their way across the rugged frontier, didn't they? She'd gotten this far on her own, hadn't she?

Feeling slightly better about the whole situation, Wynne picked up her valise and hobbled across the street toward the stable.

The blacksmith was busy shoeing a horse as she walked up and smiled brightly at him. He was a huge, burly sort of man with a big gold front tooth. Sweat shone on his wide face, and he towered over her small frame from an eminent height.

Combined with the heat of the day, the forge made the inside of the stable oppressive. Not a thread of the smith's clothing was dry. Rivulets of sweat poured freely off him and ran in streams down his body, and his muscles bunched and relaxed in rhythm as his hammer beat a steady tattoo to shape a red-hot horseshoe. Glancing at her only briefly, the smithy kept his attention trained on his work.

Clearing her throat, Wynne smiled again and said, "Good morning, sir."

His answer was barely more than a passing grunt.

"It's extremely warm," she said pleasantly, then realized how ridiculous a comment that had been.

Again he grunted and moved away to pick up more shoeing nails and put them in his large, soiled apron.

"Could you perhaps tell me how far it is to Kansas City from here?"

"Over two hundred miles."

Wynne's face fell. "That many miles?"

He nodded and kept on working.

She cleared her throat nervously and looked

about the stable. There was a lovely horse standing in one of the stalls. It was large, *and* sturdy-looking, and the most beautiful rust shade. It looked as if it would be easy to ride and as if it were gentle, and she desperately hoped the horse was both if she was going to travel 200 miles!

Wynne cleared her throat again. "Sir, I was wondering. Would that horse over there happen to be for sale?"

The blacksmith's gaze followed to where she was pointing. "It is." Then he returned to the job of shaping another horseshoe.

Wynne set down her valise and walked over to the stall. The horse stuck its nose over the gate and whuffed at her. Wynne smiled and rubbed its nose. "Pretty boy," she murmured. *Oh, yes, this one would do nicely,* she thought.

Stiffening her resolve, she quickly turned back to the smithy. "Well." She spoke again, more loudly.

"Well, I'm sure you've heard about the stage being robbed. I was on that stage and the thieves took all my money and now I have no way to travel on to Kansas City," she explained all in one breath. "But I do have this lovely pearl ring I'm sure you'd like. I would trade it in even exchange for this horse—"

The blacksmith's eyes promptly narrowed, and his mouth firmed with obvious resentment that she would think he would be interested in a pearl ring!

Wynne's eyes widened, and her mouth went suddenly dry. "Uh, oh, no! I didn't mean that *you* might be interested in the ring," she said hurriedly. "I thought perhaps you might know someone you would like to give it to. . . ." She trailed off hopefully as she saw the man's attention unwillingly focus on the ring that was on her hand. Quickly she thrust it out toward him, willing her trembling to stop.

His dark eyes took in the fragile object with little sign of any real interest. Leaning forward a fraction more, he surveyed the piece of jewelry more closely, and Wynne held her breath.

Her heart beat so strongly she was sure he must see it beneath the thin fabric of her dress. If he wouldn't trade the horse for the ring, she'd have no choice but to go to Hattie's and ask for a job.

Straightening, the smithy scowled at her sourly. "What'll I do with a little play pretty like that?"

"Oh, you could give it to your wife—"

"Don't have no wife." He interrupted curtly.

"Oh. Well, you could give it to—to a lady friend," she suggested cheerfully.

She waited for him to deny he had a lady friend, realizing instantly that had been a bad suggestion. It would be a miracle if he had such a female acquaintance.

But apparently he didn't find the suggestion that preposterous because his gaze had gone back to the ring and was lingering there as he seemed to be seriously considering the offer. Finally he spit out a stream of tobacco juice that whizzed by her ear as if it had been fired out of a cannon. The spittle had come so close to her cheek she was sure she could feel a remnant of the repulsive moisture still lingering wetly on the side of her face. It was all she could do to refrain from wiping her cheek with her hand.

"Well . . . I don't know . . ." he said thoughtfully.

Trying to keep from gagging, because Miss Fielding had repeatedly warned that a lady does not gag in public, Wynne fumbled hastily in her pocket for her handkerchief and smiled at him brightly.

Hell's bells and fiery damnation! She had to have that horse!

"Any lady would looove the ring," she said encouragingly, turning her hand from one side to another to make the ring glow in the dim light of the stable.

Fifteen minutes later she came riding out of the stable on the back of a glorious white mule, grinning ear to ear. She'd made a good deal and she'd done it all on her own.

The blacksmith wouldn't trade the horse for the ring, but he would trade the old mule for it. It seemed the animal had wandered into town on its own a couple of weeks ago. It was speculated that a prospector had previously owned it. Perhaps he'd died somewhere out on the trail and the mule had wandered wild for a while. The animal was of no value to the smithy, just one more mouth to feed, and the ring had miraculously caught his eye.

The trade had come complete with the prospector's pack equipment. There were two dirty old blankets, various mismatched eating utensils, a pick and a shovel, three pie-shaped pans, for gold panning—should she happen to run across any gold—and even an old rusty gun. The unexpected weapon would be a godsend if she were to complete her mission successfully, for she had wondered where she would get a gun. After all, she was sure she couldn't run Cass down and club him to death, although if it had come to that alternative, she'd have done it.

There was also various other paraphernalia that Wynne couldn't readily identify, but she was sure it all would come in handy once she was out on the trail. All in all, she thought with a satisfied smile, she'd driven a very shrewd bargain.

The only problem at the moment was that she'd always ridden sidesaddle. Because she suspected he had felt sorry for her, the blacksmith had thrown in a very worn saddle with the deal, and she had to ride astride. Getting accustomed to that was going to be a little tricky, and the animal had a strange gait, more of a lurching from side to side than the smooth stride of the horses she was accustomed to at Moss Oak.

The blacksmith had helped her mount. At first she thought about insisting upon riding properly like a lady, hooking her knee around the saddlehorn to make it a kind of sidesaddle, but the smith had warned her that would be a poor choice. "You'd better set like a man," he'd said, "or th' gall dern thing will pitch you right in the middle of the road."

Of course, she didn't want the "gall dern thing" to do that, so she'd primly tucked her skirt up

around her legs and shinnied up on the back of the
mule as gracefully as the situation would allow.

"Uh, just exactly what direction is Kansas City?"
she asked just before she started out on her long
journey.

The blacksmith scratched his head absently,
then sent another brown stream of juice flying by
the mule's head. "You sure you ought to be doin'
this, lady?" If she didn't even know what direction
Kansas City was in, he didn't think she should be
setting out for it all alone.

"Thank you for your concern, but if you would
just kindly point the way."

He shook his head again worriedly. "Just keep
bearin' north, little lady. Just keep bearin' north."

Oh, what a glorious feeling it was to ride down
the center of town, knowing she was once again a
woman in charge of her own destiny.

The colorful procession of two made a good deal
of noise as it progressed down the main street. The
pack was tied firmly behind the saddle, but the
utensils were tied on loosely and clanged together
noisily as the mule and its rider ambled slowly out
of town.

The only thing that spoiled her newfound para-
dise was the fact that *he* was there to witness it.

Cole was standing outside the general store, taking note of her departure with irritatingly cool detachment. Leaning insolently against the porch railing, he calmly placed a cheroot between his teeth and watched indifferently as she rattled her way past him.

Wynne ignored how blue his eyes were against the dark tan of his face. It didn't matter that the white muslin shirt was open at the neck to reveal the shadow of dark hair across his chest. Or that his sleeves were rolled back to reveal corded forearms. His hat was tilted rakishly to the back of his head, and a fringe of hair that was a bit too long framed his strong face, and he was so handsome it nearly took her breath away.

None of that made any difference, she told herself. Cole Claxton was ill-tempered, arrogant, and a completely egotistical old goat. But there was something about him that commanded her respect too. There was no way she could get around that. There were strong family feelings among the Claxtons. That alone was enviable. They'd come from a background of wealth and gentility. Their home had reflected that as much as had the ingrained southern mannerisms Lilly had exhibited.

From listening to conversations around the dinner table, she'd learned the Claxtons had indeed come from Georgia. They were even from near her home, not far from Savannah. When Cole and Beau were very young, Samuel Claxton and his wife had liquidated all their assets and moved to the West. They'd found the fertile Ozarks mountain area and had been taken by its beauty. They had settled there, determined to raise a family without the blight of slavery, and they'd succeeded.

Another painful stab of resentment attacked her as Wynne thought about the different natures of the handsome Claxton men.

Cole, at thirty, was the eldest. The strong, silent one, he made Wynne incredibly angry by being so practical, but she knew Lilly depended on him to be the strength and steady hand of the family. Beau, at twenty-five, was beguiling and charming, always out to help and please. But at twenty-two, Cass Claxton was rotten through and through. Oh, he'd been as genteel and well mannered as his two brothers—actually more so. A perfect "southern" gentleman at all times. Apparently he'd been the only one of the family to cling to its Georgia roots and fight for the South—when he'd finally decided to fight. *The miserable wretch*, Wynne thought. He'd been a handsome devil and, oh, so cleverly charming.

It was a constant thorn in her side that Cole and Cass bore such a striking resemblance to each other.

But she wasn't going to let him dampen her enthusiasm. She was back on course, and nothing would stop her now from completing her mission. Before long there would be only two Claxton men for the women of the world to defend themselves against.

With a decided lifting of her nose she nudged the old mule to a faster gait and loped past the general store with not so much as a glance in his direction.

And the last Cole Claxton saw of Wynne Elliot was her fanny bouncing along in the saddle like a proud little prairie hen flouncing over the horizon, heading west.

Chapter 9

"Weelll, guess we could always go cross the street and wet our whistles," the old-timer suggested as he shot a wad of tobacco juice cleanly off the porch, then wiped the remainder of the brown stain still lining his mouth on the shoulder of his shirt.

It never ceased to amaze Bertram how a man could be so neat yet so untidy at the same time.

"No, we was over there earlier." He winced and shifted his broken leg around to a more comfortable position. The splint was cumbersome, and his leg was beginning to itch like crazy. And the insufferable heat wasn't making it any easier on him.

"Weelll, we could go wet a line, if you was a mind to." For some reason, ever since Bertram had fallen off that blamed porch a couple of weeks ago, Jake seemed to think it was his responsibility to take care of him. From the day he had broken his leg, the old man had befriended him even to the point of insisting that he stay at his home until the leg mended. Since Bertram was once more at the mercy of fate and low finances, he had little choice but to accept the generous offer.

Jake lived by himself in nothing more than a shack on the outskirts of town. His wife had died back in '51, and his only son had been killed in a gunfight the year after. In short, Jake was lonely, and he welcomed the young stranger's company. And it hadn't been too bad for Bertram either, except Jake talked a lot and got on his nerves every once in a while. Still, the old man was good to him, so he couldn't complain.

"I could put you on back of ol' Millhouse and walk you down to the river," Jake was saying.

Every morning Bertram was put unceremoniously on the old horse's back, and Jake led it into town. The rest of the day they sat on the plank porch in front of one of the local establishments and whittled with the other idle citizens of Springfield. It was not a comfortable journey, but it was better than lying in bed all day with nothing to do and no one to talk to.

"No, thanks, Jake." Bertram refused listlessly. "I'll just sit here and finish this cow I started." He held up for inspection a piece of wood that was poorly fashioned in the form of a four-legged animal. It wasn't that he didn't appreciate Jake's efforts to keep him busy; it was just that he was getting awfully bored. He wanted to get on with his mission of finding that fool Elliot woman. Once he got his business with her finished, then maybe he would be able to resume a normal life.

"Why, that's right nice, boy." Jake paternally praised the misshapen image Bertram was holding.

Well, it wasn't, and Bertram knew it. The miniature carving didn't look anything like a cow. More like just an old notched-out piece of pine. But Jake had tried so hard to teach him to whittle that Bertram didn't have the heart not to try at least to master the art.

This afternoon the porch was full of Jake's counterparts, all whittling and spitting periodically. Bertram hadn't taken up tobacco chewing yet, but he suspected that would be next if he didn't get out of there pretty quickly.

All eyes centered on the white mule that came lumbering through town just before noon. A young, pretty red-headed girl wearing a silly little hat with a bird on it was riding the animal or at least making a stab at it. She seemed to be having a hard time getting the beast to do what she wanted.

Rising slowly to his feet, Bertram winced as he heard the woman shout an unladylike command to the mule as it suddenly stopped dead still in the middle of the road. The girl almost pitched forward on her head but finally managed to keep astride.

You filthy, stubborn piece of dog meat! I ought to —Wynne fumed, then glanced around her in embarrassment. Lord, there was a whole porchful of men staring at her! And one in particular whom she noticed leaning against a post, with a splint on his leg. Quickly regaining her composure, she pushed her hat back out of her heat-flushed face and smiled cordially at the men staring at her from the porch. "Afternoon, gentlemen," she called sweetly.

They all hurriedly tipped their hats and gave her friendly, toothless grins.

For the next few moments she sat on the mule, jabbing it in the sides with her toes and bouncing up and down just as if she were actually going somewhere.

Leaning against the post, Bertram grinned at her obvious dilemma. "Need any help, ma'am?"

The girl shot him a lame smile, but about that

time the mule decided to move on, and it did in such a rapid fashion that the last Bertram saw of the girl was a white streak bounding out of town amid a loud clamor of pots and pans.

Shaking his head in amusement, Bertram hobbled back to his chair and picked up the wooden cow once more.

"Here comes that Fancy Biggers woman," Jake said out of the corner of his mouth a few minutes later.

All heads snapped up to watch the young woman coming across the street. She worked at the saloon, and Bertram had noticed in the two weeks he had been there how the other women of the town picked up the hems of their skirts and made sure they didn't touch any part of Fancy's gown as they passed her.

Bertram didn't like that. Fancy Biggers might not be living exactly by the Good Book, but he didn't think it gave the other women cause to treat her so badly.

She couldn't have been much older than eighteen, maybe nineteen, Bertram guessed. Couldn't hardly tell with all that war paint on her face. But she was pretty. He was sure of that. She had really nice red hair, too, that shone like a shiny new copper penny in the afternoon sunlight. Her eyes were a sort of brownish yellow, kind of strange-looking but pretty.

She was thinner than she should be. Looked to him as if she could stand a few more square meals under her belt. And the dress she was wearing was indecent. He couldn't argue that. It was bright red satin and made her waist look like about the tiniest thing he had ever seen. Why, his hands could span her waistline and still have room left over. And the neckline—well, it dipped deep in front to reveal small, firm breasts. There was a small brown mole on her left one. Course, he didn't mind the dress all that much, but he could see where the other womenfolk might get a little upset with her prancing around in front of their men the way she did sometimes. She was carrying a matching red umbrella and twirling it absently around her head as she walked, sort of in a flirty manner.

All in all, Bertram liked Fancy Biggers. In the two weeks he had been in Springfield, she had been nice to him.

Fancy stepped up onto the porch, and the men's chairs came back down on all four legs with loud thuds. "Afternoon, gentlemen," she said pleasantly.

There was another outbreak of toothless grins

and nervous twittering as the men made their appropriate responses.

She turned her attention to Bertram and smiled. "Afternoon, Bertram."

"Afternoon, Miss Biggers." Bertram had managed to rise respectfully to his feet again as she had stepped up onto the porch. He felt his stomach flutter nervously, and he didn't know why.

"Lovely day," she remarked conversationally.

"A little hot."

"Yes. We could certainly use a good rain."

"We sure could, Miss Biggers. Looks kinda cloudy back in the west. Maybe we'll get a shower before the day's over." He grinned at her warmly and forced his eyes off the small mole he had located almost immediately.

"I wouldn't mind at all, but it's still a lovely day for a drive, wouldn't you think?" Fancy smiled at him again, and Bertram felt his face flush deep red as he heard the other men's knowing chuckles behind him.

"Uh, yes, I guess it is. Real nice." Was she asking him to take her for a ride?

"I know you're not exactly up to driving a team at the moment; but the saloon has a buckboard I could borrow, and I was wondering if you might like to go for a ride with me," she asked boldly.

Fancy Biggers had always had to ask for everything she got, so it didn't bother her in the least to extend such an invitation to Bertram. They had talked many times since he'd come to town, sitting out in front of the saloon while she was taking a break from the fast-drinking, fist-fighting patrons who frequented the establishment.

He was the only man she had ever met who didn't seem to want anything from her, although he was at liberty to buy her favors just like any other man. But he never once suggested such a thing. Bertram was always polite and extremely nice to her. He told her about his family and what he'd been doing since he left his home in Savannah. He was older than she was, nearly twenty-eight, but that didn't bother her either. She loved to hear him talk. He had such a nice, deep, rich voice, and she could listen for hours when he told her about how his mother used to bake apple pies for him three times a week because she knew that was his very favorite.

Fancy couldn't imagine having someone bake a pie specially for her. She'd been an orphan since birth, being raised by first one stranger, then another. Most of the women had been mean to her, and the men had taken her youth and innocence away before she was fourteen years old. Bertram

Mallory was like a breath of spring air to her with his genteel manners and soft-spoken conversation.

"Well, yes . . . a ride might be real nice," Bertram said quickly, wishing the other men would stop their dad-blasted giggling! They were worse than a bunch of old women.

"Fine." Her wide grin couldn't hide her pleasure. "I'll get the buckboard and be back for you in a few minutes."

Bertram had to take a lot of ribbing before Fancy finally appeared again, but he decided it was worth it. The old-timers got him loaded in the buckboard, and soon he and Fancy were leaving the town behind them for a pleasant afternoon in the countryside.

Those old geezers could laugh all they wanted to, Bertram thought as he stole a secret glance in Fancy's direction. A day in the countryside with Fancy Biggers was a whole lot better than trying to carve out another one of those blasted cows.

A little more than two miles away another young woman was spending the day in the countryside, but it wasn't quite as pleasant.

The mule had been nothing but trouble from the moment Wynne left River Run. It didn't want to walk, and it didn't want to sit down. It just seemed to want to exist—nothing else.

Two miles out of Springfield she'd had to slide off the mule and practically drag it another few feet before she realized they were going to have to get a few things straight, one being that she was the boss and the mule was going to have to bow to that fact.

By now the heat was unbearable. Wynne angrily jerked off her hat and fanned her face for a moment. The blister was paining her again, so she hobbled over to a grassy patch and took off both shoes. Relieved, she wriggled her toes for a moment, then hobbled back and stuffed her shoes into her valise, which she had tied on the mule's back.

Now she felt a little better, and after a sip of tepid water out of the canteen, she turned her attention back to the problem at hand: the mule.

Perhaps if she tried to explain her predicament to the animal, it just might listen to reason. At least it was worth a try. The horses at home had liked to have her talk to them.

"Now, mule, you and I have got to have an understandin'." Wynne began in her most cajoling voice. "I've got a job to do, and you're here to help me do it."

It didn't seem overly interested.

"Now I know you had a nice stall in that stable, but I've brought you out here in the hot sunshine, and we're goin' on an adventure." That was it. Lie to it. Perhaps . . . Oh, fie! It didn't really matter what she said. The danged animal didn't understand a word she was saying!

Besides, whom was she trying to fool, herself? Adventure, ha! She was out to kill a man, and she was beginning to wonder if she was really equipped to handle the job.

Wynne sat down again, one hand holding one rein while the mule sat facing her with a simple placid look on its face.

Cold reality was beginning to appear, and some of her earlier enthusiasm for the task she'd set herself was beginning to seep away. "If the truth be known, mule, I think I may have bitten off more than I can chew," she confided.

"Miss Fielding was very strict about things like servin' tea properly and carryin' on a charmin' conversation, but how do you kill a man? Even one you hate with all your bein'?" She was quite sure *Godey's Lady's Book* had absolutely nothing to say about the way to handle that task. In fact, it said quite the opposite. A proper young woman did not attempt revenge. She was above that.

"Such triflin' with a lady's heart should be avenged by the men in her family," Wynne assured the mule. A deep sigh escaped her. There were no men in the Elliot family now. They all were gone, and a tear dampened her eye.

A long, low roll of thunder rumbled across the western horizon. "Oh, flitter, mule. If it rains, I don't know what I'll do." She stood up and tugged on the reins. "Come on. Please, please cooperate," Wynne begged but the mule didn't budge.

She shielded her eyes against the bright sunlight and looked around her. Other than the ominous-looking dark clouds on the horizon there was nothing but trees and scrub brush and hundreds of grasshoppers surrounding her. The lack of rain had made the pesky creatures abundant this year. They clung to her skirt and hopped around her feet with the most unnerving exuberance as she scanned the grove of hickory trees off to the right. Her eyes narrowed when they focused on what seemed to be some sort of shelter nestled between the trees. The dense foliage almost hid the old building, but on closer inspection Wynne decided that it must be an old log cabin.

Perhaps if she were lucky, the owners wouldn't mind her taking refuge when the storm broke. But the first thing she had to do was get the darned mule to move.

Turning her attention back to the animal, she tugged on the rope halter and tried once again to force the beast to move its feet. The beast, of course, was not inclined to do so. "Ohhh!" Wynne jerked on the halter and was rewarded with a long, loud bawl which split the air with a sound resembling Gabriel's last trumpet's blast. "Oh, my Lord!" And she dropped the reins to cover her ears, completely unaware of the lone rider who appeared in the distance.

Cole slowed his horse to a walk as he surveyed the scene below him. The blue of his eyes turned to a deep indigo as he rested his forearm across his saddlehorn and watched with growing amazement.

Wynne was standing in front of the mule, which had set itself squarely in the middle of the trail. They hadn't made it much past two miles out of Springfield, but somehow that didn't surprise him.

What did surprise him was that she was standing there shaking her finger in the animal's face and from the look of it preaching it a sermon.

Damn fool woman, he thought irritably. Reaching into his shirt pocket for a smoke, Cole asked himself once more why he was wasting precious time following her, time that could well be spent on a hundred other things. Since he'd been gone, the farm had gone steadily downhill. Ma had done her best, and he'd hoped Cass would stay there to help out, but he'd gone off to Savannah and then the war. There were fences to be mended, ground to be tilled, crops to be planted, and what was he doing?

Chasing a crazy woman, that's what. He'd cursed himself all afternoon for even giving her a second thought. When he'd seen her in town, he'd laughed at the spectacle she'd been, bouncing around on the back of that mule, pans clattering. He'd told himself then that whatever happened to her was her just due. But as the day wore on, her pitiful plight kept coming back to him. It didn't matter that she was a woman unused to the roughness of the Ozarks, but it had suddenly occurred to him that she might be more dangerous than he was giving her credit for.

Oh, he didn't actually think she had the skill it would take to kill his brother, even on the remote possibility that she could find him. But there was always the chance she could accidentally kill him if she came upon him unexpectedly. Not with any expertise, but through sheer clumsiness!

The thought had nagged at him all day, and by

late afternoon he'd decided that since he was the only one who knew what she was up to, he would have to make sure that didn't happen. So, instead of working to get the farm back into shape, here he was trailing Wynne at a discreet distance, and it was getting ready to rain.

Damned woman. She'd been nothing but trouble from the day he and Beau had come across her, and now he was going to be following her across the state for the next few weeks. His purpose was not to protect her—whatever happened to her was her own blamed fault—but there was Cass to consider. He found it hard to believe Cass was the man who'd left Wynne at the altar, but if he were, he would be made to answer to Cole when he found him. Cass was the youngest, and Cole had always been protective of him since he'd never known their pa; but he'd brook no such actions from either of his brothers. If a Claxton man gave his word, then it was to be honored.

But it seemed there was no end to the trouble that Elliot woman caused. Not only had Wynne delayed their arrival at home, but she'd made him lie to Ma. It was ridiculous, but having to lie to Lilly made him feel like a kid again. He'd had to make up some farfetched story about needing to ride to Kansas City to conduct unexpected business.

Beau had looked at him as if he had suddenly taken leave of his senses. Cole had refused to offer any other explanation and had promptly gathered his supplies, saddled his horse, and ridden off without another word, leaving a puzzled mother and brother gaping after him.

He drew on the cigar in annoyance and shook his head disbelievingly at the scene continuing below him. The little twit sat in the grass, her feet firmly planted as she pulled on the mule's halter. The animal suddenly lurched forward, knocking Wynne flat on her stylish fanny, then stood over her, braying.

A tiny grin threatened Cole's stern features as he heard Wynne's screech of angry indignation. She was living up to the reputation of redheads' having a bad temper. At first he wanted to applaud the mule, but on second thought he nudged his horse forward and walked it down the slope.

Wynne might have guessed the rider approaching was none other than that miserable Cole Claxton. Squinting up at him, she was never more aware of her rumpled dress, the dirt on her hands, which had probably been transferred to her face, and the strands of hair which were falling about her face. Her shoulders slumped in dejection.

Eyeing her bare feet coolly, Cole reined the horse to a stop and peered down at her in ill-concealed amusement. Taking another drag on his cigar, he inquired in a pleasant voice, "Having a little trouble, Miss Elliot?"

"What are you doing here?" she snapped.

Once again the smile teased the corners of his mouth. "Why, Miss Elliot, you act as if you're not happy to see me," he said dryly.

"How astute of you. I'm not." Wynne jumped to her feet and tried to brush the dust and grasshoppers off her skirt while trying to conceal her toes beneath the hem.

Cole watched while she fussed with her appearance and muttered what sounded suspiciously like some very unladylike obscenities under her breath. Her hair had come totally loose from its pins, and limp curls hung down her back.

"I thought you were going to take the stage to Kansas City," he said provokingly.

"I decided it would be better to travel by . . . mule," she replied curtly. She would die before she would let him know she hadn't had a choice in the matter. "If I'd gone by stage, I might have missed Cass on his way back," she added defensively.

"Oh? Well, here I was thinkin' maybe you couldn't get a loan at the bank, so you went all over town tryin' to sell your pearl ring and that didn't work either, so you finally had to go over to the stable and swap the fool thing off for this old mule and backpack."

"Well, obviously you thought wrong," she said huffily. Now how did he know all that? There undoubtedly was a bunch of busybodies in River Run!

Shifting in his saddle, Cole had to grin at her growing frustration. "Where's your little bird hat?"

She had had about enough of his sarcasm! Jerking the hat out of her valise, she flung it at him hotly. "Right here!"

Cole ducked when the hat came sailing past his head, but he was still grinning as he straightened up and clicked his tongue. "Did anyone ever tell you you have a nasty temper, Miss Elliot?"

"Mr. Claxton, I'm sure you have not ridden all the way out here to discuss my personality traits," she replied icily. He was just trying to get under her skin, and she was dismayed to find out he was well on his way to accomplishing his purpose. "What do you want?"

Those devastatingly blue eyes skimmed over her lightly as he placed the cigar back in his mouth. "Oh, I don't know. Maybe I missed you and I decided to ride out and see how you were doin'," he answered.

"Very amusing." She wasn't buying that in the least.

"Maybe I wanted to make sure you had a rain slicker." He was delighted by the way her green eyes sparkled brighter with anger by the moment. He motioned with his eyes toward the west. "Looks to me like it's gonna rain, and maybe I got to worryin' about that little bird on your hat," he lied. "I sure wouldn't want that little bird to get all wet, so maybe I come ridin' out here to—"

Once more he was forced to duck quickly as a woman's black shoe came flying past his head.

"Oh, my!" He clucked. "There you go gettin' all riled again. And I'm just tryin' to be nice to you," he said patiently as he sat up straight again.

"Ha! That's a laugh!" He'd never been nice to her willingly, and she was quite sure he wasn't starting now. "Now will you kindly move on, Mr. Claxton, and leave me be?" she demanded. She turned her attention back to the stubborn mule.

"No." His weight shifting in the saddle made it creak. All humor left his face as she stared up at him. "I can't do that, Miss Elliot."

"And why can't you do that, Mr. Claxton?"

"Because now that I know you're out to kill my brother, I have to do somethin' about it."

"Such as?"

"Protect him from your . . . oh, shall we say, ineptitude as a gunslinger?"

Her mouth dropped open in outrage. "How dare you imply that I'm inept with a gun?" She was, of course. In fact, she didn't recall ever having actually shot a gun. But he didn't know that. She glanced around, searching for an example of her shooting abilities. "I'll have you know I can shoot a—a grasshopper's eye out at a hundred feet!" she boasted, and prayed he wouldn't insist that she prove it.

He gave a whistle of mock admiration. "A grasshopper's eye at a hundred feet, huh? Well, I have to admit, that's pretty fancy shootin'," he said with growing amusement.

"That's right. It certainly is," she replied smugly as their gazes locked stubbornly.

"But you'll have to do better than that, Miss Elliot, because I can shoot out a grasshopper's eye at a hundred and fifty feet."

No one would argue that Cole Claxton was not deadly accurate with a gun, but he seriously doubted anyone could *see* a grasshopper from that far away.

Of course, neither one pointed out the fact that there would be nothing left of the grasshopper as evidence to support this boasting should they actually engage in such a childish duel.

Wynne stared at Cole belligerently, his amused face like a needle in her flesh. "I do not want your despicable company on this trip."

"I don't want yours either," he stated calmly. "And don't make the mistake of thinkin' I'm here for you. I'm here for Cass. So don't come runnin' to me when you get yourself in a peck of trouble you can't get out of. I'll be right behind you all the way, Miss Elliot. I want you to be aware of that. And if you do happen to run into my brother, I'll be there lookin' over your shoulder," he said, all trace of teasing now gone from his voice. "I'm givin' you fair warning, Miss Elliot, I will not stand by and watch my brother killed, even if it means one of us gets hurt in the process."

Wynne paused in rearranging the pack on her mule as a shiver of apprehension moved slowly up her spine. By the tone of his voice she knew Cole was not making idle threats. He would prevent her from shooting Cass any way he had to. She studied him again at length. Cole's gaze met hers steadily.

If she was guessing, Cole Claxton was a superb poker player. There was not one flicker in his eye to which she could pin a hope he wouldn't do exactly what he said. He held all the cards, and obviously he had just upped the ante.

A small warning voice from deep within wondered if it wouldn't be smarter to fold while she was ahead.

Chapter 10

If she didn't beat all he'd ever seen. She was crazy! A silly, inexperienced woman who was going to get herself killed—if she didn't starve to death first.

For two days he'd been following Wynne Elliot, and in that short span of time she'd been caught in a brief but drenching rain, had fallen in the river twice, and, when shouting at her mule, used words that matched anything he'd heard in the war. All that had been just a prelude to the screaming fit she'd pitched when she discovered she couldn't start a campfire because she had insisted on swimming her mule through the deepest part of the streams during river crossings and invariably got everything wet, including her matches, and her clothes, and bedding.

She must have slept in wet blankets every night

since leaving River Run, Cole guessed. True, he admitted to himself with a small smile, the fool mule wouldn't walk half the time. Its stubbornness, he decided, could be bested only by its mistress's.

Cole rested easily on his horse and watched Wynne ahead of him on the trail. As far as he knew, the woman hadn't eaten a bite since her trip began. If she had, it would have had to have come from that dirty-looking pack strapped in a lumpy bundle behind her saddle.

She was a mess by now, clothes limp and seemingly permanently wet, her hair hastily thrown up on top of her head. But he was bound and determined he wasn't going to help her.

He had followed her from a safe distance during the day. Every night they had made camp not 200 yards from each other. But while his fire was easily built, with coffee bubbling over the coals and bacon and beans sizzling, the simple but filling fare's aroma wafting toward her, Wynne had steadfastly ignored his presence. And he had ignored hers.

Tonight was a little different, though. Tipping his hat forward, Cole noted with disgust where Wynne had chosen to camp and kicked his horse into a walk.

Naturally she'd pick an open space, too far from

water and without a shelter should something dangerous approach. If she did happen to get a fire started, anyone could see it from miles away.

Why couldn't she just give up this whole thing? Why was she so stubborn about killing Cass? And why was she so blamed certain he was the man who'd jilted her? Such action was unlike his younger brother, at least the brother he knew.

When Cole chose his own campsite, Wynne had already pulled her pack off the mule and spread her blankets. From the way they sagged heavily when she tried to spread them, they were still sopping wet. Cole concealed another unwilling grin. Her hair was falling down again, her dress was dirty a good two inches up from the hem, and the rip in the skirt had increased and was raveling.

It reminded him of that night in the cherry orchard when she'd accidentally unstitched her skirt from her bodice and stood there in her frilly underwear. In spite of himself, Cole hesitated in building his fire and allowed his mind to dwell on the memory. There she'd stood, that unruly cloud of reddish hair making her face appear even younger than the nineteen years she admitted to, in her bodice and white cotton bloomers. He'd never seen a woman look more vulnerable or more attractive.

Later Cole clasped his hands behind his head as he leaned back against his saddle and closed his eyes. The gentle hissing of the campfire was a soothing balm to his weary body as he felt his muscles slowly begin to relax.

Overhead the stars glistened like tiny diamonds, while back to the west there were occasional flashes of heat lightning. The tantalizing smell of rabbit roasting over the fire, and coffee boiling in the pot, drifted delectably through the air.

For some reason he felt guilty that she was sitting in the dark beside an unlit pile of sticks, hungry and probably scared. But if she was, it wasn't his fault.

He shifted against the hard ground uncomfortably, unwilling to admit his conscience was bothering him just a little. He'd warned her about making this useless trip, but she'd refused to listen. The chances that she would find Cass were close to nil, and every day he expected her to give up her crazy vendetta and go back to Savannah.

Maybe after she'd spent one more night of being hungry and listening to the coyote's howl while she sat alone in the dark, she would reconsider what she was bent on doing.

Cole let his thoughts drift aimlessly. He couldn't imagine what had gotten into his younger brother.

If anything, Cass was like Beau, generous to a fault. He wouldn't think of stealing a woman's money. The Claxton men had been raised to be gentlemen, with Cass being the gentlest of the three.

Beau had his tender side. He was always the one to take in injured animals and defend the smallest child in school. Then again, like Cole, he could be angered when provoked. Cole had to admit, though, that Cass was the ladies' man of the three. Ma had spent more time with him as the youngest, had taught him more of the "southern" way of living than he and Beau had absorbed. That was one reason Cass had gone to Savannah to visit relatives he and Beau had never met and the reason Cass had joined the southern sympathizers when he'd enlisted.

Cole sat up and tested the rabbit on the spit; it was almost ready to be eaten, and his stomach rumbled with hunger. As he settled back against his saddle again, his thoughts returned to his family. He guessed that of the three, he was just about the orneriest. Being the oldest, he'd appointed himself the defender of his younger brothers, becoming the man of the family too early to enjoy a childhood.

But none of that could explain why Wynne believed Cass Claxton had been the man she'd been about to marry. There had to be some reasonable explanation. Maybe someone using Cass's name had deceived her. Yes, Cole decided, that had to be it.

Feeling better now, he tested the rabbit on the spit and decided it was done. He gingerly tipped the cross stick loose and off the forked stands, blowing on his scorched fingers. Someone had been posing as Cass. That was the only logical answer, but if that was the case, where was his brother now? Cole shook his head in dismissal. Cass could take care of himself.

Whoever had taken advantage of Wynne had not been a Claxton. He would bet money on that.

The meat popped and sizzled as the fat dropped in the fire, which flared brightly for a moment as Cole pulled a leg free and tasted the succulent meat. His conscience tugged at him so he could barely enjoy the tasty fare. She had to be hungry. And while the days were blistering, the night air could seep uncomfortably into the bones without a fire. Maybe he should give her a few of his matches.

That couldn't hurt anything. It wouldn't be contributing to the approaching murder of his brother. She could build a fire and—no! Cole snapped his thoughts stubbornly back to his previous ones. The quicker she gave up this ridiculous escapade, the sooner he could get back home to rebuilding the farm and the sooner Wynne Elliot would be heading back to Georgia where she belonged.

Wynne was miserably hungry—wretchedly, pathetically starved!

The tempting aroma of roasting rabbit drifted toward her on a gentle breeze as she sat huddled next to a large rock and watched the glow of Cole's campfire flickering in the night. It looked so warm, so comforting.

Her stomach growled painfully as she drew the thin blankets she had found in the pack up around her tighter. Their dampness kept the warmth from being any comfort, and her skin felt clammy and dirty. Her head itched, and her face felt gritty, and her dress was destroyed. All because of that damned mule!

She glared at it as it stood not ten feet away, placid and docile. "Why can't you look like that in the morning when I'm ready to ride instead of being so blamed stubborn? Stupid mule," Wynne muttered, and pulled the blanket tighter around her shoulders.

Her stomach rumbled again. That meat smelled

so good, and the coffee's rich, full aroma filled the air with fragrance, making her mouth water. It was probably some old stuff he had made with chicory, she told herself. But she wouldn't have minded having a cup. For the last two days she'd lived on nothing but the tough jerky she had found in the miner's supplies.

At first she had been too squeamish to think about eating it, but as the hours wore on and her stomach began to hurt from being empty, she'd decided that trying to chew the leathery stuff was better than starving to death.

Wynne rested her head against the rock and fought back the urge to cry. She wasn't one of those crying ninnies, she reminded herself. It took a lot to make Wynne Elliot cry, and it sure wouldn't be over the smell of Cole Claxton's old coffee.

Rebel tears trickled down the sides of her cheeks as she sniffed and pulled the blanket up tighter. Why was he following her anyway? Did he think he could keep her from killing that worthless brother of his? If so, then he'd never dealt with an Elliot before.

Tomorrow she would practice shooting her gun. The blacksmith had been kind enough to include plenty of bullets in the trade, so she didn't need to worry about running out. And she couldn't argue that she needed the practice. She had to make sure that when she found Cass, she could outshoot him and his contrary brother.

Her gaze was drawn back resentfully to his firelight as she absently licked the salty wetness creasing the corners of her mouth.

By tomorrow night she would be a good enough shot to kill her own supper and then she'd just see whose mouth was watering!

If it killed her, she would get a fire started, even if she had to resort to rubbing two sticks together. Of course, she'd already tried that numerous times in the past two days, and it had not yet worked for her.

But if she did kill a rabbit, she would get a fire started one way or another, she vowed.

He was not about to get the best of her. She jerked at the blanket again and winced as she felt the water ooze down her neck. In exasperation she flung the wet material away from her and huddled down closer to the rock.

The next morning Cole was awakened by the sound of a gunshot and a bullet loudly ricocheting off his coffeepot.

With movements finely honed by years of sleeping lightly with an ear tuned to the sounds of battle, he scrambled behind the large log he'd drawn up beside his fire and pressed as close to the ground as a man his size could. After a moment, when no further sound was heard, he peered cautiously over the log toward the fire. "Damn!" He muttered. Black liquid was trickling out of the gaping hole in the coffeepot into the faintly glowing ashes of his fire.

When his gaze swiveled upward again, Wynne stood before him. Her red hair was tumbled wildly about her head, her green eyes sparkled angrily, and her mouth was set with determination. "Give me what's left of that rabbit!" she demanded.

"Wha—" Cole was wide-awake now, but he stared back at her blankly. Every muscle in his body was taut and ready for a fight, but instead of a bushwhacker or some other burly miscreant standing before him, there was merely a five-foot piece of fluff. And she was pointing a gun straight at his head.

"Don't argue with me!" She took a menacing step forward, the metal of her gun barrel glinting wickedly in the early-morning sun. "I said, hand me that rabbit!"

Still trying to figure out what was going on, Cole cautiously stood.

"Don't come any closer," she said warningly, her eyes glittering wildly.

Immediately Cole's steps faltered. Deciding he'd better do as she said, while the gun was waved about dangerously, he picked up what was left of his dinner and what would have been his breakfast. "All right, here's the rabbit. Now put that gun down before you hurt someone."

"Now pour me a cup of that coffee before it all seeps out," she ordered, hefting the barrel of the gun higher.

"Well, hell!" Cole said heatedly. "How do you expect me to pour you a cup of coffee when you've just shot a hole the size of Texas right in the middle of the pot?" He jammed his hands on his hip irritably. "Just what am I supposed to do for coffee now, Miss Elliot!"

"You'll do just what I've been doing," she said without the slightest trace of pity, "without. Now, pour that coffee before it all runs out on the ground."

If it hadn't been for the fact that she had the gun, he would have put a stop to this nonsense once and for all. But he valued his life more than he did the coffee, so he obliged her request grudgingly.

When he handed her the tin cup, Wynne nodded and started slowly backing away from his camp.

Cole stood with his hands still on his hips, watching her irritably. Robbed by a woman. It was too much.

"Oh . . ." She paused in flight. "I want some matches too."

"What!"

"You heard me!" She stamped her foot authoritatively. "I want some matches!"

Cole forgot all about the fact he'd been ready to give her matches the night before. "I'll be damned if I will give you any matches!"

Leveling the gun barrel directly at his chest, Wynne repeated her order in a low, ominous growl. "I said I want some matches please." She waved the gun at him, her finger on the trigger.

Cole wasn't certain how tight that trigger was set. If it was loose, he could be dead where he stood before the fool woman realized what she'd done.

With a grunt of disgust Cole bent and flipped open his own pack. He tossed a small packet of carefully wrapped matches toward her. But when they landed in the dust, Wynne waved the gun at him again.

"Pick them up and hand them to me. Carefully."

Moments later she had her matches and was backing her way out of camp. When she was in safe running distance of her own camp, she turned around and fled the enemy territory.

Cole stood watching her, disbelief still dominating his handsome features. "Damn!" he muttered. She'd done it again. The woman was a menace to society!

As she hurriedly sat down on the rock and began to eat the cold meat, Wynne had to admit that what she'd done was not very nice. But at the moment she really didn't care.

It was only after she had eaten her fill of the delicious fare and drunk the barely warm, bitter coffee that remorse began to set in.

It seemed her life of crime was increasing every day. She sighed hopelessly as she licked the remnants of the tasty rabbit off her fingers.

It had started with her simple, and completely understandable, determination to avenge herself and get her money back. Then she had decided to kill the man in the process, and now she had resorted to robbery.

Lordy, lordy, Miss Marelda Fielding would have a fit.

* * *

Having a woman best him just wasn't sitting well with Cole Claxton. The very thought that a pint-size woman weighing a hundred pounds less than he did could waltz into his camp and demand he hand over his food at gunpoint was nothing short of humiliating.

Had she been a man, she would have lived just long enough to see the muzzle of his gun pointed at her chest. Cole squirmed uncomfortably in his saddle as he reached in his shirt pocket for a smoke.

Damn. He was hungry. He had purposely eaten only half that rabbit last night so he could have the remainder for breakfast. But Miss Elliot had taken care of that.

Well, she wouldn't take him by surprise again. And the next time the fact that she was a woman, a pretty woman, would make no difference.

By evening both riders were exhausted. The heat had sapped their spirits along with their energy, and when Cole noticed Wynne making camp earlier than usual, he was relieved.

At least this time she'd chosen a decent camping space. She had halted in a grove of trees with a clear stream of water running through it. The peaceful setting looked cool and inviting. Much more so than the bare expanse of dusty ground he would have to bed down on if he were to keep her in his sights. Of course, there was nothing to stop him from taking advantage of the better location. Contemplating the thought, Cole sat on his horse. Why should he be uncomfortable just because she was in the lead?

Having made a decision, he rode to within fifty feet of where Wynne was bent over trying to start a fire. Noting the new arrival with only a passing interest, she quickly turned her attention back to her quarrelsome task.

She was no longer concerned Cole would take action against her for stealing his breakfast. If he had intended to do that, he surely would have done so earlier. There'd been plenty of opportunity. He'd followed her more closely today than before.

If the egotistical boor wanted to camp next to her, Wynne supposed there was little she could do to stop him.

With an efficiency that galled her, Cole made camp and had a good fire going long before she had fanned her tiny flame to life.

Moments later he remounted his horse and rode out of camp. Two clear shots rang out over the quiet countryside, and in a few minutes he returned with two plump rabbits dangling from his saddlehorn.

She supposed he was going to sit over there and stuff his face with two rabbits tonight just to annoy her. But he was only fooling himself if he thought she would even notice. So he'd got lucky and killed the rabbits on the first two shots! So what? Wynne carefully kept her face emotionless as she calmly went about spreading her bedroll beside the frail wisp of smoke just beginning to rise from her fire.

No doubt he had heard her trying to kill her own supper all day. All the rounds of ammunition she had shot would have been pretty hard to miss, especially as closely as he had been trailing her. And he could clearly see that she'd failed to come up with any fresh meat. He had probably snickered and laughed at her revolting lack of expertise with a gun, but that didn't bother her. She would get better. That's what he had better be concerned about. Then they would see who was laughing at whom!

Placing her hand at the small of her aching back, Wynne straightened up and watched as Cole took the rabbits down to the edge of the stream and began to clean them. She didn't watch the process, knowing it would only upset her stomach and ruin any success she might have in killing her own dinner.

But the stream was inviting. She was tired and dirty. Her hair was whipped and matted by the dry wind, and her skin felt about to crack from the heat. She felt as if she had never been clean.

Deciding that since she would obviously be going to bed hungry again tonight, she could at least be clean, she gathered up a tiny bar of soap she had packed in the valise and the last of her clean clothing and walked downstream in search of privacy.

While he worked, Cole watched from the corner of his eye as Wynne picked her way along the bank of the river. It was clear she wasn't going to be eating again tonight, but that was her own fault, he told himself. Anyone who wasted twenty rounds of ammunition to try to kill one rabbit deserved to go hungry.

Several minutes later, when she still hadn't returned, Cole found himself unwillingly glancing downstream, wondering what she was up to. Finally he wandered in the same direction. No telling what sort of trouble she had gotten into this time.

Around a small bend in the stream there was an inviting clear stream. Cole stood hidden in a patch of bushes not far from the edge and watched as she waded out into the water.

The setting sun was bathing the tranquil waters in a fiery orange glow as his gaze followed her graceful motions. Her clothes were in a small pile lying on the bank, and she wore only a thin chemise. The water had dampened the delicate material, which now clung suggestively to her rounded breasts as she began to lather with the piece of soap. The lowering sun bathed her dampened skin in gold, and with her body half turned from him the swell of her breast drew him strongly. His gaze was riveted to her. He watched her feminine movements as her hands cupped water and let it flow over her shoulders and arms. He swallowed hard as rivulets flowed between her breasts, making the material of her only scrap of clothing almost transparent. It was as if someone had unexpectedly rammed a fist into his middle. He sucked in his breath, and he swallowed the groan which began low in his throat.

It had been a long time since he'd seen a woman like that and even longer since he'd held a woman close. His mouth went dry as Wynne bent and wet her hair, working the soap into a lather. Eyes as blue as sapphires traveled from the tip of her head to the curve of her waist to the gentle flare of her hips, and he swallowed again. He could only imagine what her skin would feel like lying softly beneath him. He forced himself to turn away, but he couldn't will his legs to ease his discomfort and remove him from the scene before him.

A few moments later he found himself watching her again beneath lowered lashes. She was still lathering her hair, working the rich creaminess through the crimson mass. She was turned fully toward him now. Her eyes were closed in pleasure, and she had a sensual look on her face as she luxuriated in her bath.

The sun had turned her fair skin to a warm honey. It occurred to him that when he had seen her this morning up close, over the muzzle of her gun, her nose had been sunburned and her cheeks were sprinkled with freckles.

Get your mind on something else, Claxton, Cole warned himself as his body made him uncomfortably aware of its reaction to her nearly nude body. She would be the last woman he would make love to even if he wanted to.

But damn, he suddenly found himself actually wanting to. *Now who's actin' like a fool, Claxton? This is the woman who is on her way to kill your brother.* There were other ways of relieving his frustration, he reminded himself as he slowly began backing away from Wynne's bath.

In a few moments he was back at his fire and spitting the rabbits, wishing he were anywhere but where he was.

When Wynne still failed to return, he made certain the meat was roasting properly, then gathered his own clean clothing and went to bathe farther downstream.

Later that night Wynne lay in her bedroll and forced herself to ignore the smell of Cole's supper lingering in the air. His campfire had been banked, and she presumed he was fast asleep by now.

They had not exchanged one word since they'd made camp, but that wasn't unusual. They rarely spoke to each other unless it was to argue.

In a way Wynne wished that weren't so. She was lonely and maybe just a little bit afraid if she would let herself admit it.

This trip was the first time she'd ever been so alone, and she wasn't sure she liked it. She glanced at the other campsite and wondered if Cole had ever felt so lonely. He was probably used to being out in the dark night, beside a campfire with only the sounds of crackling bushes and wild animals.

Did he ever wonder what those strange sounds

were or if they were dangerous? No, probably not. He was a man of experience. She could tell that. A man who'd experienced war, death, killing, and probably love. Love of a woman, of many women. Wynne stared up at the stars. How many times had he lain out on the battlefield wondering if he would see another day? It was difficult to imagine Cole Claxton as a man who had natural fears, but surely he did. The only reason he was following her now was concern for his brother.

She could understand why Cole would feel resentful toward her, why he must hate her. She would have felt the same way if someone were trying to kill one of her kin, yet it would seem that since they were traveling in the same direction, maybe it wouldn't hurt for them to talk a little once in a while. They could discuss the weather, or he could tell her where he had fought in the war, or maybe they could just talk about nothing in particular.

Once more the ache in her stomach reminded her of how hungry she was. And the thought that Cole still had one whole rabbit left over there for his breakfast the next morning didn't help any.

She knew she didn't dare try to take it from him again. He had let her get away with it once, but she probably wouldn't be as lucky the next time, especially since he had witnessed her deplorable accuracy with a gun today. He'd probably laughed all day at her bumbling antics. How embarrassing. Her cheeks burned in the darkness. How utterly stupid he must think her.

Propping herself up on her elbow, she squinted toward his campfire. She tried to locate the left-over rabbit. It was lying next to the fire—all brown and juicy-looking.

No, get your mind off that rabbit! She scolded herself as she let her head drop back down on the lumpy bedroll. *He would break your arm if you tried to steal it from him again. Surely tomorrow you'll be able to kill your own,* she told herself.

But her gaze drifted involuntarily back over to Cole's camp a few minutes later, and she sighed wistfully. She was so hungry! He had at least enough rabbit left for two people, and if he were any kind of gentleman at all, he would have offered to share it with her.

She bit her lower lip pensively. Maybe she could just sort of sneak over there and take a small piece of the meat while he was sleeping. He would never miss it. She would take a piece so tiny he would never even know it was gone.

After slipping out of her blanket, Wynne tiptoed on bare feet across the short space between her camp and Cole's. Holding her breath, she crept closer to where he lay sleeping peacefully. The sound of soft snores helped still her growing apprehension of what she was about to do.

Once again her steps faltered uneasily. She'd better make sure he was actually asleep. He could be trying to trick her. She certainly wouldn't put it past him. She leaned over and studied his sleeping features intently. No, he wasn't trying to trick her. He was asleep.

The plump rabbit drew her magnetically as Wynne tiptoed closer to the fire. Just one teensy little piece. He would never know the difference, but it would mean that she wouldn't have to lie awake all night with an empty stomach.

Holding her breath nervously, Wynne reached out to capture a plump, succulent morsel.

Her fingertips were actually touching the rabbit when, from out of nowhere, a bolt of lightning slammed into her and knocked her flat on her back. "Oh, no, you don't, Miss Elliot!"

For a moment Wynne was so stunned by the impact that she couldn't see straight. Her ears were still ringing when her vision finally cleared. She swallowed hard and looked up into Cole's angry face, his weight pinning her squarely to the ground.

"Get off me, you fool!" she demanded hotly when she finally managed to regain her voice.

"You were trying to steal my rabbit again, weren't you?" he asked curtly. He grabbed her flailing arms and held them over her head.

Their bodies strained against each other, and Cole knew immediately he'd made a mistake by controlling her in this manner. She lay beneath him, her small body tense with surprise, then with anger. But now he was more aware of the softness of her breasts, the warmth of her feminine body than of the straining pull of her arms against his confining grip. It was as if they both held their breaths for a moment, but then Wynne broke the tense moment.

"I most certainly was not!" she said indignantly. Their eyes bore into each other's defiantly.

"Oh, yes, you were," he said accusingly. "And this time you're going to get your fanny whipped for it."

She glared at him defiantly. "You wouldn't dare!"

Turning a deaf ear to her angry shrieks, he calmly flipped her over his knee and began to paddle her squirming behind. Amid all the screams and threats of dire consequences that she supposedly was going to inflict on him in the future, he taught her her first valuable lesson on the inadvisability of stealing another man's meat.

When it was over, she sat before him sobbing, tears rolling down her cheeks, shooting him looks that would singe the hair on his chest.

"Now"—he reached in his back pocket to take out his handkerchief—"from now on, if you want anything that's mine, you come and ask me— nicely." He was gently wiping the crocodile tears from her cheeks as he talked.

"You're . . . a . . . big . . . bully," she said, sniffling.

"No, I'm not. I know that's what you think, but I'm only trying to help you. You can't just go through life snatching things that're not yours from other people. You're goin' to get yourself killed."

"But I was hungry and you wouldn't let—"

"I know. And I'm sorry I wouldn't help you shoot your meat." He replaced the handkerchief back in his pocket and reached out to place his hands on her shoulders. His eyes met hers almost tenderly. "From now on I'll see that you have enough to eat, okay?"

She sniffed and nodded. "And a fire?"

This time he couldn't hold back the grin. "And a

fire." His gaze focused on her mouth. Damn! It looked so kissable.

She stared back at him longingly. Her bottom still smarted from his big, rough hand, but that didn't make him any less handsome at the moment.

Back off, right now, Cole warned himself, but it was too late. Slowly his head leaned forward, and his mouth touched hers.

She sighed, a soft, kittenish sound as her arms automatically wound around his neck and he pulled her nearer. Then his mouth closed over hers in a deep, hungry kiss that left them both pale and shaken a few moments later. His touch had been electrifying and exciting, so much so that it left her breathless.

"Uh." Cole cleared his throat nervously as he forced himself to release her. "Sorry about that, Miss Elliot." He had no idea why he had done that!

Wynne quickly jumped to her feet and began to fuss with her hair. "It's—it's quite all right, Mr. Claxton." Whooee! Cass had never kissed her that way!

"Listen." He stood up and moved over to the fire to retrieve the extra rabbit. "You take this and go on back to bed."

"No, I couldn't," she said nicely. "It's your breakfast."

He glanced at her in disbelief. Women! Ten minutes ago she was ready to steal it from him. "No, I insist." He generously extended the meat to her.

Her hand immediately flew out to accept it before he could have second thoughts. "Well, if you're sure . . ."

"Yeah," he said dryly. There was that grin again. "I insist."

He watched as she hurriedly carried the rabbit back to her camp with an air of triumph and a sneaky smile on her face.

Ha! She thought smugly. *I guess I finally brought him to heel!*

Ha! Cole was echoing, with his own smug grin. *Little did she know that I killed the rabbit for her in the first place.*

Chapter 11

The following morning Wynne was awake long before the sky slowly began to shed its heavy mantle of darkness. She lay in her bedroll, watching the eastern horizon with a strange sense of detachment from the beauty unfolding before her.

Her mind was still on the kiss Cole had given her last night. "Taken" would be a more appropriate description. For she would never willingly have allowed that man such liberties with her!

It never occurred that she'd done very little to stop the unexpected embrace or, in fact, that she might have actually encouraged him in the matter. Instead, she chose to think of herself as the victim who had once more been made to suffer at the hands of a Claxton.

The longer she lay and thought about what had happened, the easier it was to convince herself that she'd had nothing to do with the kiss and that Cole had had everything to do with contributing to her damaged pride.

Oh, she would grudgingly admit the kiss had been nice. But certainly not pleasant by any means, a bit stimulating, perhaps, but only mildly so.

Most gentlemen would not kiss a woman in the way Cole Claxton had kissed her! All fiery and hungry . . .

The man should be ashamed of acting like such an—an animal!

Still . . . Her hand came up gingerly to touch her mouth, which was still bruised from his virile assault. She had to admit she had never, in all her nineteen years, been kissed that way.

But the only reason the kiss had stimulated her in the least was that Cole resembled Cass so strongly. That was the only reason why her mouth still tingled and she grew slightly breathless when she thought about the night before, the only reason her body grew warm and liquid with the memory. Fool. Cole Claxton had probably had a hundred women.

Wynne rolled over onto her side and glared in the direction of his camp. She couldn't see him, couldn't see that devilishly handsome face. But she could see in her mind those penetrating blue eyes, that thick hair which curled at the slightest provocation.

Oh, yes, Cole Claxton was breathtakingly handsome—Wynne groaned aloud with frustration—but he was also cruel, unrefined, uncivilized, and a big bully with little regard for a woman's gentle nature.

But considering her own eagerness to fall under the spell of his younger brother, it was little wonder that she was probably only one of a number of women intrigued by Cole.

Still, she wasn't about to make the same mistake twice. She wanted Cole Claxton out of her life. She was good and tired of his following her day after day, taunting her, laughing at her lack of experience in the wild. And she intended to do something about it, starting today.

She rolled out of her bedroll, talking to herself as she folded the blankets and tried to smooth some of the wrinkles out of her dress. She was going to lose that scoundrel if it was the last thing she did. She was more than capable of taking care of herself, no matter what he thought.

Once she had made up her mind, it took very little time to wash her face and hands, change into a fresh dress, and break camp. In a few minutes

Wynne was urging the mule out of the grove of trees just as the sun started to rise over the hilltops.

"Giddeyup, you ornery mule!" she commanded in a hushed tone, giving the animal a smart kick in the ribs. For once the animal complied with her wishes and set off in the bone-jarring trot which rattled her teeth and jerked her neck about painfully.

Leaning against a spreading oak, whose base was shielded by a thick undergrowth of wild grapevines, Cole watched the mule lope away with its ungainly rider. He shook his head tolerantly as he reached in his shirt pocket for a smoke.

Now what in the hell was she up to? he wondered wearily.

He'd had a hunch she would try to make a run for it this morning. From where he'd concealed himself he'd been fully aware of the moment she'd awakened and had watched in amusement as she'd studied his camp and mumbled to herself.

He'd almost laughed aloud as she'd carefully smoothed her hair and perched that silly hat back on top of her head. Why on earth she insisted upon wearing that hat and the corset he knew was beneath that Sunday dress he'd never understand.

Pushing himself away from the tree trunk, Cole moved toward his camp in his easy stride. What he ought to do was turn around and go home, he told himself. He was tired of sleeping on the ground and having to hunt for every meal. He'd lived like that for the past four years, and he was tired of it.

Going home was such a tempting thought that it almost brought him pain, but then another equally disturbing one worked its way back into his mind. For a brief moment Cole let himself think about how good Wynne had felt lying beneath him last night. All soft and fragrant, all woman. Even having been on the trail for days, she still smelled feminine and nice, like the lilac bushes that grew wild across the countryside. And her hair. The crimson strands had felt like that piece of material he'd bought Lilly for Christmas one year. The tinker had had a bolt of it in the back of his wagon. Silk he'd called it, and it was really pretty. Yes, her hair had lain across his bare arm like rich, elegant silk, and it made a man long to run his fingers through it.

Cole irritably slapped his bedroll onto the back of his horse and stared in the direction she had taken. His body followed the direction of his mind, and for the first time he found himself wishing Wynne had been one of the new girls Hattie had hired. That way he could have followed through

on his instincts without thought of the consequences.

Pulling his thoughts back to the problems at
hand, Cole sighed and flipped his half-smoked cigar out into the stream. He was tired, tired of
responsibility, tired of duty.

Just once he wished there were a simple answer
to a problem. But he'd looked after Beau and Cass
since the day Pa died, and he guessed he wouldn't
be stopping now.

Not—and a smile curved his mouth—when
Wynne Elliot was running around the countryside,
threatening to blow one of his brothers' brains out.

It was truly a glorious morning. The birds were
chattering in the trees, and the sound of an occasional woodpecker held Wynne's attention as the
mule trotted along.

Taking a deep breath, she turned her face up
and smiled happily. It felt marvelous to be free of
the specter of Cole Claxton following her within
hailing distance.

Urging the mule in a more northerly direction,
Wynne concentrated on making her trail harder to
follow. By the time he woke up, she wanted to be
only a memory.

She prayed she could keep her sense of direction and not become hopelessly lost. The blacksmith had said to steer north, and that's what she had been doing.

She had to laugh when she thought about how incensed Cole would be when he realized how easily she had rid herself of him.

It only served him right, she thought smugly. It was high time he was made aware he wasn't dealing with a complete imbecile. No sir, Mr. Cole Claxton was dealing with Wynne Elliot, a courageous woman who had survived the deaths of her parents, who had held a plantation together, if only for a little while, and who could take care of herself on the trail and could do just fine without a man's help.

Her delighted laughter rang out clearly and sweetly over the hillsides. He might not believe she was capable of anything other than making a fool of herself, but Mr. Claxton would know differently soon enough. Oh, would he ever!

By midafternoon the sun was a blistering red ball again, the heat so oppressive that Wynne could hardly breathe. The mule had slowed to barely a walk now as it picked its way along a narrow path that was overgrown with prickly briars and thickets. Vines trailed across the path, brushed at her face, and caught her hair. She had abandoned the main road hours ago to ensure her getaway but was still careful to travel northward.

Periodically she reached up to swipe halfheartedly at the moisture continuously beading on her flushed features. She would have given anything she still owned for a drink of cool water, but in her haste to break camp she had forgotten to fill the canteen.

Ordinarily water shouldn't have been that hard to come by, but with the recent lack of rain, most streams and gullies she had crossed had been bone-dry.

And she thought she really should stop and throw this blasted corset away before she fainted clean away from the heat. She wasn't sure what was causing her the most agony: the pantaloons, the corset, the layers of petticoats, or the lack of water. But she wasn't about to part with any of the three items of apparel. A woman must maintain some bit of propriety even in this wilderness, she told herself as she dabbed daintily at her cheeks and throat.

If and when she ran into Cass, she wanted to look her best, although she had to admit her dress was becoming wilted and dirty.

Of course, she had two other dresses packed away in the valise, but they were not nearly as nice as the one she was wearing. It was foolish to dress so nicely every day just on the remote chance she might actually encounter Cass, but her pride prevented her from traveling in comfort. Her hand absently reached up to readjust her hat, and a thin layer of dust trickled off the brim and brought forth a sneeze that resounded loudly around the still countryside. When he saw how beautiful she looked, Cass would be absolutely sick that he had walked out on her just before he became absolutely dead, that is.

There were still several hours of daylight left when Wynne finally admitted she couldn't go another mile. She halted the mule on a hill which overlooked a deep valley. A growing sense of despair threatened to sap what little fortitude remained. She was tired, hot, sticky, and convinced by now that she had no idea where she was or if she was even going in the right direction.

Dominating the air now were gnats, which flew around her face and stuck to her bare skin. The sun had burned her face and cheeks in spite of the hat, and the tops of her hands were beet red too. The tip of her nose itched and was peeling, and she didn't even want to guess what it looked like. It was impossible to go on, yet she didn't know what else to do.

The combination of heat and the lack of food and water made her head swim. It was all she could do to hold herself upright in the saddle, and she still had to make camp and try to find something to eat before darkness fell.

For a moment she almost wished the "pompous ass" were still following her. She turned in the saddle and peered almost longingly back in the direction from which she'd just come. He wasn't behind her, of course. She had been too thorough in her escape. By now he was probably on his way back to River Run, where in a few days he would have a wonderfully clean bed to sleep in and huge plateful of Willa's chicken and dumplings to gorge himself on. The thought of all those rich dumplings swimming around in a golden gravy with plump pieces of tender chicken made Wynne's stomach rumble with protest.

Well, this was no time to start feeling sorry for herself, she thought. Straightening her shoulders with some effort, she forced herself to think. She had a goal, and she was going to reach it come hell or high water.

There were two remaining matches and plenty of bullets left. Surely to goodness she would be able to kill one small rabbit for her supper. She was getting better at hitting the targets she chose.

Nudging the mule with her heels, she urged it down a steep incline and held on tightly. Rocks tumbled over the mountainside and hit the walls of the lower canyon, but she refused to look down. She was dizzy enough as it was. It was all she could do to hold on because the fool mule kept trying to brush her off on the trees which crowded close to the narrow path. Vines and limbs reached out and snatched at her clothes and hair. At one point the mule nearly succeeded in knocking her off against an old oak just covered with strange-looking vines.

Wynne decided to plan her next steps as a means of keeping her wits about her. She would camp at the bottom of the valley tonight. With luck there would be water available. She closed her eyes and prayed that would be the case. Then she would try to find something to eat, a rabbit or a squirrel, but most likely just berries again. Her mouth watered at the thought of fresh meat roasting over a fire.

It seemed it took forever for the mule to make its descent, but the path finally widened and became more level.

The air was a bit cooler down there. The tall limestone bluffs gave partial shelter from the sun's burning rays. She pushed at the thick mass of hair on her neck and vowed to find something to tie it away from her face before she started out again in the morning, even if it meant ripping a piece of cloth from her petticoat. She brushed at the leaves which had settled and caught in the material of her dress.

By now she had removed the hat, her one concession to ease her agony, and tied it on the saddlehorn. She could always put it back on should she run into Cass unexpectedly, and it was sheer heaven to let the small breeze that was faintly stirring blow freely through her heavy mass of hair.

Suddenly there was a new aroma permeating the air. Her nose lifted slightly as the unmistakable smell of fatback sizzling over an open fire filled her senses.

Cole! He had followed her! But jubilation quickly turned to smoldering resentment. How dare the man continue to follow her when she had made it perfectly clear she didn't want his company?

Still, the aroma of his dinner tempered her anger somewhat as she urged her mule into a faster gait. Perhaps he would be kind enough to share his meal with her tonight, although that might be pushing optimism to the very limit.

In her eagerness for food she let the mule break

through the clearing with the grace of a runaway stage. But she quickly yanked the animal to a halt as six revolvers were whipped out of their holsters with astonishing speed and pointed directly at the center of her chest.

Wynne's eyes widened as she stared almost openmouthed at the tattered, dirty men standing before her. The realization slowly dawned on her that it was not Cole's fatback she had smelled cooking, but rather these frightening-looking men's.

"Oh, lordy!" she muttered, and yanked the mule's head around and kicked his flanks. While she knew it was futile, she at least had to try to correct this newest blunder.

The mule hadn't taken three strides before she was hauled off and flung roughly to the ground. With another part of her mind, Wynne was aware that the sleeve of her dress was ripped from the bodice and the buttons down the front torn loose with the violence of her fighting. Kicking and screaming, she tried to scratch out the eyes of the ruffian holding her down, but to no avail. Recognizing defeat, Wynne lay still, staring up at the bearded face of her captor.

"Well, well, boys, look what we got here," the assailant crowed as the other men slowly slid their guns back in their holsters. His dark eyes stared at her face. Then his gaze slid over her shoulders and to the shadow between her breasts. Her heart beat so heavily that her skin moved with it, and she struggled to control her breathing so he would look somewhere else. His thin mouth smiled knowingly as he noted her efforts and the reason for them. A strange gleam came into his eyes, and his face tightened. A thread of real fear raced down Wynne's spine.

She twisted and kicked as the bully hauled her over his shoulder and carried her to where the others stood around the campfire, drinking coffee. The odor of his unwashed body was so strong it made her empty stomach roll, and she had to swallow hard several times to fight the growing nausea that threatened to overcome her.

"Why, looks like you got yourself a little hellcat, Sonny." The other men laughed as Sonny flung Wynne down on the ground like a bag of grain and eyed his new possession greedily.

For the first time in her life Wynne lost her voice as cold, paralyzing fear rendered her speechless. The men surrounding her were a terrifying sight to a lone woman. Besides the one standing over her, four stood around the fire, with another sitting on a large rock. He caught her attention momentarily. It looked as if he were reading a book!

A fifth man, stood away from the group. He was almost hidden in the shadows at the edge of the small clearing. Apparently he was on watch while the others ate their supper.

Wynne swallowed hard and sat up a little straighter, determined to look death right in the eye. Even while she willed her pounding heart to quiet down, her mind took in impressions automatically. None of the men looked more than twenty-five at the oldest. But they were dirty and unkempt, their clothes worn and dusty. Their hair was long, and their beards were untrimmed. They stared at her with a callous observation that made her feel like a "thing" rather than a woman. She was afraid even to guess what they might be thinking.

One of the men called out, "Right pretty-lookin' red-headed she-devil, Sonny. You gonna share her with us?" The man stepped over to examine Wynne more closely. Her breath caught as he reached a dirty hand out toward her. He took a lock of her hair and slid the shiny mass through his fingers absently, all the while staring into her terrified eyes. "Real pretty," he murmured again, and there was something in his eyes which compelled her to study him a little closer. He looked young, terribly young.

"Please," she finally managed to say, "let me go—"

"Ah, Jesse, you'd think anybody was purty after that woman in Kentucky. Why, she was ugly 'nough to vomit a buzzard," one of the other men said, chortling.

They all broke out in a new round of laughter, but the young man holding a lock of Wynne's hair was unruffled by their friendly jesting.

"That may be rightly so, but this one's real purty." He seemed to be speaking more to her than to the men, and his voice was soft and soothing.

"Now, look, Jesse, I got her first," Sonny whined when he noticed the way Jesse was looking at her.

"Yeah, maybe so, but I'm not sure I'm gonna let you have her first," Jesse said over his shoulder. He kept his attention centered on the frightened girl standing before him. "Where ya goin' in such a hurry, honey?"

"Nowhere—to Kansas City." She corrected herself hurriedly when his eyes narrowed warningly.

"Kansas City? That's a mighty long way for a woman to travel alone," he said chidingly.

"Well, I'm not exactly alone," Wynne lied. "I—I

have this man with me. He'll—he'll be along any moment now, so I really must be running along."

The men laughed again at her attempt at bravado.

"I'm supposed to be making camp while he hunts our supper." She continued her bluff. "And he probably would be quite upset if he finds out you have detained me, gentlemen. He's a big, short-tempered jackass—uh, man"—she hurriedly corrected herself again—"and he doesn't put up with a lot of nonsense." She began to edge slowly back toward the mule.

"Ohhh, me, oh, my! He probably will be real upset if we detained her, gentlemen." One of the men mocked her in a feminine voice. They all roared again and once more goose bumps rose on Wynne's skin.

The man reading the book glanced up at all the boisterous laughter and frowned. Laying the book down carefully on the rock, he stood up and stretched.

Wynne's eyes widened in disbelief as she noticed the title of the book was *Venus and Adonis* by William Shakespeare.

Jesse turned and grinned at his brother good-naturedly. "Where ya going, Frank?"

Frank and Jesse. The names rang a bell in

Wynne's muddled mind, yet she couldn't think where she had heard them before. But she knew she had.

"Thought I'd check the horses," Frank announced.

"Ah. Did we bother you?"

"No," he said. "Just thought I'd stretch my legs for a bit."

"Do you mind if I go with you?" Wynne piped up in a shaky voice.

She had no idea if this man was as bad as or possibly worse than the rest of them, but anyone who read Shakespeare didn't seem as frightening to her.

"No! You can't go with him," Sonny exclaimed indignantly as he jerked her back to him. "You're staying right here, sugar face."

Having regained some of her spirit, Wynne sent him a sour look. She'd sugar his face. First chance she got.

But Sonny was only amused by her dour expression as he dragged her over next to the fire and shoved her down onto an old blanket. "How about some supper, honey pie? We was jest about to 'dine' when you dropped in."

"No, thanks."

"Aw, have we spoiled your appetite?" Sonny

grinned at her. "Better eat a bite so's you'll have some strength." He glanced at his buddies, and they all laughed again. "I have a feelin' you might need it later on."

Jesse smiled with the other men but decided to let the issue of who had first claim on her lie for the moment. He went back to his watch, but she still sensed his gaze lingering on her.

Fear had eliminated her hunger, and she shook her head mutely at Sonny's urgings to eat something. Staring into the fire, Wynne tried to bite back the urge to cry.

"Better eat, woman. You're gonna need it." He taunted again wickedly, for her ears only.

Wynne shivered. At her stony silence Sonny shrugged and turned his attention to his meal.

Turning her back to the men, she sought to fasten her bodice again with the few buttons left and plucked ineffectually at the torn threads of her sleeve. Hell and damnation, what was going to happen to her now? Tears were again very near the surface, and she blinked them back. These horrible men, every last grimy one of them, were most likely going to rape her, and then leave her for dead. And there would be no way she could prevent it.

The gun was in the saddlebags on the mule, and

the one they had called Frank had led it away a few minutes earlier. There was no way she could get to it without drawing their attention.

It hurt her pride even more when Cole's numerous warnings about the likelihood of such an occurrence began bouncing loudly in her head.

A small sob almost escaped. Oh, why hadn't she listened to him? Why had she undertaken such a ridiculous venture in the first place? And this time she couldn't hold back the tears.

It was growing dark when the men finally had eaten their fill. Some had stretched out on the ground to let their meal settle while the others continued to drink coffee. They had eaten like swine, belching and smacking, eating with their fingers since there apparently were no utensils.

She had found herself comparing the motley group before her with the way Cole and Beau had looked the first time she had met them. Actually there was no comparison. The Claxton brothers had been dirty but not bone-deep nasty, the way these men were.

Cole's image kept recurring in her mind, and she suddenly, desperately wished she hadn't been so foolish that morning. Even if he did annoy her and she got on his nerves something powerful, and she had to take food away from him by gunpoint, and he had taken her over his knee and whipped her soundly, she knew he would have protected her from a fate like this, no matter how much he disliked her.

A low rumble of thunder broke into her miserable thoughts. She glanced up at the sky and saw that dark storm clouds were beginning to roll overhead. The thought of rain held no elation for her now. It would never be able to wash away the pain and degradation she was about to experience.

And the reminder of what was about to happen caused her to bury her face in her hands and weep in silent despair as a sharp bolt of lightning streaked across the ever-darkening sky, and the storm moved in.

Chapter 12

With the thunder and lightning came the wind. Cool, blessedly welcome gusts of air snaked through the treetops and sent showers of red sparks from the campfire skipping across the parched earth.

"Looks like we're in for a big one," one of the men shouted above the roar of the approaching storm.

Jesse scanned the ever-darkening sky with troubled eyes. The clouds looked ominous. They boiled and churned and puffed out periodic gusts of wind that bent the tops of the trees nearly to the ground.

Wynne's hair whipped wildly around her face as she tried to knock the sparks from the fire off her dress. The men were running about, trying to quiet the animals, which were becoming increasingly spooked by the thunder and lightning.

Chaos reigned as the wind began to reach almost gale force. Realizing that the men's attention had been momentarily diverted, Wynne whirled and started to run toward the canyon. But before she'd taken two steps, a burly arm reached out and wrapped itself around her waist.

"Let me go!" she screamed, fear and desperation giving her the strength of a wildcat. She struggled wildly, scratching and kicking, as Sonny dragged her back to the camp. His maniacal laugh blended with the howling wind as his hands bit cruelly into the tender flesh of her arms.

"No need to run, honey. Ol' Sonny'll take care of you!" Again he laughed, raising his voice to the sky and whooping loudly as his hand reached out to squeeze her breast.

Wynne screamed in protest and sank her teeth into the meat of his forearm. But he only laughed harder and jerked her up against his hard body, his eyes glittering with aroused passion. "That's it, honey pie. Fight me. I love it when my women fight me."

She spit in his face, then gasped as his broad hand connected sharply with her cheek. For a moment the sound of the wind was forgotten as she actually saw stars.

"I think that'll be about enough." A new voice

had entered the fracas now as a tall man stepped into the clearing, a Springfield rifle leveled squarely at Sonny's head.

"Let her go, Morgan," he commanded calmly.

Cole's ice blue gaze swept the group, making certain the six he'd seen from where he had been hiding were well within the range of his rifle. Wynne couldn't have picked a worse group to fall into. He counted Frank and Jesse James and several others who'd ridden with a splinter group of Quantrill's Raiders during the war as some of the orneriest men around. And of course, she had found them.

Wynne moaned and sagged with relief when she saw Cole standing not ten feet away. He looked unusually tall and commanding, and she couldn't remember ever being so glad to see anyone. The pompous ass looked incredibly beautiful to her.

Sonny Morgan was startled by the new arrival and slow to comprehend what was taking place. "Claxton, what the hell you doin' here?" he demanded irritably. Now there was gonna be another one he'd have to share her with!

The other men had begun to move in closer when Cole stepped back and motioned for them to throw down their guns. Belts were reluctantly unbuckled and quickly dropped to the ground.

Cole chanced a hurried glance at Wynne, his snapping blue eyes sending a clear message that she had foolishly gotten them into this sticky situation and she was going to hear about it if they made it out alive. "Are you all right?" he asked curtly.

She nodded sheepishly.

"Okay, Morgan. Just let her go, and there won't be any trouble."

"Ah, hell, Claxton, what's it to you?" Sonny argued, pulling Wynne possessively to his chest. "I found the little woman first, and I figure that makes her mine."

Cole's gaze never wavered, and his gun was steady as he raised it a fraction more to encompass all of Sonny's broad chest. "Well, you figured wrong this time."

Comprehension was still slow to dawn on Sonny. "How come?"

"Perhaps what Cole is tryin' to say is that the little lady is his." Jesse spoke up as he tipped his head in a mock salute to the man holding the gun on him.

Jesse James had met Captain Cole Claxton during the war. He knew him to be a fair man when it came to a fight, but a deadly force when he was threatened, so he knew it was best to hand the girl

256

over to him without a fight. Especially in view of the fact Cole had a rifle and he didn't.

Sonny looked at Cole resentfully. "She your woman?"

That was a tricky question, one that Cole didn't know how to answer. The first drops of rain began to fall as he shrugged noncommittally. "Let's just say I'm lookin' after her interests at the moment." His hand never wavered. "Just hand her over real gentlelike, Morgan, and we'll be on our way."

Sonny glanced expectantly at Jesse, who nodded his silent agreement. After weighing the situation for a few moments longer, Sonny finally shoved Wynne roughly away from him. "Well, hell! take her then. She weren't nothin' but a peck of trouble anyways."

"You noticed that too?" Cole noted dryly.

Wynne shot him a look that should have struck him dead in his tracks. But moments later she found herself edging next to his towering bulk. When it came to choices, she'd rather be with Cole than against him in this situation.

Slipping his arm around Wynne's waist, Cole started backing out of the camp slowly. "Nice to see you again, Jesse," Cole said pleasantly.

"Nice to see you, Claxton." The blue-eyed young man wore a slight grin, but there was that air of danger about him which spoke louder than the smile.

"Frank doin' all right?"

"I'm fine, Cole." The man standing to the side answered quietly. "Good to see ya again."

Cole nodded briefly at Frank James and kept on retreating in measured steps. He could feel Wynne trembling in his arms, and he squeezed her waist in quiet assurance.

"Looks like we're goin' to get a good rain," he continued conversationally, and Wynne thought she was going to scream. The tension in the air was so thick you could have cut it with a knife and *he* was talking as if they were at a Saturday night social!

"Sure could use it," Jesse agreed mildly.

The rain was beginning to pepper down on them now as Cole reached his horse. Never taking his eyes off the other men for a moment, he helped Wynne into the saddle and then swung up behind her, still keeping the gun leveled at the group that stood looking on.

Tipping his hat politely, he said. "Take care now."

"You do the same . . ." came Jesse's reply.

Reining his horse around, Cole spurred the animal into action, and they left the camp just as the sky opened up in a thunderous deluge.

"My mule!" Wynne shouted above the pounding rain.

"What about it?" Cole yelled back as he raced the horse at breakneck speed through the canyon. He doubted any of the men would try to follow, but he wanted to make sure there was plenty of distance covered in the shortest possible time should they saddle their horses and decide to try to take back their "property."

"It's back there!"

"You want to go back and get it?" Cole asked.

"No! But now I won't have anything to ride or wear. And my gun! What about my gun?" she yelled, trying to keep the pouring rain out of her mouth. "Hell and damnation! I'm about to drown," she exclaimed irritably. "Can't you slow down a little?"

"Just pipe down, lady!" he yelled back. "I'm a little out of sorts with you as it is."

"Me!"

"Yes! You! That was a crazy trick you pulled this morning, and you're damn lucky I was around to save your little tail!"

"Why, of all the nerve!" she said, bristling. "I didn't need your help in the least!"

"Oh, no? Well, it sure looked to me like you did!"

"Well, I didn't! I was just getting ready to make a run for it when you showed up," she said.

"Yes, I saw how well you made the break," he snapped.

She sucked in her breath indignantly. Her pride wouldn't let her concede the argument. "Just how long had you been standing there, Cole Claxton?"

He'd been there almost from the first moment she had been captured, but he'd decided to teach her a valuable lesson, provided she wasn't in any real danger. Perhaps from now on she'd listen to what he said. "Long enough to see you were in over your head." His arm tightened around her waist.

It suddenly dawned on her they were riding back in the same direction they had just come from. "Stop!" she screeched.

For one brief moment Cole automatically pulled back on the reins, and the horse slowed. "What in the hell is the matter this time?"

"You're going back the same way we came," she said.

"Oh, for—just dry up, will you!" Cole spurred his horse forward, but she continued to complain.

"We've already covered this ground," she said,

grousing. "Now we'll have to travel it all over again."

That's right, Cole thought smugly. If he could delay her silly mission by even an hour, he'd jump at the chance.

The horse raced through the dark night, carrying its two riders as if the hounds of hell were chasing them. Deafening claps of thunder shook the earth, and lightning zigzagged angrily across the sky as they rode on. Wynne's clothes were plastered wetly against her skin, and her hair flapped wildly about her head as Cole pushed the horse harder. She could feel the imprint of his maleness pressed tightly against her spine as she struggled to scoot up closer in the saddle.

"Sit still," he commanded gruffly, fully aware of what she was trying to escape.

He would just as soon not be in such close proximity with her either, but at the moment he had no choice. He could only hope he wouldn't make a fool out of himself by letting her see how she was affecting him.

Although her experience with men had been limited, she knew that the ride was taking its toll on Cole as a man. She could feel the strength of him at her back, the warmth of his breath against her cheek as his strong arm held her against him.

Unbidden, the memory of his kiss the night before, of his mouth touching hers, pushed its way to the forefront of her mind.

A tiny shiver sent goose bumps popping out all over her when she thought about his making love to a woman. No doubt he would be masterful and exciting, she was forced to admit. He would hold her, and his low voice would murmur words she could only imagine, and when his body . . .

She blushed when she realized where her thoughts had led her. It was only because he reminded her so much of Cass that she let herself think about such things, she told herself again. Yet she found herself smiling with smug satisfaction a few minutes later as the evidence of his discomfort continued to mount to almost alarming proportions, and now it was Cole moving restlessly against her. By his every action he had denied that he was aware that she was a woman. Instead, he had treated her like some pesky fly that he couldn't shake.

Her smile widened mischievously as she purposely squirmed in the saddle and caused him to be the one to back away this time.

"I told you to sit still," he growled.

"Sorry. I was uncomfortable," she replied innocently.

Yes, Cole reminded her of Cass quite often, but the two brothers were as different in nature as corn and sweet rolls, she found herself thinking a few moments later. And she had also come to the conclusion that their looks weren't all that much alike either. Now that she had been around Cole more, she saw that he was the handsomer of the two brothers. He had a certain maturity about him that Cass had yet to achieve, and his hair was thicker, curlier, and coarser than Cass's.

And their eyes—well, they both were blue, but Cole's had a deeper, more vibrant hue than Cass's. And Cole was taller and heavier while Cass had the body of a young man yet to develop fully.

It suddenly occurred to her had she met Cole first, she might never have given Cass a second glance.

Except she could never put up with his ill-tempered, old-goat personality, Wynne reminded herself. Cass had him beaten in that respect.

The mere thought of how he had treated her prompted Wynne to decide to torment him a little more. It wouldn't be the thing most ladies would do, but then he deserved a lesson in humility. After all, he'd just stood cruelly outside that clearing and watched those men mistreat her. And she bet he'd enjoyed every minute of seeing her frightened and shaking in her boots!

She wiggled again. Miss Fielding would surely understand, given the circumstances.

Snuggling back against the warmth of his chest, she faked a graceful yawn and settled her head in the curve of his shoulder. "I do declare I'm plumb tuckered out from all this rowdiness."

Behind her, Cole stiffened with surprise as he reined the horse to a slower pace. The storm was beginning to abate now. There were still distant, low rumbles of thunder, but the rain had slowed to where it was falling only in a fine mist.

He wasn't sure what to make of her unexpected friendliness. She was lying in his arms, totally relaxed, humming softly under her breath. It was as if they were two lovers out on a moonlit ride instead of making a run for their lives. The feel of her against him was unnerving. The ache in his loins was so intense he was in complete misery now. At one point he had about decided to stop the horse and switch her to his back so he could get some relief. But now she was lying against him like a soft, purring kitten, and he couldn't for the life of him make himself move a muscle. It had been too long since a woman had been in his arms this way. Way too long.

And it didn't help matters any that her dress was soaked to the skin and the outline of her small breasts were much more clearly defined than they should be. He carefully moved his hand an inch lower on her waist so there would be no chance of encountering anything he shouldn't. But he couldn't make himself let go of her.

Wynne wiggled again and smiled to herself at his quick, soft intake of breath. She turned and peered up at him beguilingly. "Am I disturbin' you by leanin' back on you this way?"

Cole shook his head mutely, not trusting his voice. *Damn! Claxton,* he told himself, *don't let her get to you this way! Whatever little game she's playing, ignore it!*

The moon peeked out from behind a dark cloud, bathing the two riders in its soft glow as she smiled up at him demurely. "You just tell me when you get uncomfortable."

Like the complete dolt he had always accused her of being, he found himself nodding he would while grinning back at her stupidly. He didn't like how she was affecting him, but he seemed powerless to prevent it! What he should do was set her little fanny right in the middle of the road and let her walk to Kansas City! That's what he should do, he thought angrily. After all, she'd been nothing but a thorn in his side from the moment he'd met her. She wouldn't listen to a word he said. She was constantly goading him. Not to mention the woman's unmitigated gall!

Taking his rabbit by gunpoint was not something he was going to forget very easily. She could count on that. Nor would he forget the reason for this asinine trip across Missouri. She was trying to kill his brother, and he wasn't about to forget that either. Even if she did smell like lilacs.

For the next few moments they rode along in silence. By now exhaustion had erased her teasing mood. Her eyes drooped, and she snuggled closer to Cole's broad chest. It felt terribly good to lie there against him and forget some of the overwhelming problems that this adventure had brought. She had no idea where they were going, but at this point she really didn't care. The horse just kept plodding down the road, and Cole wasn't saying anything.

Only his body continued to relay the silent message that he was aware she was still there. The memory of the kiss they had shared the night before made her pulse suddenly beat faster, and she forced her thoughts back to her newest dilemma.

Now her mule was gone. So were her clothes

and even her gun. She supposed she should be frantic, but strangely she wasn't.

If Cole had been decent enough to save her from a fate worse than death from those horrible men, then he would surely see that she was taken care, at least for tonight. Tomorrow she could start worrying again.

Having a nice man around might not be all that bad, she thought as she grew drowsier. That is, if a woman was lucky enough to find the right man. Where Cass was concerned, she was beginning to realize that she might have just made a bad error in judgment, that's all. Surely all the men in the world weren't like Cass Claxton.

Wynne sighed softly. Perhaps she would reconsider going into a convent when this was all over. Perhaps she would find a man someday who would love her and respect her the way Beau did Betsy.

For the first time Wynne noticed that her resentment of Cass was actually beginning to be more trouble than it was worth. Try as she would, she couldn't seem to summon that terrible, gut-wrenching agony she had experienced toward him only a few days before. There wasn't even the anger she'd clung to so desperately the past few days.

"You haven't eaten again today, have you?" Cole's stern voice broke into her daydreaming.

"No, how did you know?"

"I've followed you all day."

This revelation should have upset her, but somehow it didn't. "You did? I didn't know that."

"I didn't mean for you to."

"If you followed me all day, how come it took you so long to come to my rescue?" she asked crisply. The knowledge that her clever plan had failed stung sharply.

"I wanted you to learn a lesson," he stated calmly.

"You would." She sighed hopelessly again. "And I'll admit I probably have learned a lesson. From now on I'll listen more closely to what you're saying."

"I'll have to see that to believe it. You want a drink of water?" He knew she'd been without that precious commodity all day too.

"Please." She'd decided to be cooperative. What choice did she have?

Cole leaned sideways to unsnap his canteen and handed it to her. "Don't drink too fast," he said.

The water was cool and delightful going down her parched throat. She drank long and greedily until he pulled the container away from her.

"That's enough for now. You'll make yourself sick."

Recognizing his authority, Wynne lay back against his chest once more and gazed up into the sky. Low clouds were racing across the horizon, and in the distance she could still see traces of lightning periodically flashing.

"Who were those horrible men?" she asked as Cole replaced the lid on the canteen.

"Frank and Jesse James, plus a few men they ride with."

Wynne shuddered. "Are those the men Lilly and Beau and Betsy were talking about at dinner the other night?"

"They're the ones."

She shuddered again. "They were disgusting. All except the one called Frank. He seemed a lot quieter than the rest of them."

"They were just a bunch of horn—" Cole caught himself before he said "horny" in front of her. "They were just a bunch of men looking for a good time," he said brusquely.

Wynne lifted her eyes back to meet his. "You mean, all men do that sort of a thing when they're out on the trail?"

"No, not all men," Cole said. "But a woman's just askin' for that kind of treatment if she's runnin' around the countryside without the protection of a man."

She could have argued with him, but the past few hours had made her realize that he was probably right. She nestled back more comfortably in his arms.

He smelled nice, like rain and warm flesh and faint cigar smoke. She nearly gagged when she thought of how those other men had looked and smelled.

"Where are we going to camp tonight?"

Cole swallowed, his mouth suddenly dry as renewed recognition of her femininity assaulted his senses. "We passed what looked like a deserted cabin earlier this afternoon. I thought we might hole up there for the night." His eyes scanned the sky briefly. "My guess is it'll rain again before morning."

"Is the cabin very far away?" She didn't recall seeing any such lodging.

"Couple of miles more."

For the rest of the trip Wynne dozed peacefully. The air was cool now and smelled of damp earth and moist vegetation, and she was so tired she couldn't think straight any longer.

When they arrived at the cabin, Cole suggested she stay on the horse while he checked to see if the dwelling was occupied. In a few moments he was back with the good news that it was empty.

As he lifted her off the horse, it occurred to Wynne that a temporary truce had apparently taken place between them. By the way he was acting, Cole planned to share the cabin with her tonight instead of camping somewhere nearby, as he usually did. And she wasn't about to complain. Her emotions were still rattled from her earlier capture, and she personally didn't plan on letting him out of her sight any sooner than she had to.

It was entirely possible that the gang of men had followed them and might attempt to take her back. She shuddered to think what would happen then. This time Jesse and Frank James might not be quite so polite, and Cole would be a captive, too, and not able to stop whatever they had in mind. She followed Cole closely as he carried the saddle into the cabin.

The cabin was barely adequate shelter. There were a few stray pieces of furniture strewn about the dirty room. Dust and cobwebs dominated the corners and rafters, and the sound of rats scurrying for cover as they entered was a bit disconcerting.

Yet it looked like a castle to Wynne. At least it would be a roof over her head tonight, and that was more than she had been used to the past several days.

Her teeth began to chatter as Cole knelt in front of the hearth and began to build a fire. Her dress clung to her uncomfortably and felt wet and clammy. Her shoes felt as if they were coming apart and pinched her toes as the leather began to dry. A fire would feel wonderful. Some other weary traveler must have used the cabin before them because the woodbox was filled with dry wood.

"You'd better get out of those wet clothes."

Wynne agreed. The rainstorm had cooled the air down until it was almost chilly. She glanced about and located an old blanket lying on a bed in the corner of the room. It wasn't clean, but it was better than wearing those wet clothes and catching her death of cold. Her nose was tickling already with a sneeze.

Her fingers paused uncertainly as she started to unbutton the front of her dress. She swallowed nervously. "Turn your head."

Cole glanced up from the fireplace. "What?"

"I said, turn your head."

"Oh."

Wynne could have sworn she saw him smile as he obediently did as he was told.

A few minutes later she had peeled off her wet dress and underthings and draped the blanket about her shoulders modestly.

By now the fire was going and the room had lost some of its dampness. She busied herself hanging her clothing around the room so it would dry. "What about you? You're soaked to the skin too."

Cole spread out his bedroll and retrieved a blanket. Wynne flushed, knowing that while his blanket had been protected by a piece of canvas, hers must have been just as wet as the clothes on her back since she'd not taken the precaution of having either oilcloth or canvas in which to wrap her things.

Wynne turned her head, pretending to be busy with the fire, while Cole slipped out of his clothes. A few minutes later they were toasting themselves by the fire.

"Have you looked around to see if anyone might have left anything we could eat?"

Gathering the blanket around her more securely, she stood and nearly tripped over the ends. Glaring at Cole, knowing he hid a grin, she went to rummage through the old cabinets. After searching each one thoroughly, she only managed to come up with a bottle of what appeared to be discarded corn liquor.

Holding it up to the firelight, she examined the contents with a frown. "It's half empty."

"Bring it over here," Cole said. "I prefer to think of it as half full."

In a moment she was seated back at the fire and he had uncorked the bottle with his teeth. Extending the bottle to her first, he noticed a slight hesitation on her part. "You first."

She eyed the bottle worriedly.

"Go ahead. Take a sip," he said encouragingly. She was huddled deep in her blanket, and he thought she needed the extra warmth. All he needed was for her to get sick.

Wynne wasn't at all sure she should drink the liquor. On rare occasions her papa had allowed her a small glass of peach brandy, but she'd never partaken of hard spirits.

"I don't know . . ."

He grinned widely, and his eyes twinkled with merriment. Wynne noticed the rare occurrence made him even more breathtakingly attractive. "It won't hurt you."

"Well . . ." She took the bottle and brought it to her mouth. She tipped it up cautiously to let a small amount of the liquid trickle down her throat, then gasped and gagged. The stuff burned like fire. Tears immediately welled up in her eyes, and she fought for breath.

Cole burst into laughter as he scooted over next to her and patted her firmly on the back. "Good, huh?"

"It's—it's . . . hor-r-ible!" Wynne croaked.

Cole shrugged and took a long swallow of the fiery whiskey. Holding the container away from him, he looked it over carefully. "Not bad. I prefer mine a little stronger."

She looked at him sourly. He chuckled again and held the bottle out to her once more. "It'll taste better the second time."

She doubted that was true, but a pleasant warmth was beginning to settle in her stomach as she took another small taste. It still felt as if she were pouring scalding water down her throat, but the liquor actually wasn't as bad as the first time.

The rain began falling again. They could hear it on the roof as they settled back to relax. The day had been long and arduous, and other than being hungry, they both began to feel pretty good. The bottle changed hands regularly, its contents slowly diminishing.

Everything was suddenly becoming quite fuzzy, and Wynne wasn't seeing well at all now. But her eyes seemed intent on lingering on the man who sat across from her. The blanket he had thrown carelessly around him covered only his hips and legs now. The top had slipped down to reveal his brown, bare torso.

Very few times had she ever seen a man with his shirt off, just her papa and a few of the slaves who worked in the cotton fields. But Papa's chest had not looked anything like Cole's. While Papa's had been broad, it had not been nearly as broad as Cole's. Wesley's chest had been rather pale and flaccid, but Cole's was firm and tanned. Papa's had only a few wisps of hair, but Cole's chest was covered by dark, thick hair that curled sleekly against his skin.

Wynne ran the tip of her tongue around the corner of her mouth and wondered what it would feel like to be pressed against him, against his potent maleness. Her mouth went dry with the images floating through her mind, and she closed her eyes momentarily to let them flow freely.

Cole was not unaware of Wynne's preoccupation with him. He was achingly aware, in fact, of the trail her gaze took over his body, uncomfortably aware. And this time he allowed his own imagination to spin.

The liquor was beginning to work its magic, and

he found himself slowly unwinding as he lay back and studied her from beneath lowered eyelids.

The firelight played across her hair, picking up the red glints as it dried. It tumbled across her shoulders and spilled down her back in glorious profusion. The creamy skin on her shoulders compelled him to follow the curve and shadow which pointed to the swell of her breast. When she moved, it was with a delicateness and quickness which reminded him of a colt just getting its legs—an uncertain, beautiful grace. The flickering shadows from the firelight played across her face, emphasizing the hollow of her cheek, the curve of her eyelashes when she lowered them over eyes that were becoming too bright from the liquor.

Cole suddenly found himself wanting to touch her. She was clutching the blanket protectively around her, yet he could discern the curve of her small waist and the following swell of her hip. For her size her legs were long, and the ankle revealed in the fold of the too-short blanket was delicately curved. Even in a dirty, tattered blanket it was painfully obvious Wynne Elliot was a lush, very desirable woman.

There were a million reasons why it was foolish to entertain such ideas of touching her, and Cole knew every one of them by heart. But the drinks had mellowed his feelings to the point where he was actually thinking of kissing her again, and he allowed the thought to linger.

He had never met a woman who could annoy him so quickly yet make him forget all about that anger when she leveled those strange-colored green eyes on him. She was feisty, unreasonable, bullheaded, and had the endurance of six women. Yet she was one of the most beautiful creations he had ever met. At least it seemed that way to him tonight.

Their gazes met and held in the soft glow of the room. Why was he looking at her so strangely? she wondered in her sensual fog. The blue of his eyes turned to dark turquoise as his gaze began slowly but thoroughly to travel over her. Wynne didn't know what to make of it. The liquor had hit her empty stomach with the impact of an oncoming train, and she found herself unable to think clearly.

His eyes were making her feel hot and flushed, and she had a funny ache deep inside. It was as if her bones had turned to water. All she did was think of how good his mouth had tasted on hers last night and that funny ache got stronger and stronger. . . .

She mustn't let her thoughts dwell on him, she

cautioned herself. She broke their eye contact and quickly turned her face toward the fire. Somewhere deep inside she remembered there was some reason why she shouldn't think such things about Cole Claxton. Yet for the life of her she couldn't remember what it was. It had to be important because the feeling was too strong.

A loud clap of thunder shook the cabin as Cole finished the last of the liquor. He set the empty bottle very carefully to one side as if it were very important not to move too quickly. Once more his gaze found hers, and he asked softly, "Are you warm enough?"

Yes, she was. In fact, she was becoming overheated, and she let the blanket slide down her arm a fraction more. "Yes . . . thank you."

He grinned at her lazily. "You might be more comfortable over here." His baritone voice was velvety and slid over her senses like silk over her skin.

She stared at him. "I'm fine . . . thank you."

"You look sleepy." He nearly whispered the words, compelling her to come nearer. She had never seen him this at ease, and the new experience was pleasant.

"I am . . . a bit."

"Why don't you come over here closer to the fire?" he suggested again lightly.

Her pulse raced faster. If she moved any closer, she would be touching him, and she wasn't certain that would be a good idea.

"I'm all right—" But her words were interrupted as Cole reached for her hand and began to pull her closer.

Unnerved, Wynne reacted more quickly than she should have and jumped to her feet. To her dismay the blanket unfolded and slipped to the floor with a brief whisper. Cole's sudden sharp intake of breath rasped in the quiet of the cabin. Instinctively she bent to retrieve the covering, but his hand snaked out to catch her arm.

Once more their eyes locked, and she felt herself growing weak when she saw the way he was looking at her.

"Wynne." He spoke her name in a husky voice as his gaze devoured the beauty before him. "You're . . . so lovely."

He could think of only one thing as he looked at her slender frame. If it had been Cass who had run out on her, then he must have lost his mind.

She was like the picture of a goddess he'd seen in a book one time. She was slender, and her womanhood was obvious against the paleness of her skin. Shadows from the firelight danced on her body, taunting and tempting. Almost unconsciously she straightened beneath his gaze, a woman answering a man's unconscious command. Her hands hung to her side, drawing attention to the soft curve of her breasts, which were small but temptingly firm. They were just the right size to fit in his hand.

"Cole . . ." She whispered his name, knowing she should pick the blanket up and move away from him. A lady would never permit a man to see her unclothed. But she didn't want to move away.

Still watching her, Cole stood up slowly. His blanket dropped away, but he ignored it as he drew her to him. Their bodies met, and he held her against him tightly as he buried his face in her hair. She smelled of freshness, rain and woods. "Wynne . . ." He breathed her name again, and his breath was warm against her skin.

Automatically her face turned toward him, her eyes drifting closed as she drank in the wonders of the feel of his body pressed up against her. His rugged strength made her even more aware of her femininity, and she began to tremble.

"Don't be afraid," he murmured. "I won't hurt you." With those simple words his mouth gently sought hers. He didn't overpower her with his passion but kissed her tenderly at first, his tongue teasing her mouth open to receive his again and again.

The ache deep within her had begun to build again, and she stretched up, draping her arms around his shoulders. Her body moved against him automatically, her breasts aching with desire as his large hands found and molded them. She touched him, moving her palms against his firm flesh. She wound her fingers through the dark hair on his chest and held on to him tightly as his kisses started to deepen. She lost all sense of propriety, forgot everything that had seemed important just a few minutes before.

Cole widened his stance and drew her even closer, pressing her hips flush against his. A groan grew deep in his chest, and he smothered it with her mouth, reveling in the freshness and immediacy of her response.

She had been kissed many times before but never been so totally consumed as she was now. And then they were lying on the floor, one of the blankets spread under them. Cole was whispering things to her she had never heard before, exciting, titillating intimacies, and his hands and mouth were building within her body a tide of passion that threatened to sweep her into oblivion.

Sighs of pleasure mixed with the occasional rolls of thunder as he took her higher and higher. She had never seen a man's bare body, and he allowed her to discover his with a sense of freedom she had never known. He was the first man to make love to her, and he took his time to make sure she found the experience one of total joy.

She pleased him beyond his wildest dreams. He discovered an earthiness about her he'd never suspected lurking beneath that prim exterior. She experimented with an almost childish curiosity, and when she discovered something which pleased him, she explored further and further until he was nearly over the edge of reason.

In return, Cole made love to Wynne as if she were the greatest treasure on earth, and she responded with an abandon that made him laugh with enjoyment and gasp with surprise and pleasure. He'd never made love with a woman who laughed, and he found it an experience he'd never forget. And when she was finally his in the completeness of their lovemaking, she was everything he had ever imagined a woman should be.

When the tides of passion finally abated, he rolled over with her in his arms, and their mouths still sipped at each other languidly. "Mmm . . . sorry about that, Miss Elliot," he murmured guiltily. He felt strangely compelled to say that. After all, a gentleman did not take a woman's virginity unless he planned to make her his wife, and Cole had no such plans at the moment.

"Oh, that's quite all right, Mr. Claxton," Wynne answered in a drowsy voice as her small hand patted his bare chest comfortingly. She wondered why he always felt that he had to apologize when he kissed her or now, after having made love to her? But she didn't let herself dwell overly long on the troubling question.

Soon they fell into an exhausted sleep as the rain pattered gently down on the rooftop and the fire flickered brightly on the hearth.

Chapter 13

She awoke the following morning to find herself cuddled tightly up against his bare chest. He was still sleeping soundly, one arm draped limply around her waist. The sun had been up for hours, but a delightfully cool breeze was blowing through the open window. She blinked her eyes a couple of times to clear her head.

When the haze slowly began to recede, her gaze focused on his hand resting on her bare stomach. It was wide and strong with blunt-cut fingernails that were clean and well cared for. His dark, work-calloused skin made a startling contrast with her alabaster coloring.

The events of the night before suddenly rushed in on her. Hell's bells, how much lower was she going to sink in her pursuit of Cass? Not only would she have to answer to the good Lord for thinking about murder and actually having committed a theft, but now she had given herself to a man without the sanctity of marriage. And they hadn't even made it to the bed!

Wynne sighed hopelessly. There wasn't a convent in the whole world that would have her after she had finished confessing all these iniquities.

Still, with a smile curving her lips, she couldn't make herself regret this newest act of sinfulness.

Tipping her head up, she looked at Cole's slumbering features, and her pulse did that funny little cadence again. Giving in to her curiosity, she let her finger lightly caress the smooth dark skin on his left cheek. Last night had been a new experience for her, one she would forever hold dear in her heart.

In those incredible hours she had forgotten all about Cole's being Cass's brother. Instead, he had been an exciting yet incredibly gentle lover who had brought her into full womanhood in a wild and wondrous way. She sensed that no matter how many men would come and go in her life, she would never forget the joy Cole had brought to her in those few magical hours.

He stirred, his arm tightening around her possessively. He looked different in sleep. The tired lines around his eyes and mouth had softened, making him look much younger. It was hard to believe this was the same man who had angered her so in the past.

It was even more painful when she thought about the fact that he was a Claxton. Perhaps, if things had been different, if Cass had not broken her heart and trampled on her pride, then she might seriously consider the idea that she might, in time, fall in love again.

That new and disturbing thought brought her foolish meanderings to an abrupt halt. Her hand reached down to scratch her arm absently. No, that was ridiculous. She couldn't be falling in love with Cass's brother! Up until last night she hadn't even liked the man, for heaven's sake. You would think that after the misery she'd been through the past few months, she would have learned her lesson concerning men. Yet, strangely, it seemed she hadn't.

That Cole and she had shared such intimacies the night before was due entirely to the liquor, she thought.

She scratched her arm harder, and it felt heavenly. She had never drunk such hard liquor, and combined with an empty stomach—well, she had been—well, taken advantage of again! That's all. The more she thought about it, the more firmly convinced she became that that was what had happened. Cole Claxton, the uncivilized, egotistical ruffian that he was, had taken advantage of her inebriated state and imposed himself upon her—again! Otherwise, she never would have succumbed to his dubious charms.

She glared at his sleeping form resentfully. The nerve of him, taking such liberties with her! Sitting up, she jerked the blanket off, then hurriedly covered her nakedness once more. She couldn't get up and go prancing around the room like this. Cole might wake up any minute, and she would die if he were to see her this way.

He stirred again, and she watched fearfully as, in his sleep, he began to scratch a small patch of redness on his chest. A moment later she found herself scratching her arm again.

Glancing down, she frowned as she surveyed the large, irritated area spreading up her arms with long pinkish fingers. Holding the arm up for a closer look, she studied the tiny, watery blisters with growing concern. What in the blue blazes was that?

Whatever it was, it was becoming quite annoying and painful. Once more she thoroughly scratched the area but found little relief in the action.

By now Cole was scratching again, mumbling unintelligibly under his breath. Bending over to examine his misery, Wynne saw the same watery blisters erupting in patches all over his chest.

When she raised her head, it was to encounter a pair of arresting blue eyes now open and staring at her. "What are you doing?"

"Uh, looking at your chest."

A slow, incredibly sexy grin spread across his drowsy features. "Oh? Well, come over here and take a closer look." He reached out without thinking and cupped the back of her head, bringing her forward to meet his mouth in a long good morning kiss.

It never occurred to her to pull away. Instead, she found herself returning the kiss and enjoying every moment of it.

Only when he began to pull her back down beside his naked length did she remember the strange rash on her arm.

"Cole, look." She hurriedly held her arm up for him to inspect. Last night had been wonderful, but she couldn't permit it to happen again.

Cole's sleepy eyes tried to focus on the arm suddenly shoved in his face. "What is it?"

"I don't know, but whatever it is, it's on your chest too," she said lamely.

"My chest?" Cole glanced down to see what she was talking about. His eyes widened in disbelief. Then he quickly grasped her arm to peer at it more closely. "Oh, hell."

"What? What is it?" she asked expectantly.

"Oh, hell!" he stated emphatically again as he sat straight up in the bed. "It looks like poison ivy!"

"Oh." She let out a sigh of relief. The way he had been acting she had halfway been expecting him to tell her it was some sort of horrible plague. A simple case of poison ivy wasn't fatal. "Oh, is that all?"

By now Cole was busily inspecting his chest for further signs of the growing affliction. It didn't take long for him to spot the trouble areas, and he swore under his breath irritably. "Oh, damn! I'm sensitive to this stuff," he complained.

"Then you should have stayed clear of it," she said, thinking at the same time it was rather endearing that there was something to which he was particularly susceptible.

"I do stay clear of it! I always have since I nearly died with it as a kid. You must have given it to me," he said accusingly.

"Me!" Once again she was put on the defensive. "Why does it always have to be me who causes all the trouble?" Jumping to her feet, Wynne jerked the blanket off him and wrapped it tightly around her. She glared down at him angrily. "Just what makes you so sure I gave you poison ivy? You could have given it to me, you know."

"No, I couldn't have given it to you because I'll ride five miles out of my way to avoid getting the juice of the damn stuff on me," Cole replied. "Can you say you've been as careful, Miss Elliot!"

Wynne felt herself blushing to the roots of her hair as she tried to avoid his indicting gaze. It was hard to keep her mind on the argument with him lying there naked and so—so . . . stunningly male. "I—I don't even know what poison ivy looks like," she said.

"Obviously not," he grunted. "To get a case this bad, you must have rolled in it somewhere!" He surveyed her arms, which were becoming puffier by the moment, with bleak resignation.

Wynne's temper was flaring, but she had to admit he could be right. The past few days had been a nightmare, and she had waded through endless thickets and briars. She'd even fallen off the mule a few times, and there had been those strange-looking vines on that old oak tree the mule had brushed her against.

Suddenly it was all too much. Nothing had gone

right since Mama and Papa died, and she burst into a fit of inconsolable tears.

Cole hastily rolled to his feet. Watching Wynne closely, he picked up his discarded pants and slid into them. "Hey, now look. Don't start cryin'. It's not the end of the world."

"But I'm—I'm for-e-ev-er doin-g su-c-h stu-pi-d th-in-gs," she sobbed. From the moment she'd met him she'd acted like a blithering idiot. No wonder he disliked her so! Now she had given him poison ivy, and he would never forgive her.

"Come on, stop getting yourself all upset." He fumbled in his back pocket for his handkerchief and handed it to her. There were very few things in Cole Claxton's life that could bring him to heel, but a woman's tears was one of them.

Wynne could tell she was making him uncomfortable by all her blubbering and sniveling, but she couldn't make herself stop. Snatching the cloth out of his hand, she buried her face in it and bawled even harder.

For a few moments he let her cry it out, casting uneasy glances in her direction every once in a while. All that squawking and bellowing were going to make her sick, but he didn't know how to put a stop to it without bringing on more of the same.

When the storm finally began to abate and Wynne lifted red-rimmed eyes to meet his, his face sagged with visible relief. "Feel better?"

"N-o," she said, and hiccuped.

"Well, you'd better hurry and get it all out of your system," he said, but in an unusually nice tone—for him. "We have work to do."

She looked at him skeptically as she blew her nose loudly. "Wh-a-t wor-k?"

"We have to find a whole lot of pokeberry leaves."

"Pokeberry leaves! What for?" She wouldn't know a pokeberry leaf if it came up and spit in her face!

"We can make poultices out of them and hope they'll keep the poison ivy from spreading." He paused and, to her growing amazement, smiled nicely at her. "Mind you, I said hope that it won't spread any farther."

"But you think it will?" She would have thought that he would be angrier than ever with her, but he seemed to be taking this newest crisis in resigned stride.

He shrugged his broad shoulders as he absent-mindedly scratched his chest again. "With my luck lately? Yes. It'll spread like wildfire. By night we'll both be as miserable as hell." The woman was a hex. There was no longer any doubt about it. He'd come through the entire war without a sign of an injury, nearly four years of unbelievable luck when he led his men into battle, day after day, watching them fall around him in droves, yet always managed to escape unharmed. But now, after having spent one, *one* measly night with her, he was faced with a threat he feared even more than death. Poison ivy. The words struck total fear in his heart.

When he was a kid, he had been flat on his back in bed with the dreaded ailment for more than three weeks. After that Lilly made sure he was dosed heavily each spring with sulfur, molasses, and a pinch of saltpeter.

He'd come to recognize the little three-leaved vine from a mile away and to avoid it. Naturally Wynne wouldn't have recognized the vines, and probably the juice had been all over her clothing. If he knew her, she'd hung her clothes on the vines, thinking they made perfect clotheslines.

Well, it was too late to worry about it now, Cole conceded silently. He could only hope there was a mess of pokeberry leaves growing somewhere nearby.

His eyes drifted back to Wynne. She was hastily trying to pin her mass of tousled hair up on top of her head with the remaining pins she had managed to hold on to.

The tempting curve of her breasts were silhouetted against the sunlight shining through the window, and he felt a swift tightening in his loins as he recalled the memory of her lying in his arms— sweet and unbelievably giving. A stab of guilt sliced through him. He should be ashamed of himself for losing control like that. She was obviously not used to drinking, and he was. He supposed he had taken unfair advantage of her, but she hadn't put up a fight. If she had, he would have stopped. He was sure of that.

But in a way she had led him on, looking at him with those wide green eyes, all soft and inviting, seductively running the tip of her tongue around her lips after each drink out of the bottle, making them wet and shiny . . . Hell. *She,* not he, was the one responsible for last night, he convinced himself. He'd been minding his own business when she started looking at him that way. Besides, how was he to know she'd never been with a man before? She had sure been acting as if she'd known what was going on.

He deliberately cast the memory aside. Whoever was at fault, last night had not been worth a case of poison ivy. Or had it been?

He was astounded to find his hand trembling as he reached in his shirt pocket for a smoke. If she had been any other woman, he would have had his answer without a second thought. Women were a dime a dozen to Cole, and the last thing he wanted was a prissy little thing who couldn't even shoot her own dinner.

But because he couldn't convince himself that last night had not left him untouched, it unnerved him even more than her crying had.

"Is the pain any better, Bertie?" The soft, familiar voice alone was soothing balm to Bertram's misery.

"I think it's gettin' bearable." He rolled to his side and tried to ease himself into a more comfortable position as Fancy gently tried to assist. "Agghhh . . ." A low groan escaped him as a sharp stab of pain ran up his spine.

"Doc said if you needed any more laudanum, he would send you over some."

"Have I taken the whole bottle already?" He peered at the brown glass container sitting on the table among all the wooden animals he had carved these past few weeks and frowned.

"Almost." Fancy plumped his pillows and fussed

over him for a few moments. "Brought you dinner. Hope you're gettin' your appetite back."

"I am." He sniffed the air appreciatively and eyed the tray covered with a red-checkered cloth she had set on the table earlier. "What'd you bring me?"

"Just some stew and corn bread."

Bertram grinned. Stew was his favorite, and she knew it. "Wouldn't happen to be a piece of blueberry pie on there, too, would there?"

Fancy grinned back at him, her features blushing a pretty pink. "There just might be."

"You're gonna spoil me, Fancy."

"I want to, Bertie."

Bertram Mallory was about the best thing that had ever happened to her. In the few weeks he had been delayed in Springfield, she'd fallen deeply in love with him. He was about the kindest, gentlest man she had ever met, and it made her want to cry when she thought about how empty her life would be when he left town.

Fancy wished she knew what was so important about his getting to River Run. That was all he talked about, getting there and finding some woman he'd been trailing for the past few months.

The fact that he was looking for a woman worried her a little. He sounded desperate at times and frustrated at others when he talked about his leg's healing so he could go on with his trip. She couldn't imagine his being on a spiteful mission. He was too kind to be an evil man. Yet every time she tried to question him on why he was looking for this woman named Wynne Elliot, his eyes narrowed and he gritted his teeth and stubbornly refused to tell her. Just said it was personal and he had to find her. If fate didn't get him first.

He talked funny like that sometimes, and she didn't really know what he meant, but she was sure it was important for Bertie to find that woman.

And he would have been on his way again right now if he hadn't stopped to help Elmo Wilson fix a wheel that had come off his buggy Sunday morning.

Bertram had been leaving for River Run really early when he come across Elmo and his wife, Sadie. They were sitting in the middle of the road all hot and sweating in their Sunday best. Bertie said he could tell Sadie was about to expire, so he got off his horse and offered to help. Elmo was grateful and he had told Bertie that if he would just lift the side of the buggy up carefullike, then Elmo would slip the wheel back in place and they all could be on their way.

Well, Bertie had agreed that was simple enough for a strong man like himself. He had proceeded to heft the left side of the carriage when all of a sudden his back went out and he screamed like a castrated bull. Said he got mad and just cussed a blue streak right then and there in the middle of the road because he knew that throwing his back out was going to delay him another few weeks.

Fancy knew his cursing must have been pretty bad that morning. He could come out with some pretty colorful phrases at times, but she never minded. In fact, she was used to that kind of talk. You could tell if a person was really mad or not by the way he sort of phrased things.

Bertie said poor Sadie like to have jumped right out of her skin he scared her so badly, but he swore the pain grabbed him around the middle something fierce. Even worse than the times he fell off the train and broke his leg combined. And he just couldn't help letting out that holler and cussing.

And what with his leg's being out of the splint just that morning, the jolt had set it aching like all get-out.

Elmo and Sadie had brought him back to Springfield and taken him to the hospital. Then they'd rushed over to get the doctor and sent someone to tell Fancy about the accident.

Although Fancy hadn't relished the idea of Bertram's being hurt again—poor man seemed to be having an ungodly run of bad luck lately—she was elated that she would have him around for a while longer.

Bertram caught her hand in the middle of all her fussing and brought it to his lips lovingly. "You're mighty good to me, Fancy."

"Ah, I'm not, Bertie. You deserve so much more than somebody like me caring for you." Her head dropped down shyly as the grasp of their hands tightened. She'd known a lot of men in her time, but somehow this quiet, almost naïve man could make her feel like a schoolgirl again.

"I don't ever want to hear you say such a thing again," he said. "Why, you're the finest woman I've ever known, Fancy."

And she was. Oh, she might let men do things to her body that Bertram didn't approve of, but he knew what made her let them do those things, and he understood. Other people might judge her harshly, but Bertram didn't. He saw beyond the saloon girl paint and glitter. He saw into her good, kind heart. Bertram loved her.

"Thank you, Bertie. It's not true about me being nice, but I surely do appreciate you thinkin' so."

Her fingers soothed his hair back from his face tenderly.

"You *are* nice," he whispered adamantly, "and as soon as I finish what I started out to do, I'm goin' to come back and get you, Fancy. Then I'm goin' to marry you and take you back home with me."

Fancy smiled. Bertram had begun to talk like that lately, making all those silly promises that made her heart start to pound with excitement. But she didn't take any of them seriously. She knew that when he left, she would probably never see him again. No one had ever cared enough about Fancy Biggers to come back for her. But she didn't mind. Bertie had been nice to her, nicer than any other man had ever been. When he made love to her, he treated her as if she were something special. He'd say such pretty words to her—just as if she were a real lady, not just that bad girl who worked down at the saloon.

And he didn't make her do things just to please him when they were making love, vile and ugly things, the way other men did. Instead, he always cared about seeing that she was pleased, and that was nice. Really nice.

He never made demands. He always seemed happy to be with her, whether he was making love to her or just holding her in his arms while they lay on an old blanket and looked up at the stars. He'd make up silly stories about people who would travel out there among the stars someday, and she would laugh and declare that he was becoming addlebrained.

No, she never let herself believe that she would someday marry Bertram G. Mallory, but lordy, how she wished that could be.

Seeing the doubt clouding her pretty features, Bertram kissed the palm of her hand and winked at her. "You just wait and see. One of these days you're goin' to be Mrs. Bertram Mallory or I'll eat my hat."

She knew it was an impossible dream, yet it seemed to her no harm would come if she let herself hold it for a bit. "And we'll live in a big house sittin' on top of the hill—"

"With a big white fence around it—"

"And lots of flowers and a big vegetable garden—"

"And kids—"

Her eyes shone brightly as she grasped his hand tighter. "At least six kids, Bertie . . . maybe more."

Bertram grinned. "However many you want, Fancy."

"And we'll have three meals a day, three big

meals with potatoes and meat and carrots—I love carrots, Bertie. Do you?" Never in her life had Fancy had enough carrots to eat.

"You'll have all the carrots you can ever eat," he said solemnly.

"Oh, Bertie." Her eyes were glistening with tears now. "It all sounds so wonderful."

"It will be. As soon as I get my business taken care of, then we'll start our new life." He had decided he was even going to change professions when this was all over. The one he had was too harrowing. "I'll take care of you, Fancy. From now on you don't ever have to worry about a thing."

Resting her head on the pillow next to his head, she sighed and let the tears slip silently from her eyes. It all sounded so wonderful. "Bertie—about you going to River Run . . ."

"Yes?"

"Well, I know you're lookin' for someone, but maybe they won't even be there anymore," she said carefully. "After all, you've been here nigh on to six weeks now, and you said this Wynne Elliot was just supposed to be visitin' there."

Bertram's brow creased worriedly. "I've thought about that."

"Well, what if this woman's gone somewhere else by now."

It was Bertram who let out the long, weary sigh this time as his hand absently stroked the top of his head. "Then I suppose I gotta keep on goin' until I catch up with her."

"Oh, Bertie, I wish you'd tell me why it's so all-fired important for you to find her!"

"Because Bertram G. Mallory is a man of his word!" he stated firmly, and she knew without asking he wasn't going to say anything more.

Chapter 14

It was hard to believe. They weren't more than twenty miles out of River Run, and they had been gone for almost a month! For the past two and a half weeks they had been holed up here, and Cole was about to go nuts.

He lay on the old bed in the cabin and stared at a wasp circling the ceiling. His face was a mass of red puffy welts, he ached all over, and he felt as if the entire Confederate army, including General Robert E. Lee himself, had tramped over him.

He could hear Wynne humming happily as she worked around the cabin. Well, she *could* hum, he thought resentfully, and gritted his teeth to keep from scratching. Her case of poison ivy had turned out to be mild, while his had raged out of control for days now.

His gaze went back to her puzzledly. He figured

she surely would have left him there to suffer a quiet death while she stole his horse and went on in search of Cass, but surprisingly she had stuck around to care for him. Each day she had fed him, bathed him, against his indignant protests, and made new pokeberry poultices to apply to his swollen body.

Not one square inch of him had been spared. Even the shaft of his manhood had oozing little blisters on it, and he thought he would die of the searing pain every time he had to stagger outside the cabin to relieve himself.

In the long, tortured hours of the night, while Wynne had slept peacefully on the floor beside him, Cole had plotted to get even with his little brother for putting him through this nightmare if it was the last thing he did!

"Hello." Wynne had noticed Cole was awake and came over to check on him. "How are you feeling?"

"Like hell," he said grouchily.

"Oh, you always say that," she replied brightly. She was getting used to his complaints, and they no longer annoyed her. "Surely you're feeling a little better today." She tried to examine the progress of his rash, but he brushed her hand away grumpily. "All right. But I'm only trying to help."

She straightened and went back to arranging a large cluster of wild daisies in the empty whiskey bottle.

While Cole slept during the heat of the day, she'd taken to searching the area, looking for wild roots and berries for their supper. Up until now she'd been successful, but all she had come across today had been the lovely flowers. She'd taken them back to the cabin in hopes of cheering up the grump, but it looked as if her efforts had been wasted.

Wynne knew the enforced illness had been extremely hard on Cole, so she didn't begrudge his being a little touchy. At any other time she would have felt the same way. But the unexpected turn of events hadn't bothered her in the least.

Actually she welcomed the short reprieve. It was wonderful to sleep with a roof over her head each night and be able to walk down to the pond and bathe each morning.

At times she even found herself forgetting why she was here in the first place. Even more amazing, there were times when she was beginning to realize she no longer really cared whether or not she ever found Cass.

The bitterness and anger were slowly ebbing away, and suddenly she found herself—well, almost happy once again. Even thinking about Cass failed to dampen her spirits now as it once had.

"What would you like for dinner tonight?" she asked chattily.

"Since when is there a choice?" For days they had eaten nothing but berries or poke greens or some sort of stew Wynne had concocted from wild roots.

"There isn't actually. I tried to catch a fish out of the pond this morning, but I'm not fast enough with my hands," she said.

He grunted and closed his eyes again. He hated being incapacitated in this way, and escape through sleep seemed the easiest way to cope with his pain and frustration at the moment.

"When I was a small girl, Papa used to take me fishing. We had this large pond that was close to the house, and it was stocked with all sorts of interesting-looking fish." Her hands carefully arranged the flowers as she talked. "You know, fish are really interesting. Have you ever noticed that?"

Cole grunted again but didn't open his eyes.

"Some of them are truly magnificent, with nice, plump bodies and charming characteristics. And then there are those poor things that are just plain ugly and have nasty dispositions—big, bloaty-looking eyes and horrendously fat lips."

Cole's stomach rolled over in disgust.

"It's just a shame people don't eat the mean ones and leave the cute ones alone." She glanced down at him. "Don't you agree?"

One blue eye opened with pained tolerance. "With what?"

"That the ugly fish should be eaten first."

"I've never thought about it."

It suddenly occurred to her he might be trying to rest. "Am I bothering you?"

"No." She was. He was trying to get to sleep so the rash wouldn't bother him so badly, but he didn't have the strength to start another argument.

"Well, as I was saying—"

"What about supper?" He interrupted hurriedly before she could continue her conversation about ugly fish.

"Oh." Her thoughts promptly returned to their earlier discussion. "Well, I could always make stew again."

He sighed. "Anything but those damned berries."

"Cole! You really should do something about that vile cursin'." She rebuked him firmly. The man had a terrible mouth on him at times.

"I'd talk if I were you."

She frowned at him guiltily. She didn't do so badly herself at times. "Well, I couldn't find any berries today, so you're in luck."

Cole didn't consider that lucky. He was sick of the berries, but she couldn't hit the broad side of a barn with a gun, so that meant they would have to eat that unappetizing root stew until he could get back on his feet and kill some fresh meat. But it didn't really matter. He'd had very little appetite lately.

"If you would lend me your gun I could go and try to kill a rabbit for our dinner," she said. It irritated her that he had hidden his gun from her and she couldn't find it.

Cole rolled over to his side, and the pain took his breath. A new round of itching assaulted him. "I'm not letting you have my gun."

"That's not fair. You're sick, and I'm the only one able to provide our food," she said argumentatively.

"And if I give you the gun, either you'll run away and leave me stuck here without a horse or way to protect myself, or you'll shoot yourself and I'll have to get up and bury you. I don't feel up to that yet."

Her hands rested on her hips in irritation. "I'm hungry, Cole. Now give me that gun. I won't run away. If I had wanted to do that, I would have left days ago!"

"I said no."

"Then I'll just have to think of another way to kill our supper because I'm not going to bed hungry again tonight!"

"Good luck."

The door trying to be slammed off its hinge signaled him the slaughter was about to begin.

For the next couple of hours he dozed off and on. The cabin became an oven, and he woke up once drenched in sweat, and the itching began all over again.

It was late afternoon when he heard a terrible ruckus erupt in the front yard. The sound of some feathered wings flailing the air and Wynne's horrified screams mixed with terrified squawks shattered the peaceful stillness.

Cole fought to clear his groggy mind as the fracas grew louder and more intense. After pulling himself weakly up onto his knees, he dragged himself over to retrieve the gun he had hidden under a loose board in the floor, then slowly back to the doorway while the fight outside raged on unchecked.

He had no idea what the woman had gotten herself into this time, but it sounded as if the Battle of Vicksburg were being fought all over again outside the doorstep.

Just as he reached the doorway, Wynne burst through, a triumphant grin on her flushed face. Her dress was even more torn and soiled than before, and her hair was matted with twigs and chicken feathers, but in her hand dangling limply was the proof of her earlier words that she would not go hungry again tonight. "Just look what I have, Mr. Claxton!"

Cole stared blankly at what looked like a chicken, minus its head, dripping blood all over the floor of the cabin. "How in the hell did you get that?"

"I ran it down," she exclaimed gleefully. "And then I swung it around and around until its head popped off!" She had seen the Moss Oak servants do that many times. Getting the head off hadn't been as easy as it looked, but she had managed. "It was wandering around in the woods and I ran until I finally caught it and then I brought it back here. Isn't that marvelous?"

"Well, I'll be—"

"I don't need your gun anymore, sir," she informed him loftily, then grinned impishly as she swirled the chicken in a wide circle as if it were one of those drawstring purses women carried.

"Why, hell's bells, I think I've finally got the hang of it!"

Cole groaned as he sank weakly back down on the floor. "God help us all."

It was another week before Cole's rash showed real signs of improvement. During their extended stay Wynne had settled in the cabin as if it were to be their permanent home.

She had ripped off the lower half of her petticoat and made several cloths to clean with. The cabin was spotless now. The old floor was scrubbed clean, and fresh flowers adorned the table each day. She'd managed to stretch the chicken over an entire week and then miraculously went out and found another one.

She had even discovered an old root cellar in the back of the house that held a leftover bushel of apples and two jars of honey. Somehow she managed to turn the fruit and sweetening into a tasty dessert.

Cole lay in bed watching her move about the cabin, and he began noticing that all of Miss Fielding's teachings had not gone astray. There was a certain beauty and elegance about her that he had failed to notice in the past. Somehow, no matter what the circumstance, she went about her work

313

with the grace and refinement befitting the most dignified southern lady, even when she was down on her hands and knees, scrubbing the rough wooden floor with a scrap of petticoat.

Instead of the clumsy, addlebrained girl he'd first encountered, she was proving every day that she was indeed the southern, genteel lady her papa had raised her to be.

They had never spoken of the night they had spent together. But it was on Cole's mind day after day as their forced confinement began to take its toll on him.

At night they lay in the dark and talked as the sounds of night filled the old cabin. Wynne told him stories of her growing up on a large cotton plantation, while he regaled her with stories about the war. They had grown so comfortable with each other that one night Wynne even found herself telling him about Cass and how they had met and fallen in love.

When she started weeping as she talked, Cole had rolled over and pulled her up beside him. He had held her tightly as she poured out all her bitterness and grief, and when the tempest had past, they had talked long into the night. Cole found he now believed that his brother was the one partly responsible for her unhappiness, but he still couldn't account for why.

He told her all about Cass and how he had been as a boy. With each word Wynne could feel more of her rancor slowly ebbing out of her. Reading between the lines, she learned that Cole was the strong one, Beau the optimist, and Cass the dreamer of the Claxton family, and she found herself feeling almost a part of his family, a family that had produced three similar yet diverse men.

Then, one morning, Cole forced himself out of bed and took Wynne outside the cabin and gave her a lesson in shooting.

"Why are you doing this now?" Wynne asked, puzzled.

"If anything happens to me, you'll be able to take care of yourself." He resisted the impulse to scratch.

"But nothing's going to happen to you," she protested, the mere thought of something bad happening to him making her grow weak.

"I don't plan on it," he assured her. "But you need to know how to take care of yourself anyway."

They were sitting in the yard, she pressed tightly up against him as he steadied her arm and aimed at the target he had constructed earlier. For a moment their gazes met and held, and each one remembered how the other tasted and smelled. Cole's face still had signs of poison ivy, but he was so handsome it fairly took her breath away.

Reflected in both eyes were admiration and yet another light, a new radiance that had encompassed both of them in the past few days. "Aren't you afraid that I'll use this new knowledge to harm Cass?"

His gaze did not waver. "I know you'll do what you have to, Wynne."

It was the closest he had ever come to saying he understood why she was doing what she was, but it was enough.

"Thank you, Cole. I appreciate your faith in me."

He nodded briefly and returned his concentration to the lesson.

But that night Wynne once again warmed water and brought it to him. Every day of his illness she had given him a sponge bath to help alleviate the pain. But the past few days he had been well enough to tend to his own needs. That was why he was taken by surprise when she set the water down before him and began to roll up the sleeves of her dress.

"What's this?"

"Your bath?"

"Oh." He waited, his breath caught in his chest, as she crossed the room to get a piece of her torn petticoat. His eyes carefully followed her movements as she returned.

"All ready?" Wynne smiled. Her voice had a whispery, excited lilt, and he wasn't quite sure what he was supposed to do.

His eyes narrowed thoughtfully as he brought his cheroot up to his mouth and studied her for a moment. "I thought I was on my own now." He was propped back in the kitchen chair, his dusty boots perched atop the table, watching her.

She moved closer, her fingers reaching out to begin unbuttoning his shirt casually.

The chair came slowly down to all four legs. "What are you doing—"

"I told you. I'm going to give you a bath." Wynne eased down onto his lap and continued her task. Her warmth seeped through, taunting him, tempting him. She smelled of green grass and creek water, and a soft wisp of hair brushed his cheek as she leaned closer. Her nimble fingers, now roughened with the scrubbing chores and from picking berries from prickly bushes, were agonizingly slow in slipping free the buttons of his shirt.

"I don't think that would be a good idea."

But she only smiled at him and concentrated on her task.

Moments later it was clear she was actually going to go through with her threat. He finally threw his cheroot into the fireplace testily. "You're a shameful woman, Wynne Elliot." His low voice caressed her senses, and she smiled again.

Dropping her eyes away from his shyly, she knew full well he spoke the truth. What she felt for Cole might be shameful, and she had no idea where all this wantonness had come from, but right now she didn't really care. She just knew she wanted him to make love to her again. Her body clamored for his touch, to feel his lips on hers again, and to know the completeness of his loving. "I know. Do you find that undesirable?" For a moment she was afraid he might not want her.

Cole shook his head, searching for the right words to tell her this had to stop before it went any farther. Making love to her once could be blamed on drinking too much liquor. But now he was stone-cold sober, and he would have to make a rational decision.

As the fabric of his shirt fell away, the dark hair across his chest unfolded before her. And it was a magnificent chest—all broad and wide and masculine. Spreading the lapels wide, Wynne placed her arms around his waist and rested her head against his comforting warmth. He felt so good. How many times had she lain awake on the floor beside him, listening to his restless movements and the soft moans of discomfort while the poison ivy was at its worst. She'd longed to reach up and touch him, longed to lie beside him, but she'd resisted for two reasons. Cole was miserably sick, and then there had been the guilt. But even while she knew it was wrong, she obeyed the impulse to risk his possible rejection. This time she wanted to make love to him.

Her hands roamed his torso absently. He was hard and strong. He was like Moss Oak, something to give shelter, to believe in, something lasting. At least that's what she wanted him to be. Whether he would or could be all those things for her was yet to be seen. But just for tonight tomorrow didn't exist. All that existed was Cole.

His arms automatically came up to enfold her as lips gently traced the edge of her hair. "Damn . . . damn . . ." he whispered. "This is all wrong . . ." but he couldn't stop himself. She was too close, too warm, too willing, and the memory of her body beneath his was too fresh and too potent.

Cole hadn't wanted this to happen. For days

he'd watched her moving about the cabin and lectured himself on how foolish it would be to let his feelings get out of hand again. The first time he had made love to her could be excused, but tonight he would be well aware of what he was doing. And God help him, he couldn't stop himself and didn't want to.

Even as he held her, Cole knew he was making a mistake which would probably follow him the rest of his life. He didn't want her in his heart—but she was already there, a small voice argued. Somewhere between here and River Run he'd fallen in love with this winsome woman/child, and he no longer had the will to ignore it. Yet he had no idea how he would deal with it. How could he have let himself fall in love with a woman who had vowed to kill his own brother?

When his arms tightened around her, Wynne smiled softly and drew back from him. She dipped the cloth into the water. Her battle was won. She knew it.

He knew it. But he still didn't like it.

Moments later he felt the first trickles of warm water dribbling down his bare chest as an involuntary shudder rippled through him.

"Wynne . . . ." His voice was nearly pleading now, but she spared him no mercy.

"I wish I had soap." She apologized as her fingers gently administered to the small patches of redness still evident among his chest hair. She wanted to do so much for him, please him, make him so painfully aware that she was all woman that he would never forget the lesson. But she was terribly inexperienced, and she didn't know where to begin.

"It doesn't matter," he said in a voice that had suddenly grown husky. He was so touched by her actions he found it hard to speak. Her small hands ran across his bare skin, sending hot surges rushing through him as he reached out hesitantly to trace the delicate curve of her jaw. It was the first time he had really touched her in the light, and her skin looked as smooth and rich as honey.

Blue eyes looked deeply into green ones. Then, as if in surrender, his mouth slowly lowered to cover hers. They kissed—a warm and lingering exploration that made both their breaths come a little bit faster. In their hunger for each other, one kiss wasn't enough. It was as if he wanted to devour her, and she him. Pausing only briefly in the gentle assault, Wynne smiled and touched Cole's face reverently with roughened fingertips. "Forgive me, Cole Claxton, but I'm truly about to become a shameful woman," she whispered, the words trembling upon lips that were becoming swollen by his passionate kisses.

Cole chuckled, a deep rumble from low within his chest, and he pulled her to him for another long kiss. Her mouth opened willingly beneath his, and he made a soft sound in his throat as he suddenly rose from his chair, swinging her up in his arms.

"Your bath," she murmured as she wrapped her arms around his neck snugly and held on.

"We'll both take one later."

Then he was carefully laying her on the old bed, and their clothes suddenly began to come off as throaty sounds of ardor were muffled by two mouths that hungrily sought each other.

Her hands explored all there was to know of Cole Claxton. He murmured her name almost incoherently and pressed moist lips to her closed eyelids, nearly drowning in the growing haze of sensuality.

Words came rushing back to him in a thunderous roar, words he had said to Beau not so very long ago: "When I find a woman who can wrestle the Indian brave and *win,* then turn around and be soft as cotton, smell as pretty as a lilac bush in May, and forget all about being a lady in bed . . ."

With a low groan Cole rolled her over onto her

back and his hand found the womanly softness of her as her breath trembled between her parted lips.

"Cole," she whispered, "I . . ." There were so many new and conflicting emotions raging inside her. His hands and his mouth were setting her on fire, and her body was crying out for fulfillment. She moved beneath him to a silent rhythm which he alone directed. His touch was exquisite torture. He found her innermost places and revealed their secrets, and she wanted more . . . more . . . more.

She had never come close to being with Cass like this. He'd been handsome and had brought her first recognition of desire. But she'd felt nothing like this. "Love me . . . Cole . . . love me . . . I can't—"

"Shh." Her cries merged with his as he built their passion to frightening proportions. She arched against him when his warm mouth suckled her breasts, then gasped as his lips teased a taunting trail across her bare stomach only to pause and tantalize her navel. His boldness fanned the fires of passion to even greater heights until she cried out and boldly drew herself up to meet his searching hunger.

He took her swiftly and without hesitation, and

the world tipped crazily as they became one. She held nothing back from him but gave of herself as if she had been waiting all her life for this moment, this hour, this man.

"Cole . . ."

The whispered word was a demand, a prayer, and he responded. "I'm here," he whispered back. "Touch me . . . stay with me. . . ."

And she did, matching him movement for movement, cry for cry.

They were in a world where nothing existed except them, and the bed beneath them was silken—and there was no tomorrow, no Cass, no problems.

When they reached that moment of total completeness, it was as if they were suspended in space for one incredible second, and they clung to it stubbornly.

"Wynne . . ." He placed delirious kisses on her mouth, and when fulfillment finally subsided, they collapsed against each, and she held and stroked him, tenderly wishing the moment never to end. Very slowly they drifted back to earth, still clasped tightly to each other.

Wynne pressed soft kisses into the curve of his neck and whispered her happiness as she felt him slowly begin to relax.

"Uh, Miss Elliot, I'm sorry about—"

She reached over and clamped her hand over his mouth. "If you tell me you're sorry one more time for making love to me, I'll—I swear I'll scream!"

Couldn't he just for once admit that what they had shared was wonderful and exciting and certainly needed no apology?

He grinned at her, a lazy, sensual grin. "All right. I'm gettin' tired of lyin' to you about that anyway. I'm not sorry. I never have been."

She sighed and smiled back at him. "That's better, Mr. Claxton. Neither have I."

His arms squeezed her lovingly. Then, moments later, he was sound asleep.

The sounds of tree frogs and katydids closed in around them as she reached over and quietly snuffed out the flickering candle, then cuddled down in his arms to sleep.

The following morning Cole was sitting at the table smoking when she finally awoke.

"Hello." She smiled.

"Hello."

"Why didn't you wake me?"

He shrugged noncommittally. "There was no need."

Wynne sat up and stretched lazily, not at all

concerned that it was broad daylight and she was stark naked. She had come to feel as comfortable in his presence as if they were man and wife. "Did you sleep well?"

"Yes."

She noticed he seemed pensive this morning, but that wasn't unusual for Cole. He was a thinker. Wynne smiled at him lovingly. "I did too. Your rash looks almost all gone this morning."

Shoving back from the table, he rose and began to pull on his boots.

"Where are you going?" She was wishing he would come back to bed for a while.

"Home."

"Home?" Wynne asked blankly. It was as if a cool breeze had brushed her skin, and she shivered.

"That's right." The boots were on, and he straightened up to face her.

"But what about me?" Her mind was whirling. If Cole left and took the horse, she would be left alone, without any transportation—without him. The thought caused a shudder to ripple through her.

Cole leveled his gaze on her, and she noticed how clear blue his eyes were in the morning sunlight. "I think you would be wise to come with me."

"But why?" Suddenly she realized that their time together was about to end, and the knowledge was incredibly painful.

His face lost some of its earlier harshness as he knelt beside her. "Give it up, Wynne. Come back to River Run with me. There's no tellin' where Cass is. By now he may be back home, and it would be crazy for you to keep on lookin' for him. You don't have a horse or a gun."

"You could stay with me," she pleaded. Cass no longer mattered to her. It was the thought that Cole would not be with her any longer that was causing her heart to pound. "And when I find Cass, you can be there to warn him about me." She was desperate, grabbing for any feeble excuse to keep him with her.

"No. I can't do that." He turned away in exasperation, running long fingers through his unruly hair.

"Why?" Her hands grabbed the sleeve of his shirt and turned him back around to face her.

"Because, dammit, I just can't." He had already gotten in deeper than he'd planned to. "Now, I'm tellin' you, Wynne, I'm leavin' in thirty minutes. If you want to go with me, then I promise to see that

327

you get back to Savannah safely. If you don't want to come"—he forced his gaze away from her—"then I guess you're on your own."

His words were so cut-and-dried, so unemotional, so final.

Tears began to gather in her eyes as she absently toyed with the end of the blanket. The past few weeks had meant nothing to him. She had been the fool, falling in love—and with another Claxton yet.

"Well?" Cole towered over her ominously as she blinked back the tears.

"All right," she said lifelessly. She kept her face carefully averted so he couldn't see her pain.

His face sagged with relief. "You'll come back with me?"

"Yes." She didn't see where she had much choice. Cass no longer mattered, and Cole had never cared.

Cole walked to the door. "I'll saddle the horse."

Chapter 15

The ride home was depressing. The weather was gray and overcast, befitting both their moods.

Although Cole rode with Wynne sheltered in his arms, they spoke very little. At night they lay beside each other, aching to touch yet not allowing themselves the pleasure. They were lost in their own private worlds, and as morning dawned after another sleepless night, they carefully avoided each other's eyes, speaking only about the mundane, going about their business as if the past few weeks had never happened.

Wynne reminded herself a thousand times a day that Cole meant no more to her than Cass did. He had used her just as cold-heartedly as his brother had, and she had only thought she had been falling in love with him. There was no longer any doubt about what she had thought she felt for Cass. She had not been in love with him. Not really. He had just been there for her to lean on in a time when there had been no one else to turn to.

Cole rode behind Wynne, repeatedly challenging his sanity as he thought about how he had let himself fall in love with this woman. Even if she were to give up the foolish idea of killing his brother, she would always bear a deep seed of resentment toward Cass. The family would be divided, something he found intolerable.

The Claxton family had stood together through thick and thin. It was inconceivable that an outsider in a crazy little bird hat could waltz into his life and come between him and his younger brother. Yet, if he were to be honest, the thought of putting Wynne on the stagecoach to return to Savannah tore him apart as much as the thought of a divided family did. After sharing the past few weeks with her, he couldn't imagine what his life would be without her.

Toward evening of the second day they stopped to water the horse. Wynne knelt beside the stream and splashed a handful of the cool water against her grimy face. The trail dust was thick and ground into her dress. She longed for a hot bath and a clean bed.

Cole watched as she closed her eyes and trickled

the water over her neck. She had been no trouble at all lately. She'd done her share of the work and never uttered a word of complaint. Instead, she'd been submissive and unusually quiet. She was not at all like the fireball he had found standing in the middle of the road one day, waving a gun at him, and the change served only to deepen his agony.

Shading her eyes against the setting sun, Wynne peered across the small stream and watched another rider approach. He carefully dismounted and led his horse to the water as her forehead crinkled with a frown.

The young man was familiar to her, and she remembered him as the man she'd seen standing on the porch leaning against the post and who had greeted her when she had passed through Springfield a few weeks earlier. Only that young man's leg had been in a splint.

The rider maneuvered himself down on his knees with stiff, careful movements to ease his thirst, and Wynne decided he must be wearing some sort of brace on his back now. He didn't turn at the waist, and bending seemed quite an effort.

"Is that someone you know?" Cole asked when her attention seemed not to leave the stranger. A well-defined stab of jealousy sliced through him when he noted Wynne's continuing interest.

"No, but I think I've seen him before," she said thoughtfully.

Cole's brow lifted sourly. "Oh?"

"Yes . . ." She watched for a few moments longer, causing Cole's growing jealousy to simmer.

A few minutes later she shrugged and dismissed the rider, deciding that she must be mistaken. It would be too much of a coincidence.

"Let's move on." Cole waded the horse out of the stream and waited while Wynne took another long drink, then rose and walked over to him slowly.

Their eyes met, and she waited for him to help her mount the horse. On her nose was a stray droplet of water and Cole's attention was drawn to it. His eyes softened and grew tender as his finger reached out to brush it away, but he suddenly changed his mind and let his hand drop back to his side.

She gazed up at him expectantly. "What's the matter?"

"You have water on your nose," he said brusquely. What he had wanted to say was she looked too damn kissable! He knew the texture of her mouth beneath his, how it tasted, how it blended with his until he thought he would take leave of what little senses he had managed to hold on to when she was in his arms.

"Oh." Disappointedly she reached up and removed the droplet, then smiled at him. "There. Is that better?"

Keeping his gaze averted, Cole nodded yes and quickly lifted her back into the saddle.

She was incredibly close, close enough for him to see the black specs in the green of her eyes. And Cole's resolve faltered. Wynne couldn't have looked elsewhere if her life depended on it. She wanted so badly for Cole to hold her again, to whisper those wonderful things he did when he made love to her.

"I wish you wouldn't look at me that way," he said uncomfortably, careful not to reveal any of the tension growing steadily inside his trousers.

"And I wish you didn't look the way you do!" she replied defensively, but both their tones were tempered with something close to affection.

Gathering up the reins, Cole turned away quickly.

"Aren't you going to ride?" she asked with surprise as he began to walk the horse at a fast pace down the rutted lane.

"No, ma'am. I'm walkin'." The last thing he needed right now was to ride in that close saddle with her molded to him as tightly as his pants were!

By the time the Claxton farm came into view the next morning, Wynne and Cole released audible sighs of relief. Their close proximity of the past few days had their nerves humming as tautly as telegraph lines.

The household seemed to be all aflutter as Cole lifted Wynne off the horse. "What's going on?" he wondered aloud, his attention focused on the tables and chairs that had been set up in the cherry grove.

"Looks like your mother's havin' a party."

Cole led the horse toward the barn while Wynne took a deep breath and tried to gather her courage. Willa was hanging wash, her large body dipping up and down rhythmically as she retrieved the wet pieces one by one and pinned them onto the line. She momentarily glanced up at the new arrivals and grinned a friendly welcome, then went back to her chore.

Wynne shuffled slowly toward the house. The thought of facing Lilly and Beau again crept over her like a dreadful blight.

But it shouldn't have as Betsy, her face alight with pleasure at seeing her new friend again, burst out through the back door.

"Wynne! I do declare, you're a sight for sore eyes!" The young woman threw her arms around her exuberantly as they hugged hello. "Where in the world did you disappear to?" Betsy demanded.

Hearing all the commotion, Lilly poked her head out the back door to see what was going on. Seeing Wynne happily ensconced in Betsy's arms, she flew out the back door, her feet barely touching the steps. "Wynne, darlin', how good to see you back!"

After a tight hug Lilly held her away from her bosom and surveyed her disreputable condition with growing distress. "Oh, dear, I suppose this means your trip has been unsuccessful. You didn't find your friend?"

Wynne's eyes fell away guiltily. "No, I wasn't able to find a sign of him."

"Oh, I'm so sorry."

"It's all right. I've changed my mind about trying to locate him." She lifted her eyes back to Lilly's. "I've decided to go back to Savannah instead."

"Well." Lilly heaved a sigh of relief. "I must say I think that would be for the best."

Amid a new round of female chatter Cole came out of the barn and was quickly caught up in the homecoming festivities.

"Land sakes alive! You're home too?" Lilly peered over his shoulder hopefully. "I don't guess you ran into your brother anywhere along the way?"

"No, Ma, but I heard Cass made it through the war." Cole smiled wearily, glad to be able to give her that small ray of hope.

"You did!" Lilly clapped her hands together gleefully. "Well, praise the Lord! I just knew he would. Surely he'll be ridin' in any day now."

Cole grinned lamely and shrugged. "I reckon anything's possible."

"Why, course, it's possible," she said. "He'll be home anytime now. You just wait and see." She turned her attention back to Wynne. "How did you get here, dear?" Lilly had heard only one rider enter the farmyard.

"I ran into Wynne a ways back on the road. Her, uh, horse had bolted and run away, so I gave her a ride," Cole said before Wynne could answer.

"Your horse ran away?" Lilly's face was instantly filled with concern as her eyes ran over the bedraggled young woman standing forlornly beside Betsy. "Why, I thought you left on the stage."

"No—no, I decided to buy a horse instead," Wynne said meekly, leaving out the fact that a quarrelsome mule had been her traveling companion.

"Great day! I'm glad I didn't know that." Lilly sighed. "I'da worried myself to death. I hope you weren't hurt when the horse threw you, dear."

Wynne smiled. "No. I'm fine." Her fingers dug into her dirty dress embarrassedly. "But the blasted thing took all my clothes with it!" she snapped heatedly. "Now I don't have a thing to wear."

Draping a protective arm around her, Betsy rushed to allay her worries. "Now don't you worry a bit." She consoled her as she led Wynne to the house. "We'll get you into a hot tub of water, and after you're bathed, you can borrow some of my things. I'm a little larger than you, but I think I have a blue calico that will look just wonderful on you!"

Wynne smiled gratefully. "Thank you, Betsy. I surely would appreciate it." She glanced at Cole, then dropped her gaze away shyly. Betsy was still chattering like an old blue jay as the two women disappeared in the house.

Wrapping an arm around her son's waist, Lilly followed at a slower pace. "You think she's really all right, dear?"

Cole's eyes had followed Wynne until he could no longer see her. "She's okay, Ma."

"Well, she's sure a lucky little ol' thing to have you coming along to save her just at the right time," Lilly said, hoping her older son might take a closer look now that Wynne was back.

"Uh-huh, I suppose," he said distractedly. "Where's Beau?"

"Mending fences. He'll be along after a while to eat his dinner. How'd your business go in Kansas City?"

"Fine." His eyes took in the cherry orchard once more. "What's goin' on?"

"Oh, Beau and Betsy was gettin' all astir to announce their engagement, so we thought we'd sort of have an informal party so's they could hint around to all their friends that the weddin' was still on."

"You were goin' to have an engagement party without me and Cass!" Cole said with mock astonishment, knowing full well Lilly would never consider such an event without having her entire family present.

"Oh, no, dear. It isn't an official engagement party! Just sort of a Saturday night shindig. The actual announcement of Beau and Betsy's weddin' won't be made until the fall sometime," she told him quickly.

Cole squeezed his mother's shoulder affectionately. "I was just teasin' you, Ma. I know you wouldn't do that."

She reached up and tugged the three-day wiry growth that lay dark and thick across her eldest son's handsome face. Sam. He was Sam Claxton all over again, and it made her want to shout for joy that the good Lord had left a small part of her deceased husband on this earth to give her such comfort. "You think I don't know you and your tomfoolery by now?" She smacked him on his backside playfully. "Now you get on into the house and tell Willa to fetch you some bath water. There's gonna be a party tonight." Her eyes sparkled brightly with anticipation of things to come. "There's gonna be singin' and dancin' the likes of which you haven't seen or heard for five long years!"

Chapter 16

Late in the afternoon a crowd began converging on the Claxton ranch. Everyone was ready for a celebration and came with a lightness of heart that left not one somber look on anyone's face. Music filled the air, and the sound of laughter bubbled over the hillsides as the party got into full swing.

Wynne could hear the sounds of women's laughter, mixed with the deeper sounds of men's baritone voices, while she finished dressing in her room. She smiled at her reflection in the mirror as she heard a woman's high squeal and a man's booming laughter.

Tonight was supposed to be a happy time, and she didn't begrudge the silly shenanigans going on down there. But her smile slowly faded as the pain of reality closed in on her once more. She wished only that she and Cole could be a part of that lightheartedness.

What a wondrous delight it would be if they could forget what lay between them, and he would swing her up in his arms and haul her off to the barn to steal a kiss from her or whatever else he might be inclined to steal. But Cole would never do that. He never teased, he never showed what he was feeling except for the brief moments when passion overrode his pride, and he would most assuredly never haul her off to the barn in front of everyone. Yet it would be nice if he were that sort of man.

Wynne's musings were interrupted by the soft tap on the door and Betsy calling her name.

They had talked long into the afternoon as Betsy had helped her bathe and dress. Betsy encouraged Wynne to stay on in River Run while she arranged her newly washed and dried hair in a mass of shiny curls on top of her head, but Wynne would not be swayed. She would leave on the morning stage, and her decision was final. There was absolutely no reason for her to remain where she was not welcome, and Cole's quiet estrangement on the ride home had assured her that he would make no effort to try to change her mind.

When she'd told him of her decision earlier this evening, he'd met her announcement with the same calm indifference he had exhibited when they first met. All he'd said was that she should be ready by first light and he would take her into town and purchase a ticket for her if that was what she had a mind to do.

So tomorrow morning she would be on her way back to Savannah with a broken heart, but at least it would be a fresh one.

Betsy and Wynne walked down the stairway together and were greeted by whistles of male admiration. But there was only one man's reaction Wynne longed for, and he was nowhere to be found. In fact, it was late in the evening before Cole finally made an appearance at the party.

Wynne's heart threatened to stop beating when she saw him walk down the stairway and pause to speak to Betsy's sister, Priscilla June. He looked unbearably handsome, and Wynne was sure her love for him was written so clearly on her face that the whole room would soon know her secret.

She wasn't the only woman in the room who had spotted his entrance. A small crowd of women had gathered by the stairway, vying for his attention, but Priscilla had already staked her claim as she cooed and fussed over Cole until Wynne wanted to march right over and snatch her hair out by the roots.

He glanced up from saying something to Priscilla and their eyes met and suddenly every other person in the room disappeared.

She fought to hide her feelings but knew she was failing miserably. She could only stare back at him with her heart in her eyes and pray he wouldn't turn away from her.

The blue of his eyes darkened as they ran lazily over the dress she was wearing. The blue dress with tiny pink flowers hugged her breasts and accentuated her tiny waist. Cole felt the ever-familiar painful tightening in his loins that inevitably occurred when he was around her.

For a moment they stood transcended in time. It was as if the world held no one else but them. And then he smiled at her, a slow, incredibly intimate smile that told her that no matter what their differences, he had not forgotten what they had shared, nor would he ever.

She smiled back, a trembling, not at all certain smile, just enough to let him know that she understood and fondly shared his remembrances.

Then the magic was broken when Priscilla took his arm. Shattered, Wynne moved on through the crowd, trying to bite back the welling tears.

The night became a blur as she danced and laughed and tried to forget that after tomorrow she would never see Cole Claxton again.

Finally around midnight she gave up all pretense and slipped quietly around the corner of the house to go to her room. Cole's voice stopped her as she reached Lilly's flower garden. "Turnin' in so early?"

The familiar aroma of his cigar permeated the air. Wynne's footsteps faltered, and she shut her eyes in emotional pain. She didn't think she could stand another encounter with him tonight. "Yes. I'm . . . a little tired."

"Uh-huh," he intoned. "I can imagine. It was a long trip, and tomorrow you have another one facin' you."

She couldn't see him, only the tip of his cheroot glowing in the shadows. "Yes." She gathered her light shawl closer to her bosom and started to walk on.

"What's your hurry, Miss Elliot?" he asked in an easy voice.

Once more her steps slowed, and she paused. "I told you. I'm very tired."

He finally stepped out of the shadows and joined her. Her breath caught and held as she gazed up at him. The rays of the silvery moonlight played across his face, and she longed to have him take her in his arms and tell her that he loved her, that it didn't matter what she had been about to do to his brother at one time, that the only thing that really mattered was that she was in love with him now and it would be so foolish to throw away that rare, wondrous miracle simply because of her past stupidities.

He could do worse in a bride, Wynne assured herself. She could make him proud. She would use all the skills Miss Fielding had taught her until one day he would look at her as a lady, not some bumbling nincompoop! If he would only give her a chance. But how did she tell him that without making another absolute fool of herself?

It was plain to see he didn't return her feelings. No, he would only laugh and tell her she obviously didn't know what man she loved. First Cass, now him.

She could never bear that.

She turned and started away again, but his hand reached out to stop her. "Dammit, Wynne, don't go in yet." His voice had suddenly lost its earlier arrogance. Instead, it held a soft, almost urgent plea. Her breath caught as he swung her roughly around and took her in his arms, his mouth hungrily seeking and finding hers.

She melted in his arms like soft butter. This was what she'd wanted, what she'd longed for all evening as she had gaily danced with first one man and then another. She returned the kiss with such fervor it made Cole groan with newly aroused need. He pulled her closer, crushing her breasts against the solid wall of his chest in an embrace that threatened to overpower her.

Where the kiss would have ended, she could only guess because it was sadly interrupted a few moments later by Beau's calling her name.

"Don't answer," Cole murmured raggedly. "We have to talk." His mouth took hers again with fierce possession.

But Beau's voice persisted as it came closer to where they stood sheltered in the shadows. "Wynne?"

"I have to answer," she whispered. "In a few more minutes he'll see us, Cole."

Cole swore under his breath as he realized the wisdom of her words and reluctantly released her. A moment later she stepped quietly out of the shadows. "Yes, Beau?"

"Oh, there you are." He came forward with a large grin on his face. "There's someone here lookin' for you."

"Me?" Wynne asked with surprise.

Beau shrugged. "Yeah. Some guy came ridin' in awhile ago. Said he would have been here earlier, but his horse threw a shoe—oh, hello, Cole. Didn't

346

see you standin' back there." Beau's grin widened knowingly.

"Who's lookin' for her?"

"Don't know. Some fellow says it's real important that he talk to Wynne."

"She's not talkin' to any man tonight," Cole stated flatly, a new round of jealousy overtaking him. "Tell him to come back tomorrow morning and call on her proper."

"Good heavens, Cole. He's not calling on me," Wynne protested lightly. She was thrilled to hear jealousy seeping into his tone, yet she couldn't imagine who her unknown visitor was. She didn't know anyone in River Run. "Where is the man, Beau?"

"Out front. Ma made him sit down and drink something cool. He looked a mite peaked when he got here."

Wynne glanced at Cole expectantly. "It wouldn't hurt for me to see what he wants, would it?" She couldn't bear the curiosity until morning.

When she looked at him like that, Cole would have given her anything she wanted. "I don't like it, but go ahead. See what he wants."

She smiled and slipped away as Cole reached in his shirt pocket for another cigar.

"Aren't you going to go with her?" Beau asked lightly.

"I got no claim on who she sees," Cole replied curtly, but his insides were tight with the thought of another man demanding her time.

The young man awaiting her managed to paste a pleasant smile on his face in spite of his discomfort as Wynne entered the parlor. The back brace the doctor had rigged up was hot and bothering him something fierce, and it was the end of a long and particularly tedious day. When Wynne approached him, his face immediately went slack with astonishment.

For a moment Wynne surveyed him quizzically. Then she smiled in recognition and moved across the room to take his hand. "Well, hello again." He was the same young man she had seen twice before, once sitting on a porch, whittling, as she had ridden through Springfield, and only yesterday, when they'd stopped to water their horses.

"*You're* Wynne Elliot!" His voice cracked and sounded as if he had just entered puberty again.

She smiled expectantly. "Yes."

She noticed his large Adam's apple bobbing up and down nervously as he tried to regain his composure. Leaping lizards! For months he'd been chasing this woman across country, and she had passed him twice already!

"Miss Elliot . . . I had no idea that was you . . ." His voice trailed off weakly.

Wynne continued to smile at the pale young man, wondering what in heaven's name he wanted with her.

Remembering his manners, Bertram wiped his hand nervously on the side of his trousers, then politely extended it to her. "Bertram G. Mallory, ma'am."

"Mr. Mallory." Wynne tipped her head and accepted his hand graciously. Perhaps this was another one of the lawyers from her father's estate, though he certainly didn't look like a lawyer.

"Oh, ma'am, you don't know how nice it is finally to meet you!"

"Why, thank you." She smiled again. "I believe you wanted to speak with me?"

"Oh, yes, ma'am." He could still hardly believe Wynne Elliot was finally standing there in front of him. "I'm with the Pinkerton Detective Agency— you've heard of us, haven't you?"

Wynne nodded. She had read about Alan Pinkerton in a paper one time. He was a man from Glasgow, Scotland, who now lived in Chicago and had made a name for himself by recovering a large sum of money for the Adams Express Company. The paper had said he was also credited for uncovering a plot to murder the late President Abraham Lincoln.

"Well, ma'am, I was hired by Mr. Claxton to return this to you." He began to search through his pockets, extracting his billfold, a comb, a pocketknife, and his gun, all which he promptly handed to her. "Excuse me, ma'am, could you hold these for a minute?"

"Yes, certainly." Wynne took the items, and he continued his search. "You said Mr. Claxton sent you?"

"Yeah . . . yeah . . . now wait . . . I know it's here somewhere." His face suddenly brightened. "Yes! Here it is!" He quickly slapped a leather pouch into her hand and immediately felt as if a ton of weight had just been lifted off his shoulders.

"Cass . . . Claxton?" she asked again as her smile began to fade.

"Yes, ma'am. It's the money you lent him."

Wynne's hand clasped the pouch and the wallet and the comb and the gun tighter as her eyes narrowed in anger. If this was someone's idea of a joke, it wasn't very funny. "The money I lent him. What are you talking about?"

"It's all there, ma'am. Every cent of it. Cass gave it to me, to give back to you, the day you two was supposed to be married." Bertram peered back at her from eyes that were bloodshot and ringed with road grime, but they were good, honest eyes. "I've tried real hard to find you, ma'am. Honest I have. I had been in bed with a bad case of the miseries the day Mr. Claxton came to my door, so I couldn't bring the money back right then. I got up early the next morning and went to your house, but you were already gone back to Miss Fielding's school, so I went lookin' for you there, but I missed you again." He sighed hopelessly. "From then on every time I got close to you, either you disappeared again or I had another one of them damn— oh, pardon my language, ma'am—accidents."

The mere thought of those flukes made his ribs, his leg, and his back begin to pain all over again. "Then I heard you was on your way to River Run, so I figured I'd try to catch you before you got to Mr. Claxton's folks, 'cause he told me River Run was where he originally came from and he had just been visitin' kinfolks in Savannah. I was afraid you'd get here ahead of me and tell them what you thought he had done to you, and it would all be a big mistake 'cause Mr. Claxton didn't really take your money like you must be thinkin' he did."

Bertram hung his head sheepishly. "Sure sorry I didn't make it in time. I know you must be thinkin' all sorts of bad things about him—and ma'am? About his marryin' you? Well, I was supposed to tell you he loved you an' all, but he just sort of got cold feet and decided maybe he wasn't quite ready to get hitched yet, only he didn't have the heart to tell you. He told me he knew he was probably makin' a big mistake 'cause you was one of the prettiest and nicest women he'd ever met, but he thought maybe he had a lot of growin' up to do before he settled down to raisin' a family."

While Bertram rattled on, Wynne's face was a mask of conflicting emotions: disbelief, jubilation, incredulity, exultation. If what this man was saying was true, then these horrendous past few months had been for nothing! She had been running around vowing revenge on a man who was guilty of nothing more serious than being afraid of the responsibility of taking a wife and of hurting her even more by going through with an ill-advised marriage.

Wynne frowned, her eyes going to the gun she was holding. Good Lord, *what* if she had been able to find Cass and actually carry out her threat? No, she realized now that she would have never actually been able to kill him. Wring his neck as she had that chicken maybe, but kill him? No, never! Then her face lit with renewed elation. In a way Cass's deserting her at the altar had been a blessing because she realized now that what she had felt for him was not love, not in comparison with what she felt for Cole. Her smile faded again. And what was *he* going to say, other than "I told you so," when he learned that his brother had made provisions for her money to be returned all along but she had been too busy seeking revenge to stop long enough for Mr. Mallory to find her?

Wynne breathed a long, deep sigh. It all was very confusing.

"Ma'am?" Bertram was keeping a careful eye on the rapid play of emotions across her face, and he wasn't quite sure how she was taking the news.

She glanced up. "Yes?"

"Are you . . . all right?"

"Oh, yes, yes. I'm just fine." Or at least she would be as soon as her mind was able to digest the past few moments. "I can't thank you enough, Mr. Mallory, for finally locating me. You've made me a happy woman."

"Oh, that's all right, ma'am." Bertram began to gather up his wallet and comb from her safekeeping. "Mr. Claxton paid me handsomely, and I'm just doin' my job." Of course, he had spent every penny Cass had given him, plus his own substantial fee while trying to locate her; but that wasn't her fault, and Bertram was too much of a gentleman to tell her about all his problems.

Outside, someone let out a loud war hoop as the sound of approaching hoofbeats thundered into the farmyard. A crescendo of voices rang out as Wynne heard "Cass! Cass is comin'!" being shouted in excited voices.

Bertram stepped over to the window and lifted the curtain. "Oh, my, looks like Mr. Claxton could have delivered the money a whole lot easier himself," Bertram said uneasily. He'd best try to slip out the back way before he had to face Cass and have him find out he had just now returned the lady's money.

Wynne suddenly came back to life, the shock of the past few moments finally wearing off. "Good heavens! Cass is home!"

Funny, an hour ago those words would have meant very little, but now all she could feel was extreme joy. Cole and Beau would have their brother back, and Lilly's youngest son would have returned home safely.

Letting out a squeal that would have shocked Miss Fielding right down to her prissy old corset, Wynne, still carrying Bertram's gun, bolted out of the room in order to be one of the first to greet him. Cass was home, and he wasn't the scoundrel she had thought him to be at all! She had to tell him she forgave him and make peace. Then maybe she and Cole . . .

Wynne skidded to a stop halfway across the parlor and whirled around to rush back over and give Bertram a large, energetic hug. "Oooooh, thank you, Mr. Mallory, thank you ever so much," then spun around again and raced out the two wide parlor doors at full speed.

"Ma'am, my gun." But Wynne had already disappeared out the doorway. With a resigned sigh he rushed out after her.

Cole was just on his way to check on Wynne when she buzzed by him like an angry hornet, flailing the gun in the air, nearly knocking him over in her hurried exit.

"Hey, what's the hurry?"

He reached out to slow her passage, but she only shrugged his hand away and yelled over her shoulder as she flew out the front door, "Can't stop now! Cass is comin'!"

"Ma'am, the gun!" Bertram said again as he hurried along to keep up with her, but to his dismay she still wasn't listening.

The smile that had been on Cole's face drained

away to a weak facsimile as the meaning of her words sank in. And she had been waving a gun. Oh, hell. His feet suddenly went into action as he tore behind her and the man following close behind.

"Wynne, wait!" he shouted.

But she ignored him, too, and kept on running. *Oh, Lord, she'll kill him!* he thought as he ran faster.

Her total being bent on reaching Cass first, Wynne, a radiant smile on her face, had burst through the crowd on the porch and down the steps, running toward the rider who had just entered the yard. All she could think of was the fact that she wanted to thank Cass for being so honest! Not only had he restored her faith in men, but maybe, just maybe he had just provided a future for Cole and her!

Bertram was making his way out of the house as Cole rushed by like a streak of lightning, nearly knocking him off his feet in his hasty exit.

"Oh, sorry, fella." Cole hurriedly steadied his swaying form. Then the front screen slammed loudly as Bertram straightened up and readjusted his hat. Oh, lordy. If he could just get out of here and be on his way back to Fancy without further injury, then he would swear he would change profession first thing tomorrow morning. He decided to forget the gun and just pray he wouldn't need it until he got back to Springfield. He pushed open the screen door and headed directly for his horse, hoping to make a quick exit from this madhouse.

Cole was gaining on Wynne as he jumped the porch railing. "Wynne!" he shouted again, drawing everyone's attention to the chase. "Stop!"

By now Wynne had nearly reached Cass, and Cole exerted every ounce of strength he had to overtake her.

Bertram had managed to get outside and to his horse. Watching the two crazy people chasing each other across the yard from the corner of his eye, Bertram got one foot in the stirrup just as his horse began to shy.

The crowd was standing still, watching the spectacle of a red-headed woman running across the yard toward the new arrival and a man following close behind, shouting for her to stop! Bertram swore irritably under his breath and fought to control his horse, trying to swing his stiff body into the saddle.

"Wynne!" Cole yelled again. "I won't let you do it."

In one huge flying leap he shouted, "No, don't,

Wynne!" then tackled her just as Cass reined his horse to a skidding halt.

Surprised by the number of people at the house this late at night, Cass watched openmouthed, trying to control his prancing horse, as a man who looked suspiciously like his older brother tackled a young red-headed woman who was waving a gun in the air. No, it couldn't be! Was that Wynne Elliot?

Bertram had managed to get one foot in the stirrup, but his horse was prancing so frantically from the unaccustomed clamor taking place around him that he couldn't finish mounting, nor could he get his foot loose.

"Oh, please, Lord! Not again." Bertram begged, still trying to convince the horse to stop jumping around. "If you're ever gonna help me, do it right now!" he beseeched, pulling the reins to get his animal at least going in a direction he could control.

With his back held immobile, Bertram couldn't bend enough to mount unless the horse stood still. With a quick glance over his shoulder, he saw the fiasco continuing and strove even harder to control his horse so he could get his foot loose. His ankle was still a little weak, and now his back was killing him again, and these fool people were intent on murdering one another in front of their own house! Once again he fervently wished he'd never met up with the Claxtons.

"Hold it, horse. Whoa, boy, whoa!" Bertram pleaded.

The impact of Cole's landing on her had not only surprised but hurt Wynne. And it made her mad! Darn mad!

"Get off me!" she screeched, kicking and elbowing him. "What in the world is the matter with you?"

"Don't do it!" Cole was trying to still her flailing limbs, fighting to gain control of the gun. His heavy body pinned her to the ground as he grasped her wrists tightly. "Don't . . . Wynne."

"Don't what?" What on earth was he babbling about? It never occurred to her that she still had possession of Mr. Mallory's gun, or that Cole had no idea what had taken place in the parlor a few moments earlier, or that she had neglected to tell him on the ride home that she no longer wanted to kill Cass, that she now loved Cole Claxton, not his brother.

"Don't shoot him—please." A "please!" From Cole Claxton! Wynne felt she'd just witnessed a miracle.

"Shoot him? Whatever are you talking about?"

Cole's eyes were locked with hers pleadingly as his words began to seep in and she finally noticed the gun was still in her hand. "Oh, darling! I wasn't going to shoot him!" she exclaimed as she flung the weapon away from her. "I was only going to thank him for being so honest and nice. . . ." Her words trailed away meekly as she saw the pleading look in Cole's eyes begin to change.

"Thank him!" Cole exploded. Here he had nearly killed himself these past few weeks trying to prevent his brother from being ambushed, by her, and now she was going to "thank" him for being so nice!

"Well, yes . . ." Wynne knew she had a bit of explaining to do as Cole slowly stood back up and pulled her to her feet. "You see that man who wanted to see me in the parlor . . ."

While she was explaining Bertram's mission, he still had one foot caught in the stirrup and was bouncing about helplessly, swearing under his breath and trying to protect his one good leg as the horse shied away from him.

As Cole listened with amazement, the sound of running horses caught their attention. With a boil of dust and a loud "Ho! Ho, there!" a buckboard driven by a rather flamboyant woman swung crazily into the yard. With a flash of red satin she bounded down and immediately rushed to Bertram's rescue.

"Fancy!" Bertram blurted, seeing his fiancée rushing toward him.

"Oh, Bertie, darlin', let me help you." Grabbing the reins of the horse, she managed to still the animal while he jerked his aching foot free from the binding stirrup.

"What are you doin' here?" he said gratefully, a big grin covering his face now that he was safely out of harm's way with no new injuries.

She reached out and touched his cheek reverently. Fully aware of Bertram's uncanny ability to harm himself, she'd followed at a close distance, curiosity as well as love prompting her. "I just sort of thought you might need me, Bertie."

Although he had faithfully promised he would return for her, she wasn't taking any chances. Bertram G. Mallory was a rare man, and he was *hers*.

"Aw, Fancy, I do need you"—Bertram grinned humbly—"for the rest of my life."

By now Cass had dismounted and was enveloped in Lilly's tearful embrace. He had no idea what was going on; but he was finally home, and that was all that mattered.

Lilly had no idea why Cole had been wallowing in the dirt with Wynne, nor did Cass, but they supposed that in good time it all would come out. Those two were going to make a fine couple, Lilly thought jubilantly as she and Cass stepped lightly around the warring couple and merged into the happy crowd.

"—and so you see, I don't hate Cass anymore," Wynne was saying lovingly. "He didn't steal my money or my heart. I just thought he did."

"Oh, honey." Cole heaved a relieved sigh. "Then you've finally got all this avenging nonsense out of your head?"

Wynne nodded repentantly.

"And you'd be willing to listen if another man said he loved you?"

She grinned. "Only if *you* say it."

"Okay, here goes, but I don't know how good I'll be at sayin' it. . . ." Cole had never told any woman he loved her, but he was going to make a stab at it.

"Just say it," she begged, her hands framing his handsome face.

"I—I love you," he admitted gruffly. "I know that you thought you had reason to doubt those words coming from a Claxton, but I mean them, Wynne." His voice lowered intimately as he pulled her up closer to him, his mouth only inches away from hers. "You know I mean them."

She wasn't sure how many surprises she could stand in one day, but this one was even more thrilling than the last. "You really do?"

Cole's face suddenly grew playful. "Are you strong as a bull moose and healthy as a horse? Can you wrestle an Indian brave, cut a rick of wood without raisin' a sweat, and forget all about being a lady in my bed?" He already knew the answer to that one.

She smiled at him sweetly. "If you want me to, I certainly can."

"Then I really do love you, lady," he said, "and I want you for my wife."

"Well, there is Moss Oak . . . I don't know . . ." She wanted ten seconds to think it over, as a matter of principle, but she knew Cole would help her settle the problem of the plantation.

"You'd better," he said with a knowing wink. " 'Cause you're gonna have my baby."

She blinked indignantly. "I am not!"

He ran the tip of his tongue around her lower lip suggestively, hoping he spoke the truth. He had made sure there was a strong chance she carried his child before they had left the cabin. "Well, we'll see come next May."

She touched her tongue to his and brought forth the low groan she was seeking. "You think that bothers me?" She would gladly settle for being his wife and having Claxton children by the dozens, rather than run around the countryside trying to avenge her honor. It *had* to be a whole lot easier.

"It doesn't? Then I suppose we'll just have to make darn sure I got the job done," he whispered suggestively against the sweetness of her mouth.

Scooping her up in his arms, he grinned and winked at his brothers as he proceeded to carry her down toward the barn, kissing her breathless with every step he took, right in front of all those people!

Well, wonders of wonders, Wynne thought, grinning at his handsome face. Cole Claxton was romantic after all!

Watch for Lori Copeland's next historical
romance, *Passion's Captive*, coming in
August 1988!

Kansas Frontier—September 1868

"Shoo! Shooeeee! Get out of here you—you miserable . . . ungrateful . . . ham hock!" Charity Burkhouser was determined to show
no pity as she swatted the old sow across its fat rump and herded it right
back out the front door. It was a sad day when a woman couldn't step out
to hang the wash without being invaded by pigs!

She slammed the heavy wooden door and leaned against it to catch
her breath. She *had* to do something about getting the fence back up.

A woman alone in the world just doesn't have a chance, she muttered
to herself. Her husband had died in the war three years ago and since
Ferrand's death, Charity had been on her own. Not that she wanted to
be—far from it. She wasn't equipped to homestead a piece of land in
this godforsaken place they called Kansas, nor had she ever had the
least desire to do so. But it was home now, her home, so she guessed
she'd best make do and quit feeling sorry for herself. Ferrand had
worked too hard in the brief time they'd been granted together for her to
be fainthearted now. She'd see this thing through. Though she had to
admit, she couldn't see how she was going to do it.

She needed a man. Oh, not for the same reason a woman usually
wanted a man. Charity needed a man from a purely practical stand-
point. She had to make improvements on the land to keep her claim, but
she simply didn't have the knowledge, the strength, or the necessary
skill.

When it had come to setting posts and planting wheat, she'd done an
atrocious job. Ashamed for anyone to see the way her fenceposts leaned
westward when they were supposed to stand straight, Charity had
ripped them out and cried herself to sleep.

No, a man was her only answer.

But a man was a rare commodity around these parts. It was unlikely
that anyone would walk up, knock on her door, and say, "Well, hello! I
hear you're looking for a husband, Mrs. Burkhouser. Take me."

Nevertheless, she was going to have to find someone soon or lose her
claim by this time next year.

She sighed in despair and turned her face upward, as she did increasingly these days. "Well, it's up to you, Lord. I'm at the end of my
row."

The lone rider slowed his horse beside the stream and paused to let the animal drink its fill. The man was unkempt and dirty. A dark blond stubble marred his handsome features. He seemed older than his twenty-eight years. Fatigue lined his face, and nature hadn't been kind. The sun had cooked his skin to a dark, golden bronze, and blue eyes that had once danced with merriment now stared in blank acceptance of a life that no longer held purpose.

Beau knew he looked bad.

He didn't eat the way he should. He was at least forty pounds lighter than he had been a year ago. Since then, he'd rambled down one winding road after another, going wherever the next road took him. He just tried to get through one day and then the next and then the next. Sometimes he'd notice when he crossed a state line, but if anyone had asked him where he was, Beau wouldn't have known or cared. Life was just one long dreary day after the next now that his wife, Betsy, was gone.

He slid from his horse. Reaching into the stream, he cupped his hands for a cool drink. When he finished, he splashed a handful of water down his neck to ease the heat.

Straightening, he prepared to mount again when his horse began to shy nervously. "Whoa, girl, easy." Beau gripped the reins and pulled himself into the saddle as the mare whinnied and sidestepped again. 'Easy   easy.' He glanced toward a wooded area, and a strange wariness came over him.

'What's the matter, girl?" Once more, his eyes scanned the area. Suddenly, Beau felt a tightness in his stomach. Standing not twenty feet away, partially hidden in the undergrowth, was one of the biggest timber wolves he'd ever seen.

The horse trumpeted in alarm and started to bolt. The wolf's lips curled back above his fangs, and he gave a low, ominous growl. His eyes had a bright, feverish sparkle to them.

Suddenly, with one tremendous lunge, the wolf sprang from his hiding place as the horse reared wildly in fright.

Some three hundred yards away, Charity stopped kneading bread and cocked her ear toward the open window. The dogs were setting up a howl on the front step, and in the distance she could hear what sounded like animals in some sort of terrible fight.

She wiped the flour from her hands and moved to the mantel. Darn pesky coyotes, she thought irritably, reaching for the rifle. They probably attacked a stray dog or calf.

The noise increased in intensity as she stepped out of the soddy and started toward the stream.

Charity's footsteps quickened as she heard a horse's shrill squeal rent the air. Good heavens! Something had attacked a horse!

Her feet faltered as she entered the clearing, her eyes grimly taking in the appalling sight. Before her, a large timber wolf was ripping a man apart as his horse danced about him wildly.

Regaining her composure, Charity hefted the rifle to her shoulder and took careful aim. Seconds later, a loud crack sliced the air, and the wolf toppled off the man into the water. The gunfire spooked the horse, and it bolted into the thicket as Charity hurriedly waded into the stream.

She flinched as she edged past the fallen wolf, but the gaping bullet hole in the center of its chest assured her that her aim had been true.

Kneeling beside the injured man, she cautiously rolled him on his side in the shallow water and cringed as she heard him moan in agony. He was so bloody she could barely make out the severity of his wounds, but she knew he was near death.

"Shhhh . . . lie still. I'm going to help you," she soothed though he could neither see nor hear her. As his eyes began to swell shut from the nasty lacerations on his face, he passed out.

It took several tries, for he wasn't as light as he looked, before she finally pulled him onto the bank. She hurriedly tore off a small portion of her petticoat and began to clean his wounds. He tossed restlessly, fighting her when her hands touched his torn flesh.

"Please, you must let me help you!" she urged.

She peeled away his torn shirt and washed the blood from the thick mat of dark blond hair that lay across his chest. Though his chest was broad, she could count his ribs. Obviously, he hadn't had a square meal in a long time. With more meat on his bones, he'd be a very large man . . . powerful . . . strong. Strong enough to build a barn and set a fence and work behind a team of oxen all day. Her hands stilled momentarily.

Good Lord. A man. Here was a man—barely alive perhaps, but a man all the same. He could be the answer to her problems.

Her hands flew about their work more feverishly. She had to save him! Not that she wouldn't have tried her best anyway, but now no matter what it would take, by all that was holy, she'd see to it that this man survived.

As far as men went, he wasn't much—pretty bedraggled, actually, but she reminded herself she wasn't in a position to be picky.

She'd nurse him back to health, and once she got him on his feet, she'd trick him into marrying her. No, she amended, she wouldn't trick him—she'd ask him first, and if that didn't work, then she'd trick him.

A new sense of confidence filled her. He *would* live. She just knew he ᵕld. The good Lord wouldn't give her such a gift and then turn ᵕnd and snatch it back, now would he?

ᵕe moaned again, and Charity lifted his head and placed it in her lap possessively.

He was a gift from God.

She was certain of that now. Who else would so unselfishly drop this complete stranger at her door?

Once more she looked down at her unexpected gift, and her face lit with a radiant smile. Closing her eyes, she lifted her face heavenward and sighed with relief. Maybe now she would be able to claim her land after all.

Then, in her most reverent tone, she humbly asked for the Lord's help in making this man strong and healthy again—or at least strong enough to drive a good, sturdy fencepost.

She closed her petition with heartfelt sincerity. "He's a little . . . well, rough looking, Lord, but I'm sure not complaining." She bit her lower lip thoughtfully as she studied the ragged, dirty, bloody man lying in her lap. With a little soap and water, maybe he'd be tolerable. She shrugged, and a big grin spread across her face. "I suppose if this is the best you have to offer, Lord, then I sure do appreciate your thoughtfulness."